INFERNO PUBLISHING COMPANY, Houston, Texas.

For more information about this book, visit Giacomo's website.

Cover design by Natasha Brown

Book design by Giacomo Giammatteo

This edition was prepared by Giacomo Giammatteo gg@giacomog.com

Print ISBN 978-1-949074-87-1

Electronic ISBN 978-1-949074-56-7

❀ Created with Vellum

MURDER IS IMMACULATE

GIACOMO GIAMMATTEO

Inferno Publishing Company

As with all of my mysteries, this book is told in a combination of first- and third-person POV. The chapters and/or scene breaks are marked with either a gun (third person) or a bullet (first person), so it should be easy to tell who is speaking.

FRIENDSHIP

True friendship is not built on words, but actions.

Chapter One

A LONG WALK HOME

Paul Campisi combed errant strands of hair into place as he dressed for the night's activity. He'd be joining his brothers at Manko's and that boded well for a shot with the ladies; there were *always* plenty of ladies at Manko's. *And the more they drink, the less they think.*

He got to the bar around seven, and his brothers—Freddy and Chooch—were already there. As he moved through the crowded floor toward his younger brothers, a nice-looking woman walked past.

"Hey, sweetheart, where are you going so fast? You should join me for a drink and maybe get educated in the process."

"Really? A chance to converse with an intellect like you *and* get educated? Let me ask my boyfriend first," she said, then smiled and walked away.

"Bitch!" Paul said. When she didn't acknowledge him, he said it again. "Bitch." This time, he yelled as loud as he could before continuing toward the bar.

"Paulie!" his brother Freddy shouted, and the greeting was echoed by Chooch, his other brother.

"I see you struck out with Janice," Chooch said.

Paul glanced over his shoulder to where she sat. "Now that I see her boyfriend, I guess it's just as well. He's a big guy."

"Not to mention the fact that you couldn't handle her," Chooch said. "She's more my speed."

Paul brushed him off. "Anything new? Anybody hear from Baltimore?"

"Talked to them earlier today. They're in as long as we guarantee a steady stream of product," Chooch said. "And that won't be a problem from our end."

"Can we trust them?" Paul asked. "You checked 'em out?"

"Can you trust anybody these days?" Freddy asked.

Chooch brushed him off. "They seem to be as reliable as anyone, Paulie. I talked to a guy I know in Pittsburgh. He's been doing business with them for ten years, and he's got no complaints; they've paid cash every time and paid in full. They even worked through a couple of mishaps with no trouble."

"Can't ask for more than that," Paul said. "I say we go for it. We gotta do the deal with somebody, and these guys seem better than most."

"I was hoping you'd agree," Chooch said. "I'll let them know tomorrow. Now, how about you relax and have a beer or two? And get your mind off sweet little Janice."

Freddy laughed. "I agree with Chooch about Janice. And as far as the Pittsburgh guys—if they don't pay, we bury them."

Paul grabbed the handle of a mug filled with beer. "Freddy, nobody's paying attention to you, so shut up." Paul turned, smiled, and spoke to Chooch. "I'm taking you up on your offer, little brother. It's been a long day."

"Glad to hear," Chooch said, "but which offer is that?"

"Hell, I don't know. I'm hoping it's one where you promised to deliver Janice to my bed for a night of long, hot sex."

"While you're dreaming, try to be realistic," Freddy said. "I would say like wishing you could beat me at darts, but we know that won't happen either. You'd have a better chance with Janice."

"Let's play, anyway," Chooch said. "I'll place my bet on Freddy."

"Fuck you," Paul said. "Let's go. Twenty a game."

The brothers played darts then pool, but most of all, they drank beer and a lot of it. By midnight, Paul was bumping into tables when he walked to the restroom.

He called the waitress for another round, but Chooch waved her off. "I think you've had enough, Paulie. You can't drive as it is."

"Like hell," Paul said. "I'm not leaving the car here."

"All right," Chooch said. "Give me the keys, and I'll bring it around front."

Paul handed him the keys, and Chooch stood to leave. He leaned down and whispered to Freddy, "I'm taking the car home. After I'm gone, bring Paulie in your car."

"He'll be pissed."

"Better than letting him drive in his condition," Chooch said, then he left.

Ten minutes later, Paul walked to the door and looked outside. "Where the hell is that asshole? It's been forever."

"It hasn't been long," Freddy said. "Besides, you're in no condition to drive. Let me take you home."

"Bullshit!" Paul said. "Nobody's driving my car."

"Too late for that," Freddy said. "Chooch took it. Looks like it's ride home with me or walk."

"You son of a bitch," Paul said, and took a swing at Freddy, who sidestepped it easily.

"Come on, Paul. That punch should tell you how bad off you are. Under normal circumstances, you'd have hit me or at least come closer."

"Screw you," Paul said. "I'll walk. I don't need you to drive me."

"Suit yourself," Freddy said. "I'm leaving. And I don't expect a call from you begging to be picked up."

"I wouldn't call you if I was dying," Paul said. "Now get the hell outta here."

———

Freddy left, driving his own car. Afterward, Paul drank several more beers before leaving to go home. He walked down Union Street to Canby Park, then cut through the woods to save time.

About a hundred yards into the woods, Paul heard something behind him—like someone walking through leaves. He turned to look but didn't see anything out of the ordinary. He stared for a moment, then continued on, but he hadn't gone twenty feet when he heard the sound again.

He spun quickly and looked longer this time. "Hey," he yelled. "I don't know who the hell is back there, but I'll kick your ass if you try anything." He waited a moment, then resumed his walk home, continually checking over his shoulder.

He walked a few feet and turned quickly, but he saw nothing, then he repeated the action after another few feet.

Ten or twenty steps later, the sound of a twig snapping stopped him. Before he turned, something slammed into his ribs, dropping him to the ground.

"Goddamn!" he yelled, and looked up. A man holding a baseball bat stood above him, and he was preparing to swing it again. "You?" Paul said. "What the hell do you want?"

The man pulled out a gun and shot Paul in the head, then he shot him in the heart. Paul groaned, and he stopped breathing.

The man swung the bat again, hitting Paul on the other side of his ribs. He continued to swing the bat, striking his knees, stomach, and finally a brutal shot to the side of his head.

Blood poured from several of the wounds and pooled on the

ground. The man with the bat sprinkled some DNA around the scene, and, after tidying up, he left, walking out the way he came.

He had half a mind to call it in, but he decided not to. Freddy and Chooch would find the body soon enough—if nobody else did. *Then the shit will hit the fan.*

Chapter Two

TROUBLE IN PARADISE

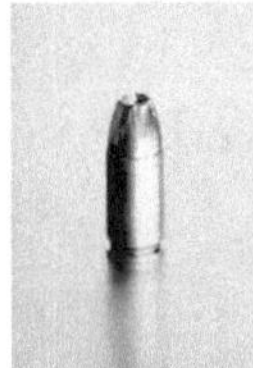

I turned left onto Sycamore Street, then drove the few blocks to the house on Beech. I parked by the curb, grabbed the present on the seat, then got out and walked inside.

The front door wasn't even closed before Dante raced across the living room, arms outstretched. "Is that for me, Dad?"

"It'll be for nobody if you slip on those hardwood floors and crack your head."

Dante laughed as he took hold of the present. "I don't fall, Dad. Besides, I'm strong."

"I know how strong you are. I felt your last punch; it almost knocked me down. Your muscles are getting big."

He laughed like little kids do. "I know you're kidding, Dad. But pretty soon I'll be able to knock you down."

I picked him up and laughed again. "I bet you will, you little devil. But for now, you'll have to settle for trying to beat me at Nerf guns. Go get a couple guns and a bunch of bullets, and we'll have a war. Only this time, I'm gonna win."

Dante ran up the stairs and raced to his bedroom. "That's what you think."

"Don't run on the stairs," I hollered but knew the warning would go unheeded, as they all did.

In less than five minutes, Dante came back down the steps holding two Nerf guns and a plastic bag filled with bullets.

"I got a lot of bullets, Dad. Let's get started. You get the dining room, and I get the living room."

"That's not fair," I said. "The living room's bigger."

"You had it last time," Dante said. "And I still beat you."

I hid behind the dining-room table and loaded my Nerf gun. After firing a few shots, I moved toward the living room as if I were sneaking up on him.

Dante peeked out from behind my chair and took several shots, then he raced forward and shot six or seven times. Three of the bullets hit me in the chest. I fell, holding my chest and moaning.

Dante laughed hard. "I got you, Dad. Again."

Angela must have heard the ruckus. She came in from the kitchen. "Dad's not very good. Is he Dante?"

"I beat him every time," Dante said.

I got up from the floor and grabbed him, then tickled his belly until he begged me to stop. "That's what you get for shooting your father," I said. "Now let's see what your mother fixed for dinner."

I scooped Dante up in my arms, and as we walked into the kitchen, I kissed Angie. "Got a kiss for a wounded soldier?" I asked.

She smiled. "Not a very good soldier. You seem to lose every time."

"You can't blame me. I'm fighting a ninja warrior," I said, and tickled Dante's belly again.

"How about you and the ninja get washed up. Dinner will be ready in five minutes."

"What are we having?"

"One of your favorites—*polpettone*."

I leaned forward and kissed her cheek. "Have I told you I loved you lately?"

"Not often enough," Angie said, then smacked me with a cooking mitt. "Now get those hands washed and tell Rosa to get down here and set the table."

We ate in silence—except for Dante—and after the meal, Rosa poured more wine for Angie and me.

"You want to play some cards tonight?" Angie asked.

I smiled. "I was thinking of that, babe, but probably not like you expected."

She frowned. "You mean you want to play cards but not with me, right?"

"Damn, but you're smart. They're having a big game at the smoke shop, and I thought I'd go up and maybe win a few bucks."

"How come I never see any of these *bucks* you win?"

"What? How about the grandfather's clock I got you? Or the necklace you love so much? Both of those were paid for with winnings from the games. Not to mention all the presents I bring that little ninja."

Yeah, Mom. Let Dad go," Dante hollered.

Angie smiled. "All right," she said. "Get out of here, but you better win." She smacked my butt as I turned. "And win big. You need to bring *me* one of those presents."

"And me," Rosa said.

"At this rate, I may not be home for days," I said.

"I'll be waiting," Dante said.

"I'll bet you will," I said, and laughed.

* * *

I got to the game early so I could get my lucky seat, but Knuckles had gotten there even earlier. "Hey, Knuckles, your fat ass is in my seat."

"Wrong, Nicky. My fat ass is in *a* seat, not your seat. I don't see a name on that chair, and I don't see a seating assignment."

"Come on, Knuckles, you know I sit there all the time."

"Correction. You *usually* sit there. Not tonight."

I pulled out another chair, but then tried one more thing. "All right, ten bucks for the seat," I said.

"Ten bucks? I wouldn't piss on you for ten bucks. Make it fifty and I'll do it."

"Fifty? Are you crazy? Fifty dollars for a seat."

"It's your lucky chair, Nicky. You said so yourself."

"How about twenty?"

"Fifty, or you take your chances with that loser chair you're ready to sit in. But remember, that chair's so bad, I don't think anyone's ever won while sitting in it. Might as well have a deuce painted on the seat."

I shook my head and frowned. "All right, for Christ's sake. Fifty it is." I pulled a wad of bills from my pocket and peeled off a Grant. "Here. I hope you lose it quick."

"Be thankful I didn't ask for a Franklin," Knuckles said.

"Fat chance you'd have had for that. I wouldn't give you a Franklin if you were dying."

"Don't I know that, which is why I settled for a Grant."

Knuckles stood and moved to what had always been Jimmy 'the Gem's' seat. "Knuckles, you know that's Jimmy's seat."

"I know whose fuckin' seat it is. I got a new plan where I'm guaranteed to win; I'm gonna sell seats instead of playing cards. I might not make as much, but I got no chance of losing."

I shook my head and laughed. "Knuckles, you're a hoot. Anything for a buck."

"No shit about that, Nicky. The way Doggs cuts this pot, you only got one winner—him. I'm out to make sure there's another one."

The game kicked off at eight on the dot, and the table was full, though I didn't know anyone but Knuckles, Doggs, and Jimmy the Gem. The rest of the players were new. A guy named Fresno, who Jimmy said was new to town, BlackJack Joe, who I knew from long ago, but he'd been away serving time, and Stud Marino, who swore his nickname derived from his sexual stamina, but everyone who knew him claimed it was due to his penchant for playing five-card stud every time he dealt.

At the first break, when all the new guys were getting a drink, I leaned toward Knuckles. "Where'd all the new blood come from?"

"Doggs has been recruiting. He makes a lot from these games—as I said—so you know damn right well he's not gonna let them slow down. I think he got most of the new blood from the north side, though a couple of them are fresh in town."

I leaned back in the chair. "North side, huh? Up where the money is, right?"

Knuckles nodded. "Suckers with money. That's what Doggs likes."

The game started up in a few minutes, and by eleven o'clock, I was up about four hundred. On the next deal, I was dealt my third seven in a five-card stud game. Much to everyone's disappointment, I was about to increase my winnings.

Jimmy the Gem bet fifty, and I raised a hundred. He hesitated, but then called—and lost. "Sorry, Jimmy," I said.

"You're one lucky son of a bitch," Jimmy said.

"Hey, it's not all bad," one of the new guys said. "I know a guy who needs to off a nice platinum ring. You deal in jewelry, right?"

"What's his name?" Jimmy asked.

"What's my cut?" the guy asked.

"The same I give everybody else," Jimmy said. "Now spit out the name."

"Some guy named Campisi."

"Campisi? From over in Canby Park?" Jimmy asked. "That son of a bitch knows me. Why didn't he come to me first?"

"I've got no idea why he didn't come to you, but don't try cutting me out. I gave you the lead."

Jimmy brushed his hand in the air. "Don't worry. I'm not interested in cutting anybody out. I'm just wondering why he didn't come to me."

"That whole family is a bunch of degenerates," I muttered. "I know all of them, and they're the same. Those sons of bitches are the reason I did ten years."

"If I recall, Nicky, you killed one of them," Knuckles said.

"Self-defense," I said. "Anyway, Knucks, it's your bet, so stop slowing down the game. And Jimmy, it's up to you, but I wouldn't do business with any of them."

"Hey, Nicky. In my business, you don't get to deal with society's elite." Gem turned to the newcomer. "What's this platinum ring holding?"

"Two carats from what I heard," the guy said.

Jimmy nodded. "All right. Send him over, and if it works out, I'll send your cut to Doggs—*after* I get rid of the ring."

"How long will that take? To get rid of it, I mean."

"As long as it takes," the Gem said. "Doggs will let you know."

The guy nodded. "Just askin'. No need to get worked up."

I continued to have a run of good cards, but then they turned a little. A little later, I decided it was time to quit—it was almost midnight, and I was up over five hundred. I called Doggs to cash in, figuring it wasn't going to get much better. Five hundred made it a good night. Even Angie would be happy—and Dante would be ecstatic.

Charlie looked at his watch. "Hey, Nicky, where you going so early; it ain't even midnight. You gotta give us a chance to win some back."

"You lost your shot at that when you charged for my seat, Knuckles." I stood and pushed the chair back. "See you guys next time."

"You won't have that seat next time," Knuckles said. "I'll make sure of that."

I smiled. "I like that seat, Knuckles. It's been good to me. But it won't matter where I sit, I'll still take your money." I laughed and pinched his cheek. "See you at the next game."

It was a nice night, and I'd won big, so I drove around for a few minutes to enjoy the fresh air. After about twenty minutes, I went home and sneaked into the house so I didn't wake anyone.

Chapter Three

MROZINSKI INVESTIGATES

Detective Ed Mrozinski stood in line waiting for coffee. It was one of those mornings when coffee was badly needed—even this coffee—and his impatience was being tested. Given the option, he'd have preferred good coffee, but that wasn't an option, at least not on the way to the office.

His phone vibrated, reminding him he had to turn the ringer on. Mrozinski looked at the Caller ID, saw it was the station, and answered it. "Detective Mrozinski."

"Detective, this is Peterson at the front desk. We've got a body, and you're up."

"Shit, that figures. The last thing I needed today was a body. Where is it, Peterson?"

"Canby Park. In the woods, halfway between the softball fields and the houses where the woods are thickest. And from what I hear, it's a mess."

"All right. I'm on my way. Tell Viola to meet me there. And in the future, at least wait until I'm done my coffee for Christ's sake."

"I hear you," Peterson said. "What should I tell them about how long you're going to be?"

"No more than twenty minutes. And remind whoever's first on the scene not to touch anything. Last thing I need is a rookie ruining the crime scene."

"Got it, Detective. I'll call Maddy now."

Detective Maddy Viola was at the scene by the time Mrozinski arrived.

"Hey, Ed. How's it going?"

"Par for the course. If you count looking at dead bodies first thing in the morning as normal. By the way, how the hell did you get here so quick?"

"I was close when Peterson called. I even skipped coffee, which you'll have to make up for as soon as we leave here."

Mrozinski approached the body, then bent down to get a closer look. "Holy shit! That's Paul Campisi."

Maddy moved closer. "Damn, Ed. You're right. I didn't notice at first, but then again I didn't know him that well."

"Understandable, Maddy. He never was one to stand out from the crowd, and considering how mangled his face is, it would be difficult for someone who *did* know him well." Mrozinski walked away from the crime scene, kicked the dirt, and cursed.

"What's the matter?" Maddy asked.

"What's the matter is that him being a Campisi raises our suspect list at least tenfold. *Nobody* likes the Campisis."

"Somebody had to not like him a hell of a lot to beat him like this."

The medical examiner arrived, walking through the woods from Canby Park. "Good morning, Detective."

"It might be a good morning for you, Fred, but not for Paul Campisi. And it's going to make things difficult because his brothers are hotheads."

"I presume you're implying you need results quickly. Is that right, Detective?"

Mrozinski smiled. "That's why I like working with you, Doc. And yes, you're right. If I don't do something to show we're progressing on this case quickly, his brothers will do their own manner of investigating."

"I'll have something as soon as I can. Now, let me get to work. Gathering DNA in a setting like this isn't easy."

"All right. We'll leave you to it. Maddy and I have to notify the family, anyway."

Mrozinski and Maddy walked to her car since it was parked closer than his, and she drove to the Campisis' house.

"The brothers are Freddy and Chooch," Mrozinski said. "Paul was the oldest and probably the calmest. The other two are hotheads."

"What are they into?" Maddy asked.

"Damn near everything," Mrozinski said. "Gambling, soft porn, bookmaking, and almost anything else you can think of. I'm not sure about drugs, but I've heard they dabble in it."

"So a nasty bunch no matter how you look at it."

"Exactly," Mrozinski said, then pointed to the side. "Don't go over the bridge, Viola. Turn left just before you get there. They live halfway down the block on the left. And when we get there, let *me* do the talking."

"You'll get no argument from me," Maddy said. "I hate doing notifications."

"Pull over," Mrozinski said. "It's right there, the fifth house on the left."

Maddy pulled to the curb, then they both got out and walked to the door. Mrozinski knocked lightly at first, then harder. He raised his hand to knock again when the door opened.

"Mrozinski, what the hell do you want?"

"Nice to see you too, Chooch. But I'm here on a serious matter."

Chooch turned to look at the clock on the wall. "Ain't nothin' serious this time of the morning."

"*This* is, Chooch. We found Paul dead this morning."

"What? Paulie dead? Where? How?"

Freddy came into the living room wearing boxers and a T-shirt. "What's going on, Chooch? Mrozinski, what are you doing here?"

"I'm here with my partner, Maddy Viola," Mrozinski said. "We came to tell you—Paulie's dead."

"Dead? How?" Freddy asked.

"We found him in the woods," Mrozinski said. "It looks like he was on his way home. He was halfway between the softball field and here."

"Son of a bitch," Freddy said. "We shouldn't have let him walk home."

"Who would do this?" Chooch asked. "I mean to Paulie? He was a nice guy."

"Back up a minute," Mrozinski said. "Freddy, what did you mean when you said 'We shouldn't have let him walk home'?"

"We were at Manko's, up on Fourth Street. Paulie was hammered and wanted to drive, so we took his keys and said if he wanted to go home he'd have to come with us or walk. He opted for the latter." Freddy shook his head. "Damn, I shouldn't have let him do it."

"You couldn't have known," Mrozinski said. "About what time did he leave?"

"I'm not positive. We left somewhere around midnight," Chooch said. "I remember checking my watch right after we left."

"What about you, Freddy? What time did you leave?"

"About the same time," Freddy said. "We normally stay till the place closes, but last night we left early. And we came straight home. When Paulie didn't come home right away, we figured he was staying till it closed."

"You know anyone who would want to do this?" Maddy asked.

"I'll do you better than that. I'll tell you who probably did it— Nicky Fusco. That son of a bitch has been after our family for more than ten years. He *killed* my oldest brother, for Christ's sake. And

I'm not sure he didn't have something to do with Bobby being killed. It's either him or that asshole Donovan."

"Did Nicky have anything against Paul?" Mrozinski asked.

"He didn't need a reason; he had something against all of us," Chooch said. "If your name is Campisi, he doesn't like you."

"Yeah," Freddy said. "And it's because he had to go to prison for killing my brother. He blames all of us for that."

"How'd Paulie die?" Chooch asked.

Mrozinski took a deep breath. "It appears as if he was beaten to death with something—a club, a stick—"

"A bat," Freddy said. "I'll bet ten bucks it was a bat."

"Why do you say that?" Maddy asked.

"Because a baseball bat is Fusco's signature weapon. Check out the guys he killed in Brooklyn a few years back."

"That wasn't Nicky," Mrozinski said. "He was never charged for those murders."

"Bullshit," Chooch said. "Maybe the law said it wasn't him, but it was him. Everybody knows. The only reason he wasn't charged is because his buddy, Donovan, was the detective doing the investigating."

"I've got to go with what the law says, Freddy, so if you think of anything else, let me know." Mrozinski handed a card to Chooch. "You can always reach me on the cell number."

"Like it'll do any fuckin' good," Chooch said.

"Just call me if you get anything," Mrozinski said, then he left.

Maddy opened the car door and slid into the passenger seat. "All right, Mrozinski, what now? The brothers didn't seem to know anything—as we suspected—so where do we start?"

"We do the normal investigative process until we hear from the medical examiner. If the report is as I expect, we then need to get some information from Brooklyn."

"And how do we do that? I know law enforcement agencies are supposed to cooperate, but they don't have a strong track record of doing that. Besides, what do you expect to find in Brooklyn?"

"As far as the cooperation, I know a detective in Brooklyn. He'll help. And as far as what I expect to find, that depends on Dr. Frederick's report. It might confirm things or it might not."

Maddy looked sideways at Mrozinski. "You think Fusco had something to do with this?"

Mrozinski shook his head. "Not necessarily, but I can't ignore facts, and the crime scene indicates he may have had something to do with it, not to mention what the brothers said—that he hated them."

"I don't know, Mrozinski, I've heard Fusco's a pretty square guy."

Mrozinski looked at Maddy and narrowed his eyes. "Depends on your definition of *square*. There are plenty of rumors about Fusco, and more than a few mention him killing people. I strongly suspect he killed more than a few when he and Monroe looked into that kidnapping case a while back."

Maddy took a sip from her bottle of water. "From what I heard of that case, I don't know if I'd blame him. Sounded like pretty nasty people were involved."

"I won't argue that," Mrozinski said, "but killing is killing, and he's been mentioned too many times in the company of dead bodies. All the murders seem justified, but there comes a time when you have to wonder."

"So we just wait on the coroner's report?"

"Not entirely," Mrozinski said. "While we wait, let's talk to the bartender where Paulie was and see if we can round up any customers who can help."

Twenty minutes later, Mrozinski parked in front of Manko's. He held the door open for Maddy, then they approached the bar.

Stan, the owner and bartender, was rinsing glasses. Maddy laid her badge on the bar. "Who was on duty last night?" she asked.

"I was. Why?"

Mrozinski showed his badge as well. "Detectives Mrozinski and—"

"I know who you are. Put the badges away. I don't want to chase away the few customers I have."

Mrozinski looked around. "If anybody's here at this time of day, I doubt they'd be scared by a badge."

"You're probably right, but let's play it safe. Tell me what you want."

Mrozinski leaned on the bar and whispered. "One of your customers—Paul Campisi—was killed after he left here."

"Whoa! I told his brothers to take his keys. If they didn't do it, it's not my fault. Besides, he . . . hey, wait a minute, his brothers *did* take his keys, and he stayed here drinking. I remember now."

"Let me rephrase my statement. Paulie was murdered. Someone beat him to death."

"No shit? Where'd this happen?"

"In the woods near the back of Canby Park. It looks like he was on his way home."

The bartender shook his head. "Son of a bitch! I knew Paulie could be an ass, but he wasn't *that* much of an ass."

"How drunk was he when he left?"

"Pretty damn drunk. He could barely walk, which is why I told his brothers to take the keys."

"He have any trouble with anyone when he was here?" Maddy asked.

The bartender shook his head. "I didn't see him piss anyone off. He didn't even argue with his brothers, and he almost always argues with them."

Maddy looked to Mrozinski, who nodded. "All right, that's all for now. If we have other questions, we'll be back."

"I'm here six days a week. Stop by anytime."

The bartender hollered to Mrozinski as he opened the door to leave. "Hey, Detective. Wait a minute."

"What?"

"It's probably nothing, but Paulie was pestering this one lady all night—hitting on her every chance he got. And she was with a pretty big guy who didn't look happy about the attention Paulie was giving her."

Mrozinski stepped back toward the bar with renewed interest. "Did you see an exchange of words between the two?

"I didn't see anything, but the guy and Janice—that's her name—left shortly after Paul did."

"Describe shortly," Maddy said.

Stan shook his head. "I don't know. Two, maybe three minutes. It wasn't long."

"You got her name? Or his?"

"I just told you, her name's Janice, but I don't know her last name. His, I don't know at all. They're usually in here two or three nights a week, though. Stop by on a Saturday night and you're bound to catch them." The bartender pointed to a table near the corner. "Usually somewhere over there."

————

"He was a help," Maddy said once they were back in the car. "More than I expected."

"I don't know," Mrozinski said. "If we buy what he said, it rules out everyone at the bar as obvious suspects. Or at least as suspects with obvious motives. Except Janice's boyfriend, of course."

"Checking on Janice and the guy who accompanied her gives us a date for Saturday night, but what besides that?" Maddy asked.

"Digging into Paul's life and waiting on Fred. So let's get back to the station and start digging."

Chapter Four

WANT TO PLAY SOME CARDS?

Tommy Nicks shuffled the deck, then dealt the hand. "Texas Hold 'em," he said. "Ante's five dollars and the blinds are ten and twenty."

The betting started with Sammy Socks, who called, then Ruffio raised fifty. The fifty-dollar bet prompted three folds, followed by a raise of a hundred by Alphonse.

"Christ's sake, Al, whataya got?"

"It only takes another one-fifty to find out, Sammy. You got the chips in front of you. Make the call." Al laughed, then mumbled. "Make the call or shut up."

Sammy looked like he was deciding whether to call when the door opened, and two masked men walked in. Both held guns.

The smaller of the two men pointed his gun from one player to the next. "Don't make any stupid moves. If you do, I'll have to shoot. And make no doubt about it, I will shoot. Now, put the money in a bag," the smaller guy said.

"All the money," the other one said. "And do it quickly or I'll do the shooting."

Sammy Socks glared at them. "You know what you're doin'? You know whose game this is?"

"I know whose game this is, and if I were you, I'd just worry about doing what I said. Now put the damn money in the bag."

The men stuffed wads of cash into a few paper bags and handed them to the robbers. "Don't forget the house money," the big man said.

It took a few more minutes for Sammy to load the bag, then the two robbers collected the money, tied everyone up, and left.

———

After leaving the card game, they rushed to the car, got in, and drove toward Red Hook.

"Why you goin' this way?" the smaller guy asked.

"Because we're not finished. We got one more stop, *then* we'll be done."

"Another game?"

The big man shook his head. "Bucky's joint. I heard he's got two days' worth, and it's all there for the taking."

A half-hour later they parked outside a bodega in Red Hook. "Put on the mask," the big guy said. Afterward, they walked inside and up to the counter, each of them pointing a gun.

The man behind the counter raised his hands and backed away from the register. "Take whatever you want. I don't need any trouble."

"And you won't get any trouble if you get the bag you have in the back room. You know which one—the one with all Manny's money in it."

The guy shook his head. "I don't—"

The big man shot him in the arm, near the shoulder. "Get it

now, or the next shot will cripple you, and the one after that will kill you."

"Okay, okay," he said. "I'm going back there now." He held his arm while walking toward the back room. "I'll only be a minute."

"Good. And if you're thinking of coming out of that room with anything but that bag, think again. There are two of us and we'll have the guns trained on you."

"I won't," he said. "Don't worry."

A moment later, he returned carrying a plain brown paper bag which looked to be filled with something.

"That it?" the big guy asked.

"This is all of it," he said. "You're lucky because it's two day's worth. They didn't pick it up yesterday."

The big guy laughed. "I guess it's our lucky night. Shame it isn't yours." After saying that, he fired two shots into the man, dropping him where he stood. He thought of ransacking the place but decided not to waste the time.

"Let's get out of here," the smaller guy said, and ran for the door.

———

Giorgio got a call from Sammy Socks around midnight. "Sammy, what's up?"

"Somebody hit the fuckin' game, Giorgio. Got everybody's bankroll and the house money too."

Giorgio slammed his fist on the counter. "Son of a bitch!"

"You better get ready to hit something else," Sammy said. "I just got a call from one of the bookies in Red Hook. He went to Bucky's to lay off a big bet, and he found Bucky dead, which makes me guess the bag is gone."

"Manny's gonna shit," Giorgio said.

"That's why I called you. I didn't want to be the one to tell him."

"I hear you, Sammy."

"So you gonna take care of it for me?"

"Yeah, I'll tell him," Giorgio said. "I'll call him right now."

He disconnected the call and dialed Manny. After half a dozen rings, he answered. "Manny, it's Giorgio. I'm sorry if you were sleeping."

"I wasn't sleeping; I was taking a piss. Christ, it's the middle of the day. But what's up? Why are you calling?"

"A bag drop was hit in Red Hook—Bucky's joint—and it sounds like the same guys hit Sammy's game maybe an hour before."

"Son of a bitch. Was it Joey?"

"I made a few calls after I heard. Turk thinks it might have been Joey. He got the call on the bodega, and witnesses in the neighborhood said there were two of them, and one had big fat hands."

"Anybody hurt?"

"Bucky's dead."

Manny slammed his fist against the wall. "That does it. 'Fat Fingers' Joey is dead."

"I thought we were giving shit like this to the cops now?"

"Fuck that. They broke the rules. Robbing the game was bad enough, but killing Bucky was uncalled for."

"Boss, I hear you, but I still think it would be better to turn it over to the cops. Hell, it's their job. Let them do the shit work. We can provide the clues if we have to, but let them handle the day-to-day stuff; besides, we don't know for sure it's Joey yet. We can't act until we know."

"I'll see about letting the cops handle this," Manny said. "It depends on how they respond. In the meantime, tell everyone to be on the lookout. I want Joey yesterday."

"You got it, boss, but just remember, we don't know for sure if it was Joey."

"I'm pretty damn sure. I'm sure enough to have him hunted down even if I don't kill him yet."

"Got it," Giorgio said. "And sorry I called this late, but I figured you'd want to know."

"You did good, Giorgio. Now get some sleep so you can find this prick for me. You don't have to take him out yet, but I want him found."

"I'll find him, Manny. Goodnight."

———

E arly in the morning, Manny called Sammy Socks. "Why didn't you call me when the game was robbed?"

"Manny, I'm sorry. I called Giorgio right away."

"What? He's got a shorter number than me? How come you called him and not me?"

"I didn't know if you were sleeping or not, and I didn't want to wake you," Sammy said.

"You knew damn right well I wasn't sleeping, but at least that answer saved your ass. From now on, anything happens, you call *me*. Not Giorgio or anyone else. Got it? And I don't give a shit what time of night it is."

"Got it."

"Good. Now get your ass busy and put everybody you got on the streets to find 'Fat Fingers' Joey. I know we aren't sure he did it yet, but I'd bet on it. And I'd bet he's hiding in the Bronx, or maybe Queens, so if you have any connections there, use 'em."

"The Bronx? What about Dominic?"

"I'll call Dominic in a little bit. He needs to know we got men looking there, and I'll see if he'll pitch in a couple pair of eyes, but don't count on it. Get busy and look on your own."

"Okay, Manny. We'll get Joey. Don't worry."

"I'm not worried. I just want him. Did he get all the money?"

"All of it," Sammy said. "House money too."

"Son of a bitch. His death just went from painless to excruciatingly painful."

Chapter Five

THE REPORT

Mrozinski got in early and gathered the files he had on the Campisi brothers. The files were full, but most of the information dealt with Paul's brothers—Freddy and Chooch. Paul had kept a clean profile.

The door opened and Maddy walked in. "Find anything interesting?"

Mrozinski shook his head and frowned. "In twenty-five years, he's had nothing more than a few traffic tickets. I can't see anything worth killing over. Hell, nothing even close."

"Who can tell what's worth killing over these days?" Maddy asked. "I've seen kids kill other kids over sneakers or sunglasses."

"But that's kids killing other kids," Mrozinski said. "I haven't seen adults do anything like that. I've seen some crazy drug crimes, but not ordinary people who were clean and sober. Not even drunks. Paul's brothers have done some things that may have warranted killing for, but not him."

"Maybe somebody made a mistake and took him for one of his brothers," Maddy said.

"Not a chance," Mrozinski said. "You saw his brothers. They

don't look anything like him, and you didn't need daylight to notice it."

The phone rang as Maddy started to speak. Mrozinski picked it up. "Hello?"

"Detective, it's Doctor—"

"Yeah, it's me, Doc. You got anything for us yet?"

"I can tell you he was beaten to death with a club-like object. Beaten beyond what was necessary, which indicates—or at least *could* indicate—it was personal."

"It looked like as much," Mrozinski said, then, "Fred, I'm going to put this on speaker so Maddy can hear. That okay?"

"Sure, go ahead."

"Okay, back to the weapon," Mrozinski asked. "Could it have been a baseball bat?"

"Not only could have, but it probably was. I didn't want to say until I was sure."

"What else?"

"Toxicology results aren't back yet, so I've got nothing there. And I don't have DNA, but I can tell you there are samples from more than a couple of people. Far more than necessary and far more than what is ordinarily found."

"More than a couple? What's that tell you?" Mrozinski asked.

"It tells me he was beaten by a gang of thugs or by a person who was smart enough to plant DNA evidence to cover up his own. It's difficult to commit such a violent crime without leaving *some* evidence, but if there are traces of evidence from a lot of people, that leaves nothing to go on."

Mrozinski nodded. "That's what I thought. Okay. Call when you get the toxicology or if anything else develops. And thanks for rushing this?"

Mrozinski almost hung up, but then he remembered something he wanted to ask. "Doc, you still there?"

"I'm here, Detective. What do you need?"

"At the scene, I noticed he was shot? What about that?"

"I almost forgot," the doc said. "He was shot in the head and chest. One shot each."

"Okay, thanks, Doc." Mrozinski hung up and leaned back in the chair. "Shit."

"Something wrong, Ed?" Maddy asked.

"What's wrong is it looks as if I have to make that call to Brooklyn after all."

"I'm sure he'll help," Maddy said.

Mrozinski laughed under his breath. "I'm *not* so sure. He's Fusco's best friend."

"You want me to make the call?"

"No, he doesn't know you, but he does know me, for all the good that will do." Mrozinski picked up the phone. "Might as well get it done."

Mrozinski dialed the number and waited while it rang.

"Donovan."

"Frankie, it's Ed Mrozinski."

"Mrozinski, what's up?"

"Paulie Campisi was murdered last night."

"No shit. Well, if you're asking, I didn't do it. I've got an alibi—my boss."

Mrozinski laughed again. "I didn't suspect you, Frankie, but I did need a favor."

"Anything. What do you need?"

"Remember those killings a few years ago in Brooklyn? The ones—"

"Hold on, Mrozinski. There's no way Nicky did this. It's not his way."

"From the looks of it so far, it's *exactly* his way. Beaten with a baseball bat, shot in the head and chest, and excessive DNA evidence. That fits doesn't it?"

"That might seem like it fits the killings here in Brooklyn, but it doesn't fit Nicky. He wouldn't do it."

"Frankie, do I get the files or not? I can go above you if I have to."

"Assume you have to, Mrozinski. I'll be damned if I'm going to help you frame my best friend."

Mrozinski sighed. "Frankie, I'm not trying to frame him. I want the files to try to clear him. I don't think it was Nicky, but I can't ignore the evidence."

"Just follow what evidence you have. You'll find out who did it."

Mrozinski cursed. "Would you do that, Frankie?"

Mrozinski heard a sound as if Frankie banged his fist on the desk. "All right, you son of a bitch, I'll send them down, but you better keep me posted on everything. I mean *everything*."

"You got it, Frankie. Thanks."

"I'll gather the files and send the package overnight. And remember, Nicky was *not* convicted of these crimes."

Mrozinski hung up and filled Maddy in on the conversation in case she missed any.

"How did Fusco get out so soon?" Maddy asked.

"He wasn't convicted of any crime," Mrozinski said. "Someone else was blamed, but everyone knows Fusco did it, just like I know he killed those people in California and the people who kidnapped Borelli's kid a few years back."

"Those killings up in Hockessin?"

"They're the ones."

"From what I heard, they were justifiable as well. A bunch of drug dealers, weren't they?"

"Maybe they were," Mrozinski said. "But there have been too many so-called *justifiable* killings involving Fusco. It's got to stop somewhere."

"Then I guess we go see Fusco," Maddy said.

Mrozinski gave her a sideways glance. "I doubt this is going to be a pleasant visit. You want to sit it out?"

"Not a chance. I'm coming. Hell, I'll even take the lead if you want."

Mrozinski chuckled. "Don't act so eager. Fusco may come

across like a nice guy, but he's probably killed a dozen or more people. He's as cold-blooded as they come, and he's more dangerous than any man I know."

Maddy narrowed her eyes. "I met him. He can't be *that* bad."

Mrozinski stopped and stared. "Maddy, he's so dangerous that his daughter can't even get mugged. From what I heard, a couple of guys tried, but when they found out who it was, they gave her back what they took."

"Get out of here!"

"Swear to God," Mrozinski said as he crossed his heart. "And this was down in Monroe's territory."

"Christ's sake," Maddy said. "This is a hell of a way to start a murder investigation."

"No shit," Mrozinski said. "Put on your fireproof suit and let's step into the lion's den."

Chapter Six

WHO ROBBED THE BODEGA?

Morreau poked his head into the coffee room. "Donovan and Miller. My office. We've got a body, and you're up."

"What's up?" Frankie asked.

"They found a body in Red Hook, the owner of a bodega there. See me for the details."

A few moments later, Frankie and Sherri entered Morreau's office and took a seat. "Other than being the owner of the bodega, do we know who this body belongs to?" Frankie asked.

"Don't know the name," Moreau said, "but he is—or was—the owner of the Roots and Chutes bodega just inside the Red Hook border south of Park Slope."

"Robbery?" Sherri asked.

"Don't know that either," Morreau said. "That's why I have detectives." He smiled and handed Frankie a folder. "Now get out there and find out."

. . .

Frankie drove past Prospect Park, then south into Red Hook. It wasn't hard to spot the crime scene due to the crowd that had already gathered.

Miller pointed to the side. "Must be there. Either that or someone's handing out free breakfasts."

Frankie and Miller pulled to the curb in front of the bodega and got out of the car.

"Must be fifty people here," Sherri said.

"Any bets on how many know anything?"

"Don't be so cynical, Donovan; you might be surprised."

Frankie chuckled. "Miller, the last time I was surprised by something on this job was on my first day when I believed people would actually cooperate. Since then, I've been suspicious." Frankie reached to light a cigarette, then put it away. "My guess is we've got fifty blind people and at least thirty deaf ones."

Sherri shut the car door and stepped to the curb. "I hope I don't become a cynic like you, Donovan. I prefer to remain an optimist and stay happy."

"A few more years on this job, and you'll lose some of that optimism. My guess is you'll probably let a little cynicism creep into your system too."

"We'll see," Sherri said. "In the meantime, let's talk to a few of these *blind* people."

Frankie grabbed her by the elbow and whispered. "Let's check out the crime scene first. At least then we'll know what questions to ask."

"I just wanted to make sure we got everybody that's here before they disappear."

"Don't worry about it," Frankie said. "When a local bodega owner dies, the crowds will hang around until we disperse them. There will be plenty of time."

Frankie and Sherri walked into the bodega, flashing their badges for the officers on the scene to see. "Where's the body?" Frankie asked.

An officer standing by the counter pointed toward the floor behind it. "Down there."

Frankie walked behind the cash register and knelt next to the body. He looked up at Sherri. "Looks like three in the chest. And from the way the body's positioned, it looks like he was coming in from the back room. Anybody check it?" he asked the officer.

"We did, sir. Didn't find anything. Didn't see any signs of struggle either."

Frankie looked to Sherri and gestured to the register. "Check it out, but be careful in case they didn't wipe it clean."

Miller used gloves to open the register. "All the cash is in there, Frankie. It doesn't look like they took anything. There are tens and twenties galore."

Frankie stood and nodded. "I'm not surprised."

Sherri appeared confused. "Not surprised? Why's that?"

"No signs of struggle or resistance. And it's bad business to kill a bodega owner, even for a junkie. I figure this guy must have been running a drop, and somebody popped him for the bag."

Sherri shook her head. "Donovan, you're talking to an ex-drug cop here. You're gonna have to speak English."

"If I'm right, this bodega was serving as a drop-off for illegal gambling money—numbers runners and such. That means that every day, the runners dropped off a bag of money for him to hold until it was picked up by one of the boss's men. Considering the location, I'm guessing that means one of Manny's men."

"Who the hell would be stupid enough to hit one of Manny's places?"

Frankie nodded. "That's what we need to find out before Manny does. If not, there will be no one to convict."

Frankie grabbed Sherri by the elbow again and tugged her arm. "You wanted to interview people? Well, now's the time we talk to the hungry masses."

Three young teenagers craned their necks from the front row of onlookers. Frankie leaned in toward what appeared to be the oldest one. "You see anything?"

He shook his head. "Can't see shit from here. Got all them cops in the way."

"I meant did you see anything before the cops got here? Anybody coming and going that wasn't from the neighborhood? Anybody who looked like they didn't belong?"

"There was—" the younger of the youths said.

The older kid kicked him. "Shut up, dude."

Frankie glanced at Sherri and nodded, then she took the younger boy to the side. Frankie pulled out a pack of cigarettes and offered one to each of the boys left with him. "Want one?"

They each grabbed a smoke and lit it. "Don't think this buys you shit," the older one said.

"You got that right," said the other.

"I wasn't trying to buy a damn thing," Frankie said. "I was just trying to figure out why anyone would want to kill old Juan."

"Bucky," the older one said. "His name was Bucky."

"So you knew him?" Frankie asked.

"We knew him," the other one said. "He was a nice guy too. Never did you wrong."

"Used to let us charge our smokes until we got the green to pay for them."

Frankie tossed his smoke to the ground and crushed it out. "That sucks. Seems like the good ones always get screwed. I'd like to get the pricks that did this. I'd—"

"You need to be lookin' for a big guy with a beard," said the older kid. "A heavy beard. Not long, but thick. Real thick."

"You think he shot him?"

"No, but he might know who did. He came by here almost every day. He seemed okay, but I didn't trust him. He used to come here, talk to Bucky for a while, then walk out carrying a bag. I asked

Bucky about him once, but Bucky just said forget I saw him, so I did."

Frankie pulled out another smoke and lit it, then offered more to the kids, which they took. "You think he did this to Bucky? If he did, his ass is mine."

Both kids shook their heads. "No way. I think he had something going on with Bucky. Maybe drugs. I don't know. But he came out here the day before yesterday, and I ain't seen him since."

Frankie inhaled a long drag and blew it out. "Okay, thanks. I'm gonna get this son of a bitch if it's the last thing I do. He handed out a card. If you hear anything, call. I'll make sure there's something in it for you. And if you get tangled up in anything small, you can use it too, but nothing major. Got it?"

Their eyes lit up like Christmas morning. "Shit, dude, you got it. Thanks."

Sherri walked away from the younger boy she'd been talking to and met Frankie, who was heading toward the car.

"Anything?" she asked.

"Big guy with a heavy beard," Frankie said.

Sherri nodded. "At least they're on the same page. I got the same, only mine said short, thick beard."

Frankie looked over at her. "Dark?"

"Dark," she said. "Let's go find him."

"I'm game, but where do we start? You gotta help me out, Donovan. I'm used to drugs, but this is new to me."

Frankie laughed. "There's not much to learn, Miller. If this was Manny's drop that was hit, there's only one place to start—Manny's house. He'll be three steps ahead of us by now, but if we're lucky, he'll cooperate."

Sherri looked at Donovan as if he were crazy. "What? You're not considering working with a gangster?"

"Hell no, Miller. I'm not *considering* it, I've already made up my mind. We're going there for breakfast."

"Going where?

"To Manny's house. Where else? Besides, he makes the best espresso in Brooklyn outside of Cataldi's. And his biscotti are to die for."

Chapter Seven

MANNY GETS HIS MAN

Giorgio took three men, and Sammy Socks took three, and they drove to the Bronx. They started by searching the coffee shops, and it wasn't long before one of Giorgio's men got a lead from a cafe on Arthur Avenue.

"I heard he was in Queens," Nino said. "And it wouldn't surprise me 'cause he ran with some mick from that part of town."

"How'd you get the info?" Giorgio asked.

"A friend of his was sittin' at a table near the back. I heard him talkin' on the phone to somebody. He was so damn loud I almost had to tell him to keep it down."

"He spot you?"

Nino shook his head. "He went straight to reading the paper when he hung up, then he left right after."

"Okay, good. We'll check it out. You did good, Nino. I'll make sure to put in a word."

Nino handed Giorgio an espresso. "Take this. And I'll make sure to give you a call if I see him again. Even if I hear anything."

For two days, Giorgio methodically went through Queens, stopping at one cafe after another and grilling the owners on Joey's whereabouts, but no one seemed to know anything. More than likely, they knew, but just weren't saying.

Giorgio knew how it worked. It was difficult to pry information out of anyone, but it was especially hard if the information was going to be used to rat someone out. Ratting out put people in a tough spot. If the cops got the person you ratted on, it likely meant prison, and if the mob got them, it likely meant death. Manny had a good shot at getting what he wanted because of who he was. The cops had no shot at all—not in this neighborhood.

———

On day three, shortly after ten, "Fat Fingers" Joey walked outside a cafe he was known to frequent while in Queens. He turned left, then saw Giorgio and reached for his pocket. Before he could make it, Giorgio pulled a gun and pointed it toward his head. "Don't try it, Joey. I'll put you down right here. Manny won't like it, but I'll do it."

"Okay," Joey said. "Gun's in the right pocket."

"Good decision," Giorgio said. "Who did the jobs with you?"

"You know I can't tell you that."

"You'll tell me, or you'll tell Manny, but you'll talk to one of us."

"Ain't happening," Joey said.

"We'll see," Giorgio said, and poked the gun in his back. "Car's across the street. Let's get going before somebody wonders why I'm holding a gun on you."

"You let me go, there's something in it for you. Could mean a lot."

Giorgio laughed. "If I let you go, Manny will cut off my balls, so I think I'll pass. I like my balls where they are."

"Hear me out, Giorgio."

"No thanks, Joey, and I don't want to hear another word until we get to Manny's."

Giorgio pulled his phone out and dialed. "Manny, we got him."

"Where'd you find him, the Bronx?"

"No, he was in Queens. I got him in the car, and I got three guys with me."

"Take him to the seaside warehouse, not my place. I'll leave in a few minutes."

"Okay, got it. See you in about an hour if traffic isn't too bad."

"I'll be waiting," Manny said. "Tell 'Fat Fingers' Joey his fingers won't be so fat when I'm through with him."

An hour later, Giorgio pulled up to an abandoned warehouse Manny often used. He bought the warehouse for near nothing from a guy who owed him money, and now he was getting a tax break on it because he was renovating it. The renovations didn't amount to much, no more than a coat of paint on a few of the walls now and then and fixing holes in the parking lot after a hard winter.

Giorgio pulled up to the garage door and beeped his horn. The door opened, and he drove in, then got Joey out. Manny greeted them with a smile.

"Joey, you're lookin' good. You won't be for long, so be happy that you are now."

"Manny, what are you gonna do? You know what I did was just business."

Manny patted his shoulder. "I know, Joey. I know. What I'm going to do is just business too." He nodded to a couple of guys standing beside him, and they grabbed Joey's hands and placed them on a wooden table. Another guy hammered nails through Joey's palms to secure them. Afterward, Manny used a meat cleaver to chop off his fingers. He did them one at a time to prolong the pain.

Halfway through the process, Manny held up a finger and laughed. "Looks like a damn sausage. Maybe I should put it in my sauce."

Joey screamed the whole time, but no one could hear him. Finally, Manny nodded. "Get rid of him. Make sure he's not found. And remove his teeth in case you fuck up, and he is found. I don't want anyone knowing who he is."

"You got it," Giorgio said. "Anything else?"

"Yeah," Manny said. "Find out where he hid the money and send it to his wife. No sense her suffering more than she has to."

Giorgio pulled the nails out of Joey's hands, him screaming each time one was removed. Afterward, they led him to a car and opened the door. "Get in, Joey. Time to go."

Joey lowered his head to get in the back seat. "Between moans of pain, Joey asked, "Giorgio, you think he meant that about giving my wife the money?"

Giorgio nodded. "Manny's a good guy. He'll give it to her. As far as he's concerned, he already lost it."

"All right, my cut is in a safe-deposit box at Central Bank, downtown. She can access it with the key in my right pocket."

"Won't she need you to get in?"

Joey shook his head. "It was opened years ago in both our names. She probably forgot we even had it."

"All right, Joey, sit tight. It's time to go."

"Hey, Giorgio, make sure I'm dead before you take out the teeth. Can you do that?"

"Consider it done, Joey. Now sit back and relax."

Joey leaned back on the headrest, and a moment later, Giorgio put two bullets in his head. "Drive over the bridge to Jersey," he said. "We need to get rid of this body."

"What about the car?"

"We'll dump him, then go somewhere and call somebody to pick us up. I don't want nobody knowing where the body is."

Chapter Eight

AN INITIAL INTERVIEW

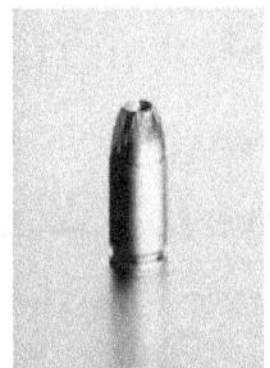

S heila knocked on the door, then opened it. "Mr. Fusco, there are two detectives here to see you."

"Show them in, please."

I was sitting behind my desk when Mrozinski and Maddy entered. "Nicky, good to see you again," Mrozinski said, as if we were old friends.

I knew why he stopped by, though. "You selling girl-scout cookies, Mrozinski, or are you here about Paulie Campisi?"

Mrozinski appeared surprised. "How'd you hear?"

"Come on, Mrozinski. Not much goes on that Doggs doesn't hear about, which means Knuckles and the Gem and a lot of others know. In other words, not much goes on that I don't hear about. So what's up? What do you want to know?"

"An alibi would be a good start. It was somewhere around midnight."

"I was playing cards till just before midnight, then I went for a short drive—fifteen or twenty minutes—then home. And no, nobody can verify that because my wife and kids were asleep when I got home."

"Shit! An airtight alibi would have made this easier. I was hoping you'd have one. At the very least *some* kind of alibi."

"Sorry to disappoint you, Mrozinski. Why? What's up?"

"Everybody knows there's bad blood between you and the Campisis. With you not having an alibi, it hurts but, as bad as that looks, the details of the crime scene make it worse. The coroner will verify it when he's done, but it looks as if Campisi was beaten to death with a baseball bat, and a surplus of DNA evidence was left at the scene. And he was shot in the head and chest."

I nodded. "So you're thinking Brooklyn?"

"I'd be a piss-poor detective if I *didn't* think Brooklyn."

"I wasn't convicted of those crimes, Mrozinski, and you know that."

"I also noted you said you 'weren't convicted,' not you didn't do them."

"Would you have believed me if I said I didn't do them?"

"Probably not."

"Then let's leave it at 'I wasn't convicted.' "

"I'd rather have your cooperation, Nicky. I don't think you did this, but I have to follow leads."

"Don't worry about leads. I'll find out who did this," I said.

"Fusco, stay out of it. This is police business."

"If I had faith in the police, I *would* stay out of it, but I have no faith, so plan on bumping into me during the investigation—if you're really conducting one."

"I'm warning you, Nicky, stay out of it."

"You said you were following leads. What brought you here to see me?"

"I already told you, there's bad blood between you and the Campisi brothers. Combine that with the way Paul was killed, and I had no choice but to stop here."

"And?"

"And Brooklyn, yeah. I wouldn't be doing my job if I didn't give it thought."

"That's bullshit, Mrozinski, and you know it. There's bad blood between the Campisi brothers and a couple dozen people. As far as Brooklyn goes, all you have are rumors. Next you'll be trying to pin Jimmy Hoffa's murder on me."

I turned and pointed to Maddy. "As for you, young lady. You should partner up with someone who might teach you how a real detective works because you sure as hell won't learn it with him."

"Fusco, I—"

"You'll have to excuse me, Detective. I have a meeting coming up. If you need to ask me anything else, make an appointment, please."

Mrozinski got up and walked toward the door. "I'm warning you, Fusco. Stay out of this."

"Warning noted, Detective. Have a nice day." I held the door as they left. "Sheila, please see the detectives out and let me know when my appointment gets here."

Maddy slid into the passenger seat just as Mrozinski put the car in gear. "Buckle up. This might be a bumpy ride."

Maddy looked over at him. "Just because you're pissed at Fusco, don't take it out on me or the car."

Mrozinski let off the gas and took a left on Fourth Street. "You're right, Maddy. I *was* pissed at Fusco. Actually, I still am."

"So where are we going?" Maddy asked.

"The smoke shop. Nicky said he was playing cards, so let's see who remembers what. I'll split up the group when we get there. You take half, and I'll take the others. We'll see if they can keep the stories straight."

"You think they will?"

Mrozinski chuckled. "I think we'll be lucky if they tell us to fuck ourselves, but it's worth a try. Stranger things have happened."

"Are these guys mobbed up?"

"We don't have much of a mob down here, and the ones we do have are like an extension of the Philly family. Those guys, however, will be at the smoke shop."

Mrozinski parked by the curb in front of the shop, then he and Maddy walked inside. He held out his badge to the guy behind the register. "I'm here to see Doggs Caputo. He in?"

The guy looked at him with suspicion, then pressed a button on the intercom. "Doggs, two cops here to see you."

"Tell them to take a fuckin' seat and wait. I'm gonna be a minute."

"Doggs, there's a woman cop with her partner."

"What the fuck do I care who's with him. Tell her to take a fuckin' seat too."

Mrozinski grabbed Maddy by the arm and led her to a chair against the wall. "Not the nicest bunch," he whispered.

Maddy smiled. "That's all right, Ed. It's not like I haven't heard the word before. I grew up with older brothers, remember?"

Five minutes later, Doggs came in, Coke-bottle glasses fogged up and sliding down the bridge of his nose. "Mrozinski? What the hell do you want?"

"I need to ask a few questions. We had a murder last night, and I need to know where Nicky Fusco was at the time."

"Nicky? Christ, he's been a saint since he got out, but you're welcome to ask away. Just know that I *do not* grant you permission to enter the back room, so if you see anything you might think of reporting, it's an illegal search." Doggs opened a door that led to a back room. He grabbed hold of Maddy's arm as she passed by. "What I told Mrozinski goes for you too," he said. "Ignore anything you might see while you're here."

Maddy nodded and followed Mrozinski inside. He pointed to a

table with two guys seated at it and tapped Maddy's shoulder. "I'll take those two; you take the two over there."

Maddy interviewed Salvatore Fonseca, also known as 'Slick Sallie,' but when she couldn't get anything out of him, she moved on to Charlie Knuckles.

"Buon giorno," Charlie said when Maddy walked up.

"Buon giorno, yourself, Charlie." She displayed her badge. "Detective Maddy Viola, Homicide."

"Viola? Viola? I knew a Viola. Your family run a pastry shop on Scott Street?"

Maddy smiled. "That's them. Been there for a long time."

"No shit about that. I used to go there when I was a kid. Must've been your grandparents running it then."

"It was. They almost closed it when *nonna* died, but then my dad took it over, and he's been running it ever since."

Knuckles eyed Maddy head to toe. "How'd you stay so thin? If I had to look at those pastries every day—tempting me all day long— I'd be as fat as Patsy the Whale was."

Maddy smiled. "It's different when you work there. You almost get sick of it."

Knuckles shook his head. "I hear what you're saying, but I don't buy it. People say the same thing about meatballs, but I can't cook a batch without eating a dozen before I'm through. Anyway, you're not here to talk about pastries or meatballs, so tell me what you want."

"Were you here last night?"

"I'm here most every night."

"Was Nicky Fusco here?"

"Who?"

Maddy cocked her head and stared. "Fusco. Nicky Fusco. I'm sure you're familiar with him."

Charlie scrunched his nose and appeared to be thinking. "I don't know no Nicky Fusco."

Maddy appeared confused. She leaned forward and looked

Knuckles in the eyes. "You have to know him. Fusco. Nicky Fusco. He's—"

Knuckles burst out laughing. "Just messin' with you. Of course I know Nicky. And yes, he was here playing cards and taking our money."

"What time did he leave?"

"Whenever he said he did."

"I don't want to know what time he said he left, I want to know what time he actually left."

Knuckles shifted in his seat, leaned forward, and whispered. "Listen, honey. You seem to be new to this, so I'll help you out. First, there ain't nobody in this joint gonna tell you anything different than what I just did. Second, Nicky Fusco don't lie. Whatever time he said he left, that's when he left."

"Oh, so Nicky's a saint?" Maddy asked.

Charlie laughed. "Far from it. He's probably closer to Satan than a saint, but he doesn't lie. You can take whatever he says to the bank."

"You must have *some* idea when he left?"

"Sure, I can help you with that. It was sometime between supper last night and breakfast this morning."

Maddy closed her notebook and stood. "Thanks for your help."

"No problem," Knuckles said. "And say hi to your folks."

Maddy leaned against the car and waited for Mrozinski. He came out five minutes later. "Get anything?" she asked.

"Probably as much as you did," he said. "That's a tight-lipped group in there."

"Did you expect anything else?" Maddy asked. "We're dealing with a bunch of dagos who are either connected or semi-connected. They're not gonna tell you who their mother is, let alone what an associate is doing."

Mrozinski opened the car door and slid behind the wheel. "I

hear what you're saying, Maddy. And I didn't expect anything else, just hoping."

"Put your hopes in your back pocket and let's figure out what we're doing next," Maddy said. "And you can start by stopping for coffee."

As Mrozinski drove down Front Street, Maddy looked over to him. "Ed, I heard you talking to those two. Why didn't you tell them that Campisi was shot in the head and heart?"

"I wanted to keep that to ourselves because that's exactly how the killings in Brooklyn were."

Maddy nodded. "So you *do* think Fusco's got something to do with it."

"I didn't say that, Maddy. I'm just not ready to rule him out as a suspect."

"Well, from what you've said, we better have a hell of a lot more than coincidence to go on if we're going after Fusco."

"Don't I know it," Mrozinski said.

Chapter Nine

NICKY NEEDS AN ALIBI

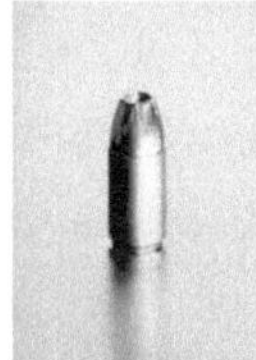

I got home from work around six, walked in the door, and ducked a few Nerf-gun bullets. "Hey, you devil, you can't ambush me. I don't even have a gun. That's not fair."

"You better get one," Dante yelled, then he shot a few more rounds, hitting me in the arm with one of the shots.

I dodged a couple more missiles, then grabbed the gun from him and set it high on the shelf. "Enough of that until after dinner. When we're done eating, you're a dead man. And this time, *I* get the living room."

Dante laughed. "That's what you think," he said, and ran upstairs.

The doorbell rang a moment later. I opened the door to see Detective Mrozinski. I was surprised to see him so soon, but I maintained composure. "What is it, Detective?"

"I had a few questions," he said.

"See me tomorrow," I said, and began to close the door.

"It can't wait, Nicky. It won't take long."

I stepped outside and closed the door. "We'll do it here," I said. "I don't want to upset the family."

"No problem. I just wanted to tell you that you need some kind of alibi. The one you gave me about the card game won't cut it."

I looked at him with my head cocked. "You talked to the guys at the game?"

"Yeah, I talked to them, but they didn't tell me anything. I mean nothing."

"Nothing? Did they say I was there?"

"Yeah, they said you were playing cards, but nobody remembered what time you left, and if they did, they weren't saying. That makes it look suspicious from my angle."

"It can look suspicious all it wants, Detective, but I told you what time I left. I could have said an hour later, and the guys would've backed that story up just as much. Do what you have to do, but I'm not changing my story. It was the truth last night, it's the truth now, and it will be the truth next week."

Mrozinski sighed. "Fusco, you know I have to follow the evidence, and so far the evidence is leading to you."

"I'm not worried, Mrozinski. I have confidence in you. Dig deep enough, and, maybe with your partner's help, you'll find out who really did this."

"Nicky, everybody knows you had a problem with the Campisi brothers. And—"

I chuckled. "If that's what you're calling a lead, you better start over. There are dozens of people who had problems with the Campisis and most of them bigger beefs than mine. Yeah, I didn't like them, but I had no problem with them, especially not Paulie. Chooch and Freddy are the pricks. Paulie wasn't bad. Paulie didn't care much about anything besides his car."

Mrozinski shifted weight to the other foot. "So that's all you've got?"

I nodded. "That's all there is. I can't have an alibi for every murder that happens. You'll have to do some work and find out who really committed the crime."

Mrozinski turned and walked to his car, and I went back inside.

Angie was standing in the living room, staring. "What was that about?"

"Nothing."

"Detectives don't stop by your house for nothing. What's going on?"

I sat in my chair and kicked my feet up on the hassock. "Paulie Campisi was murdered a few nights ago. Naturally, they're asking me for alibis."

"Do you have one?"

"I was playing cards, then I came home."

"I'm sure the guys at the card game will back that up," Angie said.

"That's part of the problem. Campisi was killed shortly after I left the game, and I have no alibi after I left, and I have nobody to say what time I got home."

"I was here," Angie said. "And Rosa."

I laughed. "And you were asleep, babe. So was Rosa. Even Dante was asleep, so none of you are alibis."

"What bad luck that he was killed at that time. I mean, it's terrible that he was killed at all, but why then?"

"I don't know if it was all bad luck. There are aspects of the murder that are similar to the murders in Brooklyn a few years ago —the ones they tried to pin on me."

"What do you mean? Are you saying somebody's trying to frame you? Who would do that?"

I pulled her close and hugged. "I don't know, babe. I just don't know."

"Maybe we should call a lawyer."

I shook my head. "I'm not wasting money on a lawyer. I'll handle this myself."

Angela wrapped her arms around me. "I don't want you handling it yourself. Every time you handle things yourself, someone gets hurt."

"Nothing's going to happen," I said. "I promise. I'll take care of it."

Rosa sat at the top of the steps, listening. She knew her father was too hardheaded to ask for help, so she figured she'd have to take charge.

She went to her room, opened the dresser, and pulled out a slip of paper with a phone number written on it. She closed her door tightly, then dialed the phone. After a few rings, it was answered.

"Donovan."

"Uncle Frankie, it's Rosa."

"Rosa, what's up? What are you doing calling?"

"It's dad, Uncle Frankie. I think he needs help."

"What kind of help?"

"A detective was just here, and he thinks dad committed a crime, a murder. I know dad didn't do it, but this detective is trying to make it look like he did."

"Is it Detective Mrozinski, the one who was Jimmy Borelli's partner?"

"Yes, it's him, and he won't listen to reason. I heard Dad talking to him on the stoop. My bedroom window was open, and I heard them."

"All right, find out what you can, and I'll call you later, probably tomorrow."

"Okay, but don't tell dad I called you. He'd be pissed."

"I won't, Rosa. And don't worry about anything, I'll take care of it. Goodnight."

"You can't just say 'goodnight' and leave it at that, Uncle Frankie. Dad needs help."

"I know he needs help, Rosa, and I won't let him down. I have to take care of a few things up here, then I'll be down to fix things. Don't worry."

"Promise?"

"I promise. I wouldn't let you down."

"Thanks, Uncle Frankie. I knew I could count on you."

Chapter Ten

QUESTIONING MANNY

Miller met Frankie at the station at 8:00. "About time you got here, Donovan. I've been waiting an hour."

"I should have let you wait another hour; besides, no way that Manny will be up at this time of day. You need to drink a few more cups of coffee before we go over there."

"What? It's the middle of the day," Miller said.

"Not for Manny. Two in the morning *is* the middle of the day for him. Sit down, and I'll pour a few more coffees, then we'll figure out how to proceed."

An hour later, Frankie and Miller pulled to the curb in front of Manny's house, and before they reached the porch, the door opened.

"Bugs! What the hell you doin' here? Somebody die?"

"Actually, somebody *did* die. A bodega owner in Red Hook."

Manny raised his brows. "What's that got to do with me? I ain't been to Red Hook in years."

"I'm sure you haven't," Frankie said. "Hey, Manny, how about we chat while drinking some of that good espresso you make?"

Manny slapped himself on the forehead. "Where the hell are my manners? Christ's sake, come inside, and I'll put a pot on the stove."

Manny held the door as Frankie and Sherri walked in. "By the way, Donovan, who's this beautiful young partner you got with you?"

Sherri turned, smiling. "Detective Miller. We met before."

"I'll be a rat's ass," Manny said. "You're more beautiful than you ever were." He grabbed her cheeks and pinched them, then he gave her a kiss on the forehead.

Manny slapped Frankie on the back. "Forgive my manners for not offering espresso earlier. Now tell me what you want."

"The guy who was murdered in Red Hook ran a bodega, and we think it was a drop spot. If I'm right about that, the location means it would be one of yours. You missing a bag of money?"

Manny laughed. "Bugs, how long have I known you? Did you expect me to tell you anything? If it wasn't mine, I'd tell you it wasn't mine. And if it *was* mine, I'd tell you it wasn't mine. So either way, the answer is the same. It wasn't mine."

Frankie smiled as he took a seat at the kitchen table. "Manny, a witness says the man who collected the bag was a big man with a heavy beard. A thick beard, not a long one. Anybody you know fit that description?"

Manny brought several espressos to the table, then he reached and grabbed a plate filled with biscotti. "Eat up, Miller. You're too skinny."

"Well, Manny?" Frankie asked.

"What if I did know somebody who fit that description?"

"We just want to talk to him. I don't give two shits about the drop bag. All I care about is the murderer, and the guy they describe doesn't fit that description. The guy witnesses are naming is a big guy with a beard who came out carrying a bag almost every day, but they're not saying he was the shooter."

"That's on the up and up? You don't care about the bag?"

"Not even a little bit," Frankie said. "But the thing is, my boss is pressuring me to solve this murder, so I gotta bring him something. If all I got is what the witnesses gave me. I gotta go with that."

Manny sipped his espresso, then said. "All right, Bugs, I'm trusting you, but don't mess around."

Frankie sat up. "You know I won't, Manny."

"Check out a guy named 'Whiskers' DeNuzzio. His real name is Bobby DeNuzzio, but he's called "Bobby Whiskers" or just Whiskers. You can usually find him at Sal's cafe after lunch. You can't miss him. He'll be the one who looks like he's got a full beard anytime after ten in the morning."

"Thanks, Manny. I won't forget it."

"And tell Whiskers I sent you or you won't get a word out of him."

"Will do, Manny," Frankie said as he stood. "And thanks for the espresso. I haven't had any as good since the last time I was here."

Manny's belly rolled as he laughed. "I know that's right, Bugs. And unless you go to Dominic's house or Cataldi's, you won't."

Frankie and Sherri got about halfway to the car when Manny called from the porch. "Don't forget to tell Whiskers I sent you. And tell him to call me if he's got any questions."

Frankie waved his hand in the air. "You're the best, Manny. Thanks." He and Sherri got into the car, then pulled away from the curb and turned toward Sal's cafe.

"Donovan, how well do you know these guys? You seemed pretty comfortable sipping coffee with them considering they are gangsters."

"Don't worry about it, Miller. I'd arrest Manny same as anyone else, but just because he's a gangster doesn't mean we can't help each other out."

"How far does the helping out go?"

"It stays legal if that's what you want to know. And I get the benefit of good information plus some damn good espresso and occasionally seafood ravioli that is to die for. The only place I've had better is at Cataldi's."

"You've eaten at Cataldi's?"

Frankie smiled. "Several times, and, before you get in an uproar, it wasn't with Manny." Frankie laughed. "It was with Dominic Mangini."

"Donovan, I'd say that borders on a bribe, especially knowing how you love to eat."

"If you knew Dominic Mangini, and if you ever tasted Cataldi's ravioli, you'd say it *was* a bribe. But forget about all that, Miller, we're almost to Sal's."

"How are we gonna handle this?" Sherri asked.

"We'll leave that to Manny. I'm sure Whiskers will want to call him to verify, so it will depend on what Manny tells him."

Frankie and Sherri walked into the cafe and spotted Whiskers right away. He was seated near the back at a table by himself. Frankie walked up and showed his badge. "Manny said you'd be willing to help us. He said to call him if you had questions."

Whiskers looked at Donovan, then Miller. "Manny said that?"

Frankie nodded.

"Forgive me if I don't trust you," Whiskers said as he pulled out a cell phone and dialed. "Manny, I got a couple of badges here that say you said to cooperate.

Whiskers nodded while staring at Frankie and Miller. "Yeah, okay. I'll tell them what I know."

Whiskers hung up the phone and put it back in his pocket. "Sit down," he said. "What do you need to know?"

"I need to know whatever you can tell me about the Roots and Chutes bodega in Red Hook. Bucky was murdered, and I need to know why."

"Bucky? Shit. He was a nice guy," Whiskers said.

"You picked up the bags from there?" Frankie asked.

Whiskers didn't answer at first. He looked at Donovan, then Miller. "I talked to Manny, but I need to hear it from you. This is all okay? It won't come back on me?"

"It's all good," Frankie said. "This is a murder investigation. We don't care about a numbers drop."

Whiskers nodded. "Okay. Yeah, I picked up the bag from Bucky every night. Sometimes every two nights. He did a pretty good business there, especially on weekends, but I'd always call him first. If he said he had a slow day, I'd wait till the next day to get the bag."

"Who else knew about it?" Miller asked.

"Shit, I don't know. Anyone who laid down a bet, I guess. And anyone they might have told. Could be hundreds or even thousands of people."

"We've got a witness who said it was two white guys wearing masks, and witnesses say one of them had big hands."

"Big hands?"

"Yeah, that mean anything to you?" Frankie asked.

"No, it's just a strange description. Never heard that in describing someone."

"If you think of anything that might help, let us know," Frankie said, and handed him a card.

———

Frankie and Sherri left the cafe and walked to the car. After they left, Whiskers dialed his phone. "Yeah, Manny, it's Whiskers. Your cop buddy said the guy had big hands.

"Yeah, that's what I thought. I'll keep my eyes open."

———

"That was a waste of time," Miller said as they drove off.

"Not entirely," Frankie said. "Did you see his expression when I mentioned 'big hands'? It rang a bell of some kind. Now we need to find out what kind of bell it rang."

"And how are we going to do that?"

"Ask Manny?"

"Ask Manny? Why didn't you just ask him when we were at his house?"

"You've got a lot to learn, Miller. Manny is not a guy who gives anything away. His expression would be the same whether you told him the sky was blue or his mother was dead. But Whiskers told us a lot. Now we can go back to Manny with something solid."

"Then I guess we go see Manny."

"We'll do that tomorrow. First, let's talk to some more people who live by the bodega. It's a snowball's chance in hell, but we might get a lead."

Chapter Eleven

MILLER GETS A NEW PARTNER

Frankie met Miller early in the morning. They had coffee and discussed how to proceed with the investigation. "Miller, I don't know how much I should be involved with this."

"What's that mean, Donovan? You're the lead detective."

"I know, but I'm going to have to take a few days off. Probably more than a few days."

"Why? What's up?"

"I've got to help a friend."

Miller stared. "Nicky?"

When Frankie didn't say anything, she asked again. "Is it Nicky? What kind of trouble is he in?"

Frankie nodded. "Yes, it's Nicky. The cops where he lives think he did something, but I know he didn't."

"So you're gonna ride in on your white horse and save the day?"

"Miller, if I recall, Nicky saved your ass one time. He's also saved mine, Kate's, and he even saved Lou's life. I owe him."

"Do what you gotta do, Donovan. But I'd appreciate it if you helped out with Manny before you left. I don't see him cooperating with me. At least not like he cooperates with you."

"You're not giving him credit, Miller, but don't worry, I won't leave you hanging. I've got to tell the lieutenant, then I'll go with you to see Manny."

Frankie walked into Morreau's office and took a seat. "What's up, Lieutenant?"

"Something's up or you wouldn't be sitting here asking, so spit it out."

"I need to take off a few days, maybe longer."

"What for?"

"A friend of mine is in trouble. I've got to see if I can help him."

"Is this one of your gangster friends? Or is this your killer friend?"

"Lieutenant, I don't know what you mean."

"Donovan, you know damn right well what I mean, and no, you can't go. You need to work that bodega murder. Miller can't do it herself, and I don't have anyone qualified to give her."

"But—"

"No damn buts. I said *no* and that's final, so you and Miller get your asses out there and solve that murder."

Frankie stormed out of Morreau's office and into the coffee room. "Come on, Miller. We're going to see Manny."

Frankie slammed the car door when he got in, and the tires screeched when he pulled away from the curb.

"Guess your talk with Morreau didn't go so well."

"All the shit I've done for that man, and he can't even give me a couple of days off. Son of a bitch. Damn son of a bitch."

"Maybe we can bust this case quickly, then you can go."

"Fat damn chance of that," Frankie said.

He pulled in front of Manny's house ten minutes later and knocked loudly on the door. Manny answered with his usual smile.

"Bugs! Back so soon? You see Whiskers?"

Frankie pushed in and headed for the kitchen. "Manny, I'd love a cup of your espresso, but more importantly, I'd like some straight answers."

"Sure to the espresso, and what the hell do you mean to the second."

"What's the significance of a big guy who has really big hands?"

Manny stood by the stove waiting for the espresso. "What's that supposed to mean?"

Frankie sighed. "Manny, I don't have time for games. Nicky is in trouble, and I need to get down there and help him, but my boss won't let me leave until I solve this case, so I've got to get whoever did this quickly. I know from talking to Whiskers that the guy having big hands is important. I need to know why."

Manny brought the pot of espresso to the table and started pouring. "I can trust you?" he asked, nodding to Miller.

"You can trust her," Frankie said.

"Hey, Bugs, I didn't ask you. I asked the girl."

Miller smiled. "*Puoi fidarti di me.*"

Manny cocked his head and laughed. "Son of a bitch. I'll be a horse's ass. That's good Italian. Where'd you learn that?"

"Grandparents," Miller said. "One was in the war in Italy, and the other was Italian."

"That settles it. I can trust you." Manny sat down and bit into a *biscotto*. "The guy you probably want is Joey 'Fat Fingers' Tomaselli. He used to work for me."

"Doing what?" Frankie asked.

Manny looked at him with a sideways glance. "I'd rather not say, Bugs. Let's leave it that he worked for me, and I had to let him go. I suspect that may have pissed him off, and this is his way of getting back at me."

"Where can we find him?" Miller asked.

"He lives in Bay Ridge, but I doubt you'll find him there. He's got to know I suspect him, so he's likely hiding out somewhere else."

"You have any notion of where?" Miller asked.

"I've got feelers out, but I'll step up the pace since it's for Nicky. It won't take long; Joey was never too smart."

"All right, we'll kick the leaves in Bay Ridge and—"

"I'll handle everywhere else," Manny said. "You cover Bay Ridge, and we'll be good. I'll let you know when I find something."

Frankie shifted uncomfortably in his seat. "Manny, I may not be here."

"Then I'll call *this* sweetheart," he said, and pinched Miller's cheeks.

"Ow! Damn, that hurt."

"Bull," Manny said. "If you had an Italian grandparent, that little pinch couldn't have hurt."

Sherri laughed. "Okay, you're right, but it's been a long time."

"That's more like it," Manny said. "Give me your phone number, and I'll call when I get something. As for you, Bugs, get your ass down there and help Nicky out of whatever jam he's in."

"And I can—"

Manny sighed. "Yes, Bugs, you can count on me to work with Miller. Now get your ass moving."

Frankie and Sherri finished the day cruising Bay Ridge and searching for Joey 'Fat Fingers' Tomaselli in all the likely places, but they had no luck.

At the end of the day, Frankie dropped Sherri off at the station. "Miller, it might be a while before I see you."

"That's no problem; it seems like Manny will be better than I expected. Just answer the phone if I call. And get Fusco out of trouble."

Frankie smiled. "You know, I actually like Manny. If he wasn't a gangster, I could really like him."

"He grows on you," Miller said.

"All right, see you when I get back."

An hour later, Kate got home and found Frankie pacing the floor.

"What's the matter, Frankie?"

"Kate, we need to talk."

Kate sat on the couch and pulled him down next to her. "About what?"

"Rosa called. She said Nicky's in trouble. She thinks he needs my help. I know—"

"Go, Frankie. Nicky didn't hesitate to come up here when you were in trouble, and he saved me from the Russians. Why the hell are you still here?"

Frankie smiled, grabbed her face in both hands, and kissed her. "I love you, Kate Donovan."

"I know you do. Now get down to that shithole of a city where you came from and help your friend."

"One more thing. Morreau doesn't want me to go."

"The hell with him. We don't need your salary anyway, just pack up and go. I'll take care of things here. Besides, I'd rather have you looking at Nicky's ass than Miller's."

"All right, I might head out tonight. Traffic will be much better."

"Then get going. I'll give Alex a kiss for you."

"You're the best, Kate."

"And don't you forget it. Drive safely."

————

Miller was drinking coffee when Morreau walked in. "Where's Donovan?"

"You know Donovan, boss. He's probably drinking a cup of *good* coffee somewhere."

"Don't try that shit with me, Miller. Where is he?"

Sherri looked up. "I don't know."

"I think you do know, and I'd bet he's on his way south."

"Want some coffee, Lieu?" Miller asked.

"Keep your damn coffee. And when you talk to Donovan, tell

him if he isn't back here tomorrow, he can stay where he is. I don't want him."

"You don't mean that, Lieu."

"I sure as hell *do* mean it. And I want you to tell him. Before you do that, though, you need a partner. Come to my office and let's see who's available."

Morreau was leafing through the assignment book when Miller walked in. "Find anyone good, Lieu?"

Morreau poked his finger at the book. "Meyers. I think he'd be good. Seven years on the job as a detective, and ten as a beat cop."

"Homicide?"

"Two years in Homicide. And both of them in Brooklyn."

Morreau picked up the phone and dialed. "Meyers, you have a new partner. Come upstairs and meet her."

Sherri stood. "Thanks, Lieu. I'll go meet him. By the way, what's his first name?"

"Jack. And, Miller, don't corrupt him. I know some of the shit Donovan and Mazetti taught you skirts the rules, but I don't want any more of that going on."

"You got it, boss. I'll play it straight and narrow."

"You better," Morreau said. "And you better solve this case."

Sherri got to the top of the stairs and noticed a freckle-faced young man coming up. "You Jack Meyers?" she asked.

"None other," he said, and stretched out his hand. "You must be Miller."

"I am. Nice to meet you. If you need coffee, grab it. If not, let's go. We have places to be."

"I'm good on the coffee," Meyers said as he turned around. "Where are we going?"

"You can't tell the lieutenant, but we're going to see some gangsters."

Meyers laughed as if she were joking.

Chapter Twelve

THE INVESTIGATION CONTINUES

I was working on a new bid when Sheila stuck her head in my office. "Sir, Detective Mrozinski is here to see you. He said you were expecting him."

Mrozinski pushed through the door before she finished. "Fusco, we need to talk."

"That will be all, Sheila," I said, then turned to Mrozinski. "Need to talk about what?"

"A car matching your car's description was seen at the crime scene when Campisi was killed."

"Since cars can't traverse Canby Woods, I'm assuming you are referring to *Freddy* Campisi's murder. Do you think I'm methodically killing the entire family?" I stood and walked to sit beside Mrozinski, where I leaned close and whispered. "Besides, Detective, do you know how many cars like mine are out there? I'm sure you've already done the math on that, so why come here?"

"The coincidences are building up, Fusco: two dead people, and you hated both of them; Paulie beaten with a bat; both of them, might I add, were shot in the head and heart; and your car was spotted at the scene—"

"Correction," I said. "A car *like* mine being spotted at the scene which happens to be one of hundreds, if not thousands, of the same model car in this small city alone. I'm sure you can check with the manufacturer to get the number sold by the dealerships."

"Point taken, Fusco; otherwise, I'd be hauling your ass in right now."

I laughed. "Detective, if you arrest me, you'll have a huge lawsuit on your hands. You can't arrest people based on coincidence alone."

"I'm waiting on DNA evidence from Paulie's crime scene. If your DNA is in there, you better get a lawyer lined up for that lawsuit."

"I've got him on speed dial," I said. "Besides, based on how these murders are being committed, it appears as if someone is going to great lengths to frame me. If that's the case, I'm sure there will be more than my DNA at the scene, and if there is, you're screwed again." I got up and walked back to my desk where I pressed the intercom button. "Sheila will you show the detective out, and if he or any of his associates show up again, *do not* let them in."

Maddy was sitting in a chair in Mrozinski's office when he got back.

"Maddy, what's up? Anything wrong?"

"I got a strange call and wanted to share it with you." She pulled her phone out and placed it on the desk. "I recorded it so you could hear it yourself."

"Who called?"

"Charlie Knuckles, the one who gave me *nothing* when we went to the smoke shop."

"Don't make me wait," Mrozinski said. "Play the recording."

Maddy turned on the recording, then sat back in the chair.

Maddy: "Hello."

Knuckles: "Maddy, this is Charlie Knuckles. You stopped by to see me the other day."

Maddy: "Sure, I remember. What's up? Did you think of something?"

Knuckles: "Nothin' about Paulie, but I do have something on Freddy's murder. I seen him driving down Union Street when I was leaving the smoke shop, and two or three cars behind him was Fusco."

Maddy: "What?"

Knuckles: "Yeah, and there's more. I can't tell you everything here, though, I got ears everywhere. If you meet me at the Columbus Inn around 7:00, I'll fill you in. I'll be at a table in the back."

Maddy: "Great, I'll see you there."

Knuckles: "Hey, Maddy. Don't make it look like no planned meeting. Come in the restaurant, ask for a table, then act surprised to see me and come over. I can't wait to sink my teeth into one of those luscious steaks."

Maddy: "No problem, Charlie. I'll make sure nobody suspects."

Mrozinski slapped his hand on the desk. "Son of a bitch, Maddy. That's golden. You need me to go with you tonight?"

"I don't think you should," Maddy said. "Charlie seemed a little paranoid, and you being there might make him uncomfortable."

"You're probably right," Mrozinski said. "Just make sure you get everything. And tell Knuckles we can keep it confidential."

Maddy gave a little laugh. "I can almost guarantee you he won't make a formal statement. No way he's going public with this. We're lucky he's telling us anything."

Mrozinski nodded. "Right again, Maddy. Let's hope he gives us something that we can follow through with and prove on our own. Which reminds me, we should check Manko's to see if Freddy was up there. If Knuckles spotted him going south on Union Street, my guess is there's a good chance he was coming from Manko's."

"Let's go," Maddy said. "That place is usually busy for lunch, so maybe we'll get lucky. Besides, we still need to talk to that lady who Paulie tried hitting on."

"Yeah," Mrozinski said. "We'll see if she's there, but I'm not too excited about that lead."

Mrozinski and Maddy walked into Manko's and up to the bar. "Stan, do you always work? You're on duty every time I come here."

Stan filled a mug with draft and slid it to a customer to Mrozinski's left. "I feel like I'm always here, but it's only six days a week."

"Were you on duty the last few nights?"

"If you mean was I here the night Freddy got killed? Yeah, I was here. And it was a good thing he left when he did, 'cause I was about to toss him out of here on his ass."

"Why's that?" Maddy asked.

"As usual, he was being a pain, trying to pick fights with everyone, about anything."

"Anyone in particular?"

"Fusco, for one. That tells you how crazy he was. Who the hell would pick a fight with Fusco?"

Mrozinski leaned forward. "What happened?"

"Nothing happened, but that was Nicky's doing. Freddy tried his best to rile him into a fight, but Nicky wouldn't take the bait. He accused Fusco of killing his brother, and when that failed to get a rise out of Nicky, Freddy even pushed him a couple of times."

"Then what?" Mrozinski asked.

"I was about to throw him out when he left on his own."

"And Fusco?"

"Nicky left a couple of minutes later. He wasn't mad or anything. He finished his beer and left. Goin' home, I guess."

Mrozinski glanced at Maddy. "Or maybe not."

"You happen to know what time this was?" Maddy asked.

"No idea. I know what time it is when I start, and I know what time it is when I get off. Other than that, don't ask."

Mrozinski and Maddy talked to at least half a dozen people at the bar. A few of them confirmed Freddy's antagonistic manner, and they claimed that Nicky kept his cool.

Forty minutes later, Mrozinski suggested they leave. "I don't think we're getting anything else from this crowd," he said. "Let's talk to some of Freddy's neighbors and see if anybody saw anything other than what we have."

"Before we leave, we may as well check and see if Janice is here."

Mrozinski shrugged. "What the hell." He walked up to the bar. "Hey, Stan, you remember telling us about that lady Paul Campisi was hitting on? I think her name was Janice."

Stan smiled. "Sure do," he said and gestured to the corner. "She's right over there. Long blonde hair and tight jeans. Can't miss her."

Mrozinski and Viola stopped at Janice's table and showed their badges.

Maddy lowered her voice and leaned into Janice. "We're investigating the murder of Paul Campisi. We understand he was in here the night he was killed, and that he was giving you trouble."

Janice laughed. "Excuse me. I'm not laughing because Paul got killed, but we didn't have anything to do with that if that's what you're implying."

"Can you vouch for the whereabouts of your boyfriend?" Mrozinski asked.

Janice nodded. "Sam came home with me, and we went to bed as usual, and we made passionate love as usual."

"That's usual?" Mrozinski asked.

"It is whenever we go out. Sam's never said anything, but I think he gets worked up when other guys hit on me, which is why he likes me dressing provocatively. I can barely hold him off after a night on the town. Not that Manko's is a night on the town, but it's something."

Maddy leaned in closer. "So he doesn't get jealous?"

"On the contrary. I think he gets excited. Actually, you can scratch that out. I *know* he gets excited."

"And he was with you all night?" Maddy asked.

Janice grinned ear to ear. "All night," she said. "Jealous?"

"Thanks for your time," Maddy said, and got up to leave.

"I hope this proved fruitful for whatever the hell you were after," Maddy said.

"Not quite. But at least we know Campisi was here with Fusco."

"And we know Fusco did nothing except attempt to defuse him. I wouldn't call that motive." Maddy stopped and stared at her partner. "Ed, what are you hoping to get?" Maddy asked. "If you're not after the truth, what *are* you after?"

"I don't know," Mrozinski said. "But whatever it was, we didn't get it. Now, let's get over to Freddy's place and see if we can get something."

"What are you hoping for there?" Maddy asked.

"A license plate would be great, but I doubt we'll get one."

"I doubt it too," Maddy said, and headed for the door.

Mrozinski and Maddy spent a couple hours canvassing the neighbors around Campisi's house, but as they suspected, they got nothing new. "Might as well call it a night," Mrozinski said. "I've got an event at my son's school, and you have to meet Knuckles."

"I've got time," Maddy said.

"No sense in pushing it," Mrozinski said. "If you're early, sit in the parking lot and read."

"All right, see you tomorrow."

———

Maddy sat in her car outside the restaurant and played games on her phone. She didn't like reading on such a small screen, but it beat the alternative. Every minute or so, she looked up to see if she spotted Charlie entering.

After a while, she checked the time and realized it was twenty past seven. *Maybe I missed him.* She got out of the car and quickly made her way to the restaurant, checking the tables near the back closely. Charlie wasn't there, so she got a table, ordered a glass of wine, and waited.

After another half hour, he still hadn't shown, and Maddy decided to call it quits. She paid her tab, left the restaurant, and drove home in a sour mood. She had been counting on Charlie coming through for her. It might have meant a big break in the case.

At the last minute, she decided to check the smoke shop, so she turned around and dropped in. "Charlie here?"

"Charlie who?" the guy up front asked.

Maddy sighed. She pulled out her badge and showed the guy. "I'm not here to bust anyone. I wanted to see Charlie Knuckles, that's all. If he's not here, let me talk to Doggs."

The guy smiled and pressed an intercom button. "Doggs, a detective is here to see you, and it's not Mrozinski; it's some broad."

Doggs came through a door leading to the back room a moment later. "What do you need?"

"I need to see Knuckles," Maddy said.

"He ain't been here all day. Why do you want to see him, anyway?"

Maddy almost said she had talked to him while he was here, but she wasn't sure that was true. She assumed it from what he said. "Nothing big. Just thought he'd be here. I wanted to verify his statements about Paulie's murder. We're trying to wrap that up."

"Since he's not here, he's gotta be at his house 'cause Knuckles doesn't go anywhere else. You know where he lives?"

Maddy shook her head.

"Up on Franklin Street, about two or three blocks north of the hospital. Hang on and I'll get the address." Doggs stepped behind the counter and opened a drawer next to the cash register, then he wrote the address on a slip of paper and handed it to Maddy. "Talk to him there. I'd rather not have you cops hanging around my shop."

Maddy smiled. "You got it, Doggs. Thanks."

S he drove to Charlie's house and knocked on the door, but no one answered. She waited a moment, then knocked again, but still no answer. *Where the hell is he?*

After a third attempt, Maddy got in her car and drove home.

Chapter Thirteen

HELP IS HERE

Frankie woke and jumped out of bed. "Holy shit," he said when he saw the time. He dressed and ran downstairs. "Mom, why the hell didn't you wake me? It's the middle of the day."

"You didn't get in till almost morning. I figured you needed sleep."

"You figured wrong. I gotta go."

"Wait, you haven't had any breakfast."

"I don't have time for breakfast. I'll grab something on the way."

"On the way to where? Where are you going? What are you doing? You haven't told me anything. Are you still married? Did you get separated?"

"No, mom. Everything's fine. I just have to run. I'll see you later and tell you all about it." Frankie rushed out the door, closing it behind him.

* * *

Sheila opened the door to Nicky's office and looked inside. "Someone is here to see you, Mr. Fusco."

"If it's that son of a bitch Mrozinski, tell him he can leave."

Frankie walked past Sheila, all smiles. "It's not that son of a bitch Mrozinski; it's that son of a bitch Donovan."

Nicky jumped up and rushed to Bugs. He threw his arms around him in a big bear hug. "You Irish prick, what the hell are you doing here?"

"Thought I'd come for a visit, you Italian prick. I haven't seen anybody in ages."

"Well, I'm glad you came. Had lunch yet? If not, we'll get some subs."

"You know I can't refuse a lunch offer that involves subs. Let's go."

Nicky grabbed his coat, and he and Bugs walked out the door. "Sheila, we're going to grab some subs. Want one?"

"I'm fine, Mr. Fusco. Enjoy."

On the drive to Casapulla's, Nicky and Frankie talked about everything, but the majority of the conversation focused on the old days. Suddenly, Nicky stopped and turned to Frankie. "Bugs, did you bring Kate and Alex?"

Frankie looked down and shook his head. "No, Kate's swamped at work, and Alex can't afford to miss school."

Suspicion was evident in Nicky's voice when he spoke. "So you just came down for a visit?"

"Yeah, I thought I'd see the family and you and Angela."

Nicky shook his head. "Bugs, you've always been full of shit, but besides that, you're a terrible liar. Why'd you really come down?"

"What the hell do you mean? Like I said—I came for a visit."

"Did Angela call you?"

"Angela? Hell no. Why would Angela call me?"

"If it wasn't Angela, then it must have been Rosa. And I'm only saying that because Dante doesn't have your number."

Frankie laughed. "All right, you shit. Yes, it was Rosa, but don't tell her I told you. She'd never forgive me."

"And what the hell do you think you can do about my predicament? You have zero jurisdiction down here and no juice unless you count Doggs, which means no juice."

Frankie pointed his finger at Nicky. "Listen up, you hard-headed dago prick, I won't know what I can or can't do until you tell me what the hell is going on."

Nicky sighed. "All right, we're almost to Casapulla's. I'll fill you in over lunch."

While we ate lunch, I filled Bugs in on the situation, including the similarities to the Brooklyn crime scenes and a car like mine being spotted at Freddy's murder.

"It sounds like someone is setting you up, Rat."

"I've thought about that, and I agree, but who's doing it and why? Not many people knew the details of the Brooklyn crimes.

Besides, who would *want* to do this. Somebody would need a powerful grudge to kill people just to frame me."

Bugs took the last bite of his sub. "Nicky, let's face it. If anyone's got enemies that fit the bill, it's you. We need to go through them and determine who it is."

"We'll have to do that later, Bugs. I've got to get back to work. I *have* to get this bid in before Friday if I want the job."

We left Casapulla's, and while I mostly drove the speed limit back to the office, I have to admit, I pushed it a few times.

After I parked, Bugs got out of the car and walked alongside me into the office. "All right, here's the deal, Rat. You get to work, and I'll start working on possibilities. You got a place to work out of at your house, or do you want me to use the office?"

I gave it some thought, then said, "I think the office works best. The less Angie knows about this, the better."

"Just so I know, how much have you told her so far. I don't want to spill the beans."

"She knows Mrozinski is looking into me for Pauli Campisi's murder. Other than that, nothing."

We got off the elevator and went to my office. We were barely settled in when Sheila buzzed me, then walked in.

"Excuse me, Mr. Fusco," Sheila said as she opened the door. "Detective Mrozinski is here again."

"Tell him to—"

Frankie held up his hand. "No, Nicky. Let him in. I want to hear what he has to say."

"All right, Sheila. Let him in."

Mrozinski and Maddy Viola walked into the office. He gave Frankie a sideways look, then took a seat. "Maddy, let me introduce you to Detective Frankie Donovan, formerly of the same neighborhood as Nicky and now a resident of Brooklyn."

Maddy reached over and shook hands.

"What's up, Mrozinski?" I asked.

"I'm going to have to ask you to come with me, Nicky."

"What for?"

"Suspicion of murder."

"Are you arresting me?" I asked.

"If I have too, I will. I'd prefer you come to the station on your own."

Frankie leaned to the side and stared at the detective. "What evidence do you have, Mrozinski?"

"You have no jurisdiction here, Donovan."

"I didn't say I did. I simply asked what evidence you had. Long gone are the days when you can just arrest somebody with no evidence."

Mrozinski sighed. "His car was spotted at the scene of the crime. He had an argument with Freddy moments before he was killed. The way both of them were killed is similar to the killings in Brooklyn. And—"

"Let me stop you right there," Frankie said. "It wasn't Nicky's car that was spotted but a car that *looked* like his according to you as reported by a 79-year-old witness—in the dark. A witness, I might add, that wears glasses but did not have them on at the time."

"And how the hell do you know that?" Mrozinski asked.

"I've got connections, and they're above your head, Mrozinski."

"Anyway, as far as arguing with Freddy Campisi, every conversation Freddy had with anyone was an argument, and I'm willing to bet he had more than a few that night, but I'm sure a talk with patrons of Manko's will verify that. As far as the murders having similarities to a crime or crimes in Brooklyn—that has nothing to do with Nicky. He was never convicted or even arrested for those crimes. If you put this in front of any judge, it will be thrown out of court before you bat an eye. And if you proceed, it *will* be put before a judge. I can guarantee that."

"What's your stake in this, Donovan. Don't you want to see these crimes solved?"

"I most certainly do. But I want them solved with the right person, not the first person you can pin it on. If you arrest Nicky for this, I'll make sure you and the department are both sued, which means you'll both lose."

Mrozinski gritted his teeth. He looked as if he wanted to say something, but he didn't. Instead, he stood. "Maddy, let's go. We're done here for now." He turned to Nicky. "But we'll be back, Fusco. Count on it."

"You'll need a warrant next time," I said. "Otherwise you won't get in."

Mrozinski slammed the car door as he got in. "That son of a bitch is going to get his."

"You really think he did it?" Maddy asked.

"I don't know, and at this point, I don't care, but I'm not going to have him make a mockery of the law."

"Excuse me for saying so, Detective, but some people would say he's simply defending his rights. Donovan was right; we don't have any real evidence. The best we've got is the potential car match, and that description is from an old man at night, and as Donovan reminded us—without his glasses; besides, even if the description is right, it fits thousands of cars."

"Damnit, what else do we have?"

"Nothing yet. And the only lead we have is Knuckles, but like I told you, he didn't show, and he wasn't home when I went there."

Mrozinski made a quick turn. "Then let's go there again. If he's not in, we'll check the smoke shop, and if he isn't there, we'll sit on his house until he comes home. I want to know why the son of a bitch told us he had something, then didn't show up at the meeting."

"Sounds like a plan," Maddy said. "Head up to North Franklin."

Mrozinski spun around to Viola. "Are you sure you were at the restaurant on time? You didn't miss him, did you?"

Maddy was appalled. "Screw you too, Mrozinski. I do my job, and I was there in plenty of time; in fact, I was early. There's no way I missed him. He simply didn't show."

"All right," Mrozinski said. "Let's find out why."

Chapter Fourteen

SKIRTING THE LAW

Miller drove the speed limit through the streets of Brooklyn, and through Prospect Park, then took a turn toward Manny's house.

"What did you mean when you said 'going to see some gangsters'?" Jack asked.

Miller laughed. "I guess you need a little clarification. I meant we were going to see some gangsters. Donovan, my partner, has more than a few unorthodox friends."

"You mean he's crooked?"

"No, I didn't say that, and I didn't mean that. I meant just what I said. Donovan sometimes does things for these friends—legal things—and they sometimes do things for him."

"Legal things too?"

Miller smiled. "Usually." Sherri reached over and patted Jack's arm. "Just follow my lead, Meyers. You'll be fine if you do that."

Manny sat on the front porch drinking espresso when Miller pulled up. "*Buon giorno, Manny. Come va?*"

Manny set his cup on the table, walked over, and pinched Miller's cheeks. "*La mia principessa preferita.*"

Sherri smiled. "Manny, this is my temporary partner, Jack Meyers. He's filling in for Frankie. And since I'm pretty sure he doesn't speak Italian, maybe we better stick to English so he doesn't think I'm dirty."

Manny laughed and shook Jack's hand. "Come inside and have an espresso, and hurry up about it. I'm gonna get a bad reputation if the neighbors keep seeing cops stop by here."

Sherri held the door while Jack Meyers walked inside. "Don't worry, Jack. Manny's espresso is so good you'll want to come back every day."

"You might want to, but don't do it," Manny said as he walked to the stove. "So what's up? Bugs go to see our friend?"

"He did," Sherri said. "And the lieutenant didn't like him going, which is part of the reason why I'm here."

"He'll get over Bugs being gone," Manny said. "If not, call me. I got some connections."

Meyers risked a glance to Miller and mouthed the word *connections.*

Sherri laughed. "Manny, don't say stuff like that; you'll get my partner all worked up."

"So what brings you today, Miller? You get anything on Tomaselli?"

"No, that's why I'm here. We went everywhere we could think of, but we found no sign of Joey. I came to see if you had any other leads, or if you had any luck. The thing is, my boss probably wouldn't be so hard on Frankie if I solved this case quickly."

Manny slurped his espresso. "Miller, I looked everywhere for Joey, but I'll tell you what. I'll ask Dominic to check the Bronx. If he's there, Dominic will find him. He can find a flea hiding on a rat's ass. And he's got a guy who could shoot that flea off its ass without doing the rat any harm."

Manny glanced at Jack, who looked in shock, and Manny smiled. "But don't worry, we'll get him. You'll have your case solved in no time."

Sherri stood. "Thanks, Manny. And don't forget, we want him alive. If he did that bodega, he's going down for murder."

"I'll take care of it, sweetheart. Don't worry." Manny kissed Sherri's cheek, then laughed. "And you better get your new partner some antacids or something. He looks like he's gonna be sick."

Sherri laughed. "He'll be fine, Manny. Thanks again."

As Sherri pulled away from the curb, Meyers said. "That was Manny Rosso?"

She smiled. "Not as bad as you thought, huh?"

"He seemed like a nice guy."

"He *is* a nice guy—if you're on his good side. It's when you cross that line that things get ugly. And trust me, you don't want to cross that line."

"So are we going to the Bronx?"

Sherri shook her head. "Not a chance in hell. Manny said he'd have Dominic check, and I'll leave it at that. Dominic's not as nice as Manny. What we're going to do is check Bay Ridge again, then we'll turn over every rock we can find in Bensonhurst and Sheepshead Bay."

"What'd this guy do?"

"He's the main suspect in our murder investigation."

"What's Manny Rosso got to do with it?" Meyers asked.

"You didn't hear this from me, Jack, but this guy hit one of Manny's drop spots, killed the owner, and took the bag. We need to get him before Manny loses patience because if that happens, we'll never find him unless we dig through the garbage dumps in New Jersey."

"So we hit Sheepshead Bay first?"

"Sounds good to me," Miller said. "We'll hit every cafe, restaurant, and hangout. If he's here, he'll have shown up at one of those places."

"And you think they're going to tell us?"

"Ordinarily no, but we can use Manny's name, and he'll verify that he approved of it. With his okay to back us up, they'll talk."

"How'd Donovan get hooked up with Manny?"

"It's a long story, Jack. One *I* don't want to talk about, and *you* probably don't want to know about."

"All right," Meyers said. "No need to say more."

Miller drove to Sheepshead Bay and stopped at the first cafe. They got out of the car and approached the owner. She flashed a picture she'd picked up of Joey. "You know him?"

The owner looked like he was going to shake his head when Sherri said, "Manny Rosso said to cooperate with us. He said to call him if you have questions."

The guy looked at her with narrowed eyes. "Manny said so?"

Miller sighed and handed him a slip of paper with Manny's number on it. "Here's his number. Call him. Tell him Miller's here asking questions."

The guy looked at the number, then handed it back to Sherri. "No need to call. That's Manny's number. Okay, so yeah, I know the guy. It's Joey 'Fat Fingers' Tomaselli."

"Have you seen him lately?"

"Saw him about a week ago. He was in here with Ricky Boxcars."

"Any idea where we can find him? Actually, either one of them?"

The guy hesitated, shifted weight from one leg to another. "Word has it he might be up in the Bronx."

"You know where in the Bronx?"

"I don't know where, but if he's in the Bronx, he'll eventually show up on Arthur Avenue."

"Okay, thanks," Sherri said.

Miller got back in the car, and she and Jack drove off.

"Where to now?" Meyers asked.

"We'll keep plugging here, but it looks like we might have to rely on Dominic."

"You think he'll do it?"

"If Manny asks him, I'm guessing he will. From what I understand, he and Manny are friends."

"You don't know Dominic?"

"I don't know him, and from what I've heard, I don't *want* to know him. Donovan's told me a few stories about him, and they were enough to convince me to steer clear. I'll let Manny deal with him. Which reminds me, I better call Manny."

She hung up and dialed the number on the slip of paper she had. "Manny, it's Sherri Miller.

"I'm fine, Manny. Listen, I just talked to a guy in Sheepshead Bay, and he claims Joey is in the Bronx.

"Okay, thanks. If he'll do it, that would be great."

Sherri hung up the phone, and Jack asked, "Well?"

"He said he'd call Dominic again. Joey's as good as ours now."

"And you're good with this?" Meyers asked.

"I'm good with anything legal that gets our man. I don't care who gives him to us."

"But these people are gangsters," Jack said.

Sherri laughed. "Don't we make deals with criminals all the time? Hell, the DAs give them plea bargains for information. This isn't costing us anything."

"Aren't they going to want something in return?"

"You've been watching too many movies, Jack. Sometimes they help for selfish reasons. Take this case." Sherri turned left and headed north. "If we didn't get this guy, Manny would have to track him down and kill him. If we convict him of murder, Manny doesn't have to do anything."

Jack nodded. "In that case, let's finish out the day going to restaurants and cafes."

Chapter Fifteen

WHERE IS KNUCKLES?

Mrozinski turned left onto Franklin Street and drove to Knuckles' address. "Let's go, Detective. Time to find out why this son of a bitch didn't show."

"Could be any reason," Maddy said. "Don't get so worked up."

"Yeah, it *could* be any reason, but I'm a suspicious type. I'm guessing something went wrong or Charlie got cold feet."

Maddy climbed the steps of the porch, knocked on the door, waited a few seconds, then knocked again.

After about ten seconds, Mrozinski stepped forward and knocked harder, much harder.

Maddy waited for almost thirty seconds, then turned. "No one home again. I guess we go to the smoke shop."

"I don't think so," Mrozinski said. "We're going inside."

"We can't do that without a warrant," Maddy said.

"I heard someone cry for help," Mrozinski said. "Maybe you didn't hear it, but I did. I'm going in." He opened the screened door and tried busting through the wooden door. It wouldn't budge. "Use your gun handle and break this window," Mrozinski said.

"Christ's sake, Ed, I can't do that."

Mrozinski drew his gun and used the butt end to break the glass close to the door handle. He then cleared away the broken glass, reached in, and unlocked the door. "Let's go."

The stench hit them quickly. Maddy stepped back, covering her nose. "Oh, my God!"

"I figured as much," Mrozinski said, and walked into the living room. Knuckles lay on the floor surrounded by a pool of congealed blood. "Looks like he's been here a while," he said.

Maddy kept her distance, and she kept her mouth and nose covered. "I guess we know why he didn't show."

Mrozinski knelt to examine the body. "Why don't you step outside and call Fred. Tell him we need this done quickly."

"Be glad too," Maddy said. "By the way, what the hell is the doc's real name?"

Mrozinski laughed. "His name is Dr. Frederick, but people call him doc or Fred."

"What should I call him?"

"Whatever the hell you want. He doesn't seem to care. Just get him over here and tell him to bring a full crime-scene unit."

Maddy stepped outside and made the call while Mrozinski finished examining the body. He came out on the porch a few moments later. "Looks the same, Maddy. Knuckles got it just like Paulie. He was beaten, and he was also shot in the head and heart."

"Doesn't look good for Fusco," Maddy said.

Mrozinski shook his head. "Not good at all."

"What I don't get," Maddy said, "Is how Fusco knew he was going to rat, assuming that's the reason Knuckles was killed."

Mrozinski nodded. "I think you can bet that's why Knuckles was killed, but as to how Fusco knew about it, I don't have a clue. You can bet he did though, and we're going to have to find out."

It took Dr. Frederick an hour to get to Knuckles' address, but he pulled up with a full crime-scene unit.

As he walked toward the house, carrying his bag, he said to Mrozinski, "What have you got, Detective?"

"You tell me, Fred. That's what I'm waiting on. Which reminds me, did you ever get the DNA evidence on the first murder, the one in the woods?"

The doctor nodded. "I had you on my list to call. It was as it looked—an excess of DNA, but a few hair samples matched the profile you gave me—that local character. The problem as I see it is other trace particles matched other characters in the database, including more than a few policemen—local ones too."

"I figured it would," Mrozinski said.

Mrozinski led Fred to Knuckles' body. "What's your initial take on this one?"

Fred shot him a quizzical look. "Good God, Detective. I'm not a magician. Give me some time."

"I'm not asking for a report, just a guess."

Fred stared at the body, then stood and looked around the house. "It looks as if he was killed in a similar manner: beaten with a blunt object and shot in the head and heart. But—and this is a big but—I can't be certain about anything until I'm through with the investigation, and that will take a few days at best."

"Nothing? You've got nothing else for me?"

Fred glanced around the house again. "Just an observation, but it looks as if the victim may have known his attacker because the body is a long way from the front door, and the way it's positioned on the floor, it appears as if the killer may have been behind him. I don't see that happening with a stranger. You don't let a stranger in the house and then have them walk behind you. At least, I wouldn't."

"Unless the killer was holding a gun on him," Maddy said. "In which case, the killer would *have* to be behind him."

Fred nodded. "That would explain it too, Detective. You're right about that. Either way, I'd say he was disabled quickly. He was a big man, and there are no signs of struggle. Give me a few days, and I'll be able to tell when I'm done."

Mrozinski got a smug look on his face. "Okay, Doc. Thanks."

The coroner's team stepped inside and they examined the body. Half an hour later, the doc walked outside.

"I know I'm repeating myself, but from a first look, Detective, it looks to be the same as the others: shot in the head and heart, beaten with a blunt object, and from what I can tell, an excessive amount of DNA. I'll let you know the details when I have them, but you wanted an early assessment, so there it is."

"That's fine. You've given me enough to start with." Mrozinski turned to Maddy. "Let's go. We have a warrant to get and then serve."

"For Fusco?"

"None other," he said, then they got in the car and drove back to the station. "Tell me again what Knuckles said to you when he called."

"Didn't you write it down when I told you?"

"No. I figured you'd be meeting him that night."

Maddy thought for a minute. "He said he had something on Freddy's murder, and that he saw Fusco following him on Union Street the night of the murder."

"Is that it?"

"He said there was more, but he couldn't talk because there were people around. I assumed he was at the smoke shop. Then he told me where to meet him."

"All right," Mrozinski said. "When we get to the station, write it all down so we have it. I'll see the boss and fill him in."

"No problem," Maddy said. "I have it on tape, just not with me."

At the station, Mrozinski told the lieutenant about Charlie's phone call and about him not showing up, then he told him about finding the body, and about what the doc said after examining the body.

"I'm going to see Judge Markham this afternoon. I'll get him to sign a warrant," the lieutenant said.

Around 2:30, the lieutenant returned and handed the warrant to Mrozinski. "Get this served right away. I don't want any more bodies."

"Thanks, Lieutenant. We'll deliver it now."

Mrozinski grabbed Maddy, then they left for Nicky's office. "Hurry up, Maddy. It's Friday, and I want to catch him before he leaves for the weekend."

"You know this isn't going over well," Maddy said.

"Ask me if I give a shit," Mrozinski said. "Then ask me again in twenty minutes."

Chapter Sixteen

YOU'RE UNDER ARREST

Mrozinski and Maddy parked outside the building, walked in, and approached Sheila's desk, then Mrozinski pulled out a warrant and placed it in front of Sheila. "Here to see Nicky."

"I'll call him," she said, and buzzed Nicky on the intercom. "Mr. Fusco, the detectives are here to see you, and they have a warrant.

"Yes, sir. Right away." Sheila looked at Mrozinski and said, "Go on up."

Mrozinski and Maddy walked into Nicky's office. Frankie was sitting in a chair by his desk.

Mrozinski handed the warrant to Nicky. "Mr. Fusco, I'm placing you under arrest for the murders of Paul and Fred Campisi and Charlie Knuckles."

Nicky stood. "Knuckles is dead? You can't think I did that."

"Read the warrant," Mrozinski said.

Nicky glared at the detective. "You're going to regret this, Mrozinski."

Frankie picked up the warrant and began reading. "What brought this on? I thought we talked about coincidence."

"We did, but the medical examiner came back with his report, and DNA at the scene matched Nicky's DNA."

"And how did you get my DNA?" Nicky asked.

"It's on file from when you were in prison," Maddy said.

"How many other people did the DNA match?" Frankie asked. "I know it wasn't just Nicky's at the scene."

"No one yet, but there is more evidence to go through." Mrozinski stepped forward and held out a pair of cuffs. "Anyway, I'm through talking, Nicky. You want to come with us?"

"I don't want to, but I guess I have no choice," he said. "Bugs, will you handle telling Angela?"

"Of course. And I'll get a lawyer, a good one. We'll have you out in no time."

It took a few hours for Frankie to get a lawyer, but he got a good one. The lawyer then arranged for a visit with Nicky in jail. Frankie went with him.

"Nicky, I'm attorney Vaughn Swayzee. I need to ask you some questions."

Nicky nodded. "Ask away; I've got nothing *but* time."

"First, do you have an alibi for *any* of the murders?"

Nicky shook his head. "Not a one. None that would hold up. Paulie was killed shortly after I left a card game at the smoke shop, but I drove around for twenty minutes before going home, and everybody was sleeping when I got there. The next one murdered was Freddy, and he was killed when I was on my way to get subs at Casapulla's, which happens to be a few blocks from his house. And I have no idea where I was when Knuckles was killed."

Swayzee shook his head. "It almost seems as if the murders were planned around your lack of an alibi."

"In other words, a frame job," Frankie said.

"Quite possibly, yes," Swayzee said. "Any idea who would want to frame you, Nicky? Or where someone might get your DNA?"

Nicky laughed. "Plenty of people might want to frame me, but I don't know anyone who wants to do it so bad they'd commit murder. As to the DNA—anyone could get it if they had access to the smoke shop, my office, my car . . . hell, a lot of places."

Swayzee nodded. "Then we need to start by making a list. Once we get the list, we'll methodically eliminate suspects, or if those suspects warrant further investigation, we'll dig into that."

"I appreciate your concern, Mr. Swayzee, but I don't have this kind of money."

Frankie leaned forward. "Pay no attention to him, Swayzee. I'll take care of the money. You concentrate on doing whatever we need to get him free."

Nicky looked to Frankie. "What? You hit the damn lottery or something? How are you gonna pay for it?"

"Don't worry about it, Nicky. I've got it taken care of. Now let's work on putting together the list."

Swayzee stood. "While you two work on that, I'm going to request files on everything the police have. We need to see what we're up against."

"I can't think of anything," Nicky said. "The list of who wanted to hurt the Campisis might go on forever, but I can't think of anyone who would want to harm them *and* who had a beef with me."

Frankie shook his head. "I can't either, Nicky."

"As for Knuckles, I have no idea who'd want to hurt him. He was a good guy. He could push your buttons when he wanted to, but it was all in fun. I don't know anyone who didn't like him. Certainly not enough to kill him, even if it was to frame me."

"We've got to do better than that," Frankie said.

The door opened, and Swayzee walked in. "You're right about that, Donovan. According to this evidence, Charlie was supposed to deliver incriminating evidence on Nicky the night he was killed."

"What!" Nicky said.

Swayzee set a file on the table in front of Nicky. "Look for yourself. He called Detective Viola during the day and asked to meet that night. He said he saw you following Freddy the night before on Union Street when Freddy was heading toward his house."

Frankie looked at Nicky. "Were you on Union Street that night?"

"Yeah. I told you I went to Casapulla's to get subs. I saw Knuckles when I passed the smoke shop. I even beeped the horn at him. I wouldn't have done that if I was following Freddy to kill him."

"Was anyone with Charlie when you saw him?"

"Hell, I don't know . . . Wait. Jimmy the Gem was there. He was right behind Knuckles. No more than ten feet away."

Swayzee took out his pen and started to write. "So you were following Freddy—"

"I wasn't following Freddy," Nicky said. "I didn't even know he was in front of me. He left the bar five or ten minutes before me. He must have stopped somewhere or sat in his car before leaving. Something like that."

Swayzee turned to Frankie. "Detective Donovan, make a note to check the patrons at the bar to confirm the time between when Freddy left and when Nicky left. Also, let's check with this Jimmy the Gem character and verify that Nicky beeped his horn at Charlie."

"I'll get on it right away," Frankie said.

Swayzee tapped his pen on the table while he looked through the files. "The thing I don't like about the murder of Charlie is that he is tied to both of the previous murders."

"How's that?" Nicky asked.

"He was your primary alibi witness for Paulie even though he wouldn't verify the time you left, and he saw you a few cars behind Freddy moments before he was killed. Neither one of them looks good."

Frankie nodded. "He's right, Nicky. It might look like he was trying to cover up for you on Paulie's murder and decided not to cover up with Freddy. Based on his call to the detective, that is."

Nicky shifted in his seat. "Talk to Jimmy. Maybe Knuckles said something to him."

"We probably should keep this to ourselves," Swayzee said. "It doesn't look like the police know Jimmy the Gem was involved."

Frankie nodded. "In case what Jimmy has to say doesn't help, you mean?"

"Why wouldn't it help?" Nicky asked. "I beeped the horn at Knuckles. I wouldn't do that if I had it in mind to kill Freddy."

"Not everyone will see it that way," Swayzee said. "Some people might think you did it just to show you had nothing to hide. It's always a guessing game when juries are involved. Hardcore evidence is what usually decides a case." Swayzee stood straighter. "That and a good lawyer."

"Let's forget the good lawyer part. As far as the evidence, you mean 'hardcore' as in DNA?" Nicky asked.

"Exactly," Swayzee said. "Which reminds me, Donovan. We need to press the coroner to find out who else's DNA was found at the scene of that first murder. From what's in this file, it has to be more than Nicky."

Frankie wrote something down in his notebook. "Got it. I'll call him in the morning."

"You know the coroner?" Nicky asked.

"No, but I'll get Kate to call him. It'll work better that way, with her being a medical examiner."

"Good idea," Nicky said.

"All right, we're set for now," Swayzee said. "Nicky, keep thinking of anything that might help and don't worry about anything else. Detective Donovan and I will do the worrying."

Nicky laughed. "Bugs has you beat hands down in the worrying department, Swayzee. He's good at that. Been doing it all his life."

"Screw you, Rat. Just relax and don't get into trouble," Frankie said. "I'll take care of things from my side."

FRANKIE INVESTIGATES

Frankie got out of his car and walked slowly up the sidewalk to Nicky's house. Angela met him at the door. "Did you hear anything, Frankie? Any news?"

"Nothing yet," Frankie said. "But we're working on it."

"Oh, God. Oh, God. It's happening again. They're going to send him to prison, aren't they? And he didn't do anything." Angela covered her face with her hands and cried.

Frankie pulled her close and hugged. "Don't worry, Angela. I'll take care of it. Don't worry."

"Don't worry? What are *you* going to do? You have no authority down here. You can't do anything."

Frankie knew Angela was right, but he was determined to do *something*. "Don't worry, Angela. I'll get him out."

That night, Frankie slept at Nicky's house, occupying the living-room sofa. The next morning, he ate a late breakfast, gulped his coffee, said goodbye to Angela, then headed for Manko's.

He decided on the drive over that he would talk to the bartender first and, if he had to, he'd go back to speak to patrons.

Stan was wiping down the bar top when Frankie walked in and showed his badge. "If it ain't Bugs Donovan. I heard you were Detective Donovan, but I didn't believe it until now. I haven't seen you in years."

"And it'll probably be years before you see me again," Frankie said. "How's it been going, Stan?"

"Same shit, Frankie. So what the hell brings a famous New York detective down to the Delaware backwoods? And once you explain that, tell me what brings you here so early?"

"I need help, Stan. Or rather, Nicky Fusco needs help. They're trying to pin Freddy Campisi's murder on him. I know he didn't do it, but things don't look good. In particular, the timeline is in question."

"How so?" Stan asked.

"The cops say they have a witness that puts Nicky only a few cars behind Freddy on Union Street that night. But as I understand it, Nicky was here for five or ten minutes after Freddy left."

"That's right," Stan said. "Freddy was being an ass—as usual— and after he left here, Nicky must have talked to three or four people before he left. I'd say it was closer to ten minutes. Maybe even more."

"You'll testify to that?"

"Hell yeah, I'll testify. And there are half a dozen others who will back me up. I'll go through and look at the receipts of who was here that night. I know Markowski was, and I'll check on who else."

Stan opened the register, lifted the drawer, and shuffled through the receipts lying under it. "And I already told that Polack asshole that came here all about it. I even told him Freddy was being an ass."

"I assume you're referring to Mrozinski when you say 'Polack.'"

Stan laughed. "How'd you guess?"

"I suspected when you said 'Polack' but the 'asshole' descriptor confirmed it."

Stan laughed, then said, "No problem, Frankie. Anything you need."

"Okay, thanks, Stan. I appreciate it." Frankie turned to leave, then said, "Stan, if you see Markowski, tell him what I want. And tell him I'll be by to ask a few questions."

"Will do, Frankie. Good to see ya."

Frankie stopped to get another coffee, then he made his way to the smoke shop. Doggs was in the front when he walked in. "Hey, Doggs, long time."

"Christ's sake, if it ain't Bugs Donovan. What the hell are you doing here?"

"Trying to help Nicky out. You heard?"

Doggs turned somber. "Yeah, Nicky and I have had our pissing matches, but no way did he do Knuckles. If it was just the Campisi brothers, I might question it, but no way he did Knuckles. They were friends."

"I agree," Frankie said. "I don't think he did the Campisis either, but definitely no way on Knuckles."

"Yeah, that fuckin' Polack needs to look somewhere else."

"Hey, Doggs, is 'the Gem' here?"

"He's in the back, why? What do you want him for?"

"Nicky said he was with Knuckles the night Freddy died. I need to chat with him about what he saw."

Doggs pressed a buzzer under the cash register. "Go on through. He's back there by himself. But make sure you're a blind man while you're back there."

"Doggs, are you going senile? Do you remember how many times I've been in that back room? For Christ's sake, it's where you gave me my nickname."

Doggs lit another smoke. "Yeah, I know, but I had to say it. Can't be too careful."

Frankie walked into the back room and saw Jimmy sitting at a table by himself. He was playing solitaire. "I see nothing's changed," Frankie said.

Jimmy pushed the chair back and stood. "Bugs Donovan, what the hell brings you here?"

"I'm here about Knuckles," Frankie said. "Nicky said he saw you with him when you were leaving the shop the night before Charlie was killed."

Jimmy laughed. "Same old Bugs. Nicky's right about that, but that's not why you're here. No way you're investigating Knuckles' murder. This is about Nicky, and I'm guessing it's off the books."

"Sharp as ever," Frankie said. "You don't miss a trick."

"When you gotta deal with conniving old weasels like Doggs, you can't afford to miss tricks."

Jimmy reached out and shook Bugs's hand. "I can't even afford to listen to the bullshit flattery you're throwing at me." The Gem sat back down. "Now tell me what you want."

Frankie sat across from him. "Nicky said he saw you and Charlie in front of the smoke shop. He said he beeped his horn at you as he passed."

"And he's right on both counts. In fact, Charlie saw Freddy, then Nicky beeped, then Charlie waved to somebody else, but I don't know who."

"Somebody else? Somebody he knew?"

"Of course it was somebody he knew. You don't wave to people you don't know. What the hell, Bugs? You're making me think all the time you spent in Brooklyn drove you bat-shit crazy. Not that I'm surprised—spending that much time in Brooklyn would make anyone bat-shit crazy."

"Now that I've heard the philosophical Jimmy 'the Gem,' how about telling me if you have any idea who it was?" Frankie asked.

"Not a clue," Jimmy said. "Charlie knew a lot of people. You know that. By the way, Donovan, what's this all about? Why is it important?"

Frankie sighed. "Mrozinski is saying Charlie called and said he saw Nicky following Freddy the night he was killed. He also said Knuckles said he had more to tell, but he couldn't do it there, that he'd meet at the Columbus Inn that night. Next thing we know, Charlie's dead."

Jimmy shook his head. "No way. No fucking way. First off, Charlie wouldn't tell the cops if he witnessed Nicky shoot Freddy—especially Freddy. Secondly, I was with Charlie that day. He was only here about an hour, and I didn't see him make any calls. I can't swear to it. I mean, he could have gone into the pisser and called someone, but I don't think he did."

"You're sure about that?" Frankie asked.

"If you mean 'am I sure' he didn't make any calls, no, I'm not sure, but I don't think so. Like I said, he could have gone to the pisser and made a call for all I know. But if you're asking me if Charlie would rat somebody out to the cops—not a fucking snow-ball's chance in hell. Not Charlie. He saw a guy shoot his cousin when he was a kid, and he didn't even rat him out. He got even for it years later, but he never ratted."

Frankie nodded. "That's what I thought. Back to the day Charlie was killed—you remember what time he was here that day?"

"I know exactly what time. I was here between nine and eleven, and Charlie left about half an hour before I did. Peg it at 10:30 or so."

Frankie smiled. "Perfect, Jimmy. I appreciate it."

"Hey, Donovan, I know you cops are always wanting people to testify to things and such. If that's still the case, then yeah, I'll testify to what I said. All of it."

"*Perfetto*, Jimmy. *Grazie*."

"All right, Donovan. You don't have to try to impress me with your Italian language skills. Just get the hell out of here and find out who killed Knuckles."

Later that night, Frankie pored over case files until he found something he thought would help. *Got it. Now I'm going to shove it up Mrozinski's ass.*

Chapter Eighteen

MROZINSKI STRIKES BACK

Frankie waited outside for Mrozinski to show up. After ten minutes, Mrozinski pulled to the curb and got out of his car. "Donovan, what are you doing here?"

"I'm here to prove that Nicky had nothing to do with these murders."

"And how are you going to do that?" Mrozinski asked.

"Because I did *real* police work and talked to *real* witnesses."

"Let's hear what you have," Mrozinski said.

Frankie filled him in on what Jimmy the Gem had told him, and then asked for the exact time of the call from Knuckles.

"I don't have the exact time," Mrozinski said.

"In other words, you're going to make up a time to coincide with when Knuckles was at the smoke shop. I got news for you," Frankie said. "I'm going to the phone company, and I'll get the records so we can verify the time."

Mrozinski smiled. "If you look at the report closer, you'll see we didn't say he was *definitely* at the smoke shop; we said he was somewhere he couldn't talk. We may have made an assumption it was the smoke shop, but we didn't clarify it."

"Just like I figured," Frankie said. "You're no better than the rest of the cops here. I thought you wanted to solve the crime, but you just want to close the case any way you can. Doesn't matter if an innocent man goes to prison."

"Donovan, even if the *wrong* man goes to prison for this one, it won't be an innocent man."

Frankie got up and headed for the door. "You fuckin' whore. You're as bad as whoever really did these crimes. And don't worry, Mrozinski, I'm gonna find who did it, and then I'll put him *and* you away."

"Good luck with that."

Frankie left and went to the phone company, but his connections were long gone. Without a court order, he had no way of getting the logs. With no recourse, he called Doggs. "Doggs, you still got connections with the phone company?"

"Are cops crooked? Don't be an ass. Of course I have connections at the phone company. Why?"

"Nicky needs help, and I need some phone records to help him."

"Give me the dates—the times if you have them—and the phone numbers," Doggs said. "It may take a day or so, but I'll get them."

Frankie gave Doggs what he wanted, then went to see Nicky. "Jimmy verifies he saw you that night, and he'll also state that Charlie saw someone else, but he doesn't know who. You got any idea who it was?"

Nicky shook his head. "Not a clue. I told you. I didn't see Freddy, and I didn't see anyone else. If somebody was there, either I didn't see him, or I didn't know him."

"Who's Charlie going to know that you don't?" Frankie asked.

"Shit, I don't know, Bugs. It could be a hundred people. I was gone for a lot of years, remember."

"Yeah, I guess so," Frankie said. "Still, it would be nice to know who he saw."

"What else have you got?" Nicky asked.

"Not much yet, but Doggs is getting me some phone records that might help. If they do, I'll be back. Mrozinski's being a prick about all this."

"He has been all along," Nicky said. "Work with Viola. She seems like a good person."

"You trust her?" Frankie asked.

"I don't know if I trust her completely, but my gut instinct tells me she's all right."

Frankie left the jail and called Viola.

"Detective Viola."

"Detective, this is Frankie Donovan, a friend of Nicky Fusco's. Remember, we—"

"I know who you are," she said.

"Can you talk? Is anyone with you?"

"I could meet you for coffee later today. Say five o'clock."

"Perfect. How about the cafe on Delaware Avenue just up from Scott Street? You should be safe from prying eyes there."

"I'll be there at five," she said.

———

"Who was that?" Mrozinski asked when Maddy hung up.

"An old friend of mine. She's in town from Philly and wants to catch up. Christ, she comes in town every month or so and wants to catch up like she's been gone for years. Drives me crazy."

"I know what you mean," Mrozinski said. "I got a cousin like that. He lives in North Jersey, and when he comes for a visit, he expects to be treated like he came in from Poland."

"Some people," Maddy said. "Anyway, did I miss anything on the case?"

"Fusco's got his lawyer and Donovan asking questions at Manko's. He's also been pestering people at the smoke shop. Donovan thinks he's got something, but we'll put a stop to that."

"Mrozinski, what makes you so sure Fusco did these crimes?"

"For God's sake, Maddy. Look at the evidence."

"I'm trying to look at it with an objective eye, but I don't see it. First off, we can't use the way these people were killed as evidence because Fusco wasn't convicted of those crimes in Brooklyn. And if he had been, would he be so stupid as to do it again?"

"Maybe that's his plan? Throwing us off by figuring that we'd think that way."

"Okay, second. If he's following Freddy to kill him, would he beep his horn to Knuckles? Chances are Knuckles would have never seen him if he hadn't beeped. And then Knuckles gets killed? I'm sorry. I don't buy it."

"What about Manko's?" Mrozinski asked.

"Let's look at the whole thing at Manko's—Nicky arguing with Freddy. Are you gonna kill somebody the same night you had an argument with him? If you're a hothead, you might do it while the argument is going on, but you're not going to wait till the guy leaves, then track him down and kill him. I don't see it. And there's the time factor. Stan said Nicky left ten minutes after Freddy, so how did he get two cars behind him by the time they got to the smoke shop?"

Mrozinski gritted his teeth. "We're still left with Knuckles."

"Yeah, we're left with Knuckles, and he's the worst. There was no reason in hell for Nicky to kill him."

"Charlie was going to tell us something about him."

"Was he?" Maddy asked. "Or did Charlie already say everything? And regardless, how did Nicky know he had talked to us? It doesn't add up, Mrozinski. None of it."

Mrozinski shook his head. "I just follow the evidence, and the evidence is pointing to Fusco."

"I don't think it is. I think you *want* it to point to him, but I don't buy it. If I were a juror, I sure as hell wouldn't convict."

"Viola, I'm lead on this, and while you're working with me, you'll do as I say. And that means keep your opinions to yourself."

"Can't do that, Mrozinski. Can't and won't. I plan on looking at all angles of the case. If it leads to Fusco, so be it, but if it leads somewhere else, I'm following it."

"Don't worry, it'll lead to Fusco," Mrozinski said.

The rest of the day, the detectives talked to people at Manko's, and they interviewed more people who might have witnessed the murders in Canby Park or at Knuckles' house on Franklin Street. Regardless of their persistence, however, they got nothing new.

"Time for me to go," Maddy said. "It's four-thirty, and I told Samantha I'd meet her at five."

Mrozinski drove to the station and dropped Maddy off to get her car. "See you in the morning, Maddy."

"Think about what I said," Maddy hollered as she got out of the car. "Be objective."

———

Maddy started the engine and drove to the coffee shop on Delaware Avenue. Frankie was inside waiting.

When Maddy walked in, Frankie got up. "Hey, Viola. What'll you have? I'll place an order."

"No worries. I'll get it. Take a seat before you lose it."

Frankie sat down and waited for her to return. "What did you call me for?" she asked.

"I've been talking to some of the guys at the smoke shop, and I'm getting information that doesn't necessarily jibe with what Mrozinski has in the reports."

"Like what?" Maddy asked.

"Like the official report states, Charlie called you from the smoke shop at about 11:30."

"Yeah?"

"He wasn't at the smoke shop at 11:30. Everyone said he left about 10:30. And even if your times are off, no one remembers him making a phone call. Especially one that lasted as long as you indicated."

Maddy seemed to think. "So what's that tell you?"

"It tells me that Knuckles wasn't at the smoke shop when he called you. And if he wasn't there, why did he make it appear as if he were by saying he had ears everywhere? Everybody knows Knuckles didn't go many places, especially places where there would be people listening. So if he wasn't at the smoke shop, where was he? And why hide where he was?"

"Good questions, Donovan."

Frankie sipped his drink. "There's something in that explanation that explains why Knuckles got killed, and we need to find out what."

Maddy stopped for a moment and whispered, "I've been wondering myself about the whole Knuckles thing. When I talked to him about Nicky's alibi for Paulie, he shut up tight as a drum, and then all of a sudden he calls about seeing Nicky following Freddy. It didn't add up."

"It also makes me wonder who else he saw on Union Street."

"What are you talking about?" Maddy asked.

Frankie appeared surprised. "I assumed Mrozinski told you. Jimmy the Gem told me that Knuckles saw somebody else drive by at the same time he saw Nicky, but Jimmy doesn't know who it was. He saw Knuckles wave to him though."

"And you told Mrozinski this?" Maddy asked.

"I told him all of this. I'm guessing he wanted to keep it to himself."

"Son of a bitch!" Maddy said.

"Maddy, listen up. You know I've been friends with Nicky for a long time. That aside, if he did these murders, I'd be the first one to say lock him up. I investigated him in Brooklyn when I was looking into a string of murders a few years ago."

"And?" Maddy asked.

"And I cleared him," Frankie said. "I'm his friend, but I'm a cop. I'm not gonna hide things from you."

Maddy wrapped her hands around the coffee cup. "Okay, good. Then you have my word I'll play this straight too. I'll make sure Mrozinski looks at, and considers, all evidence."

Frankie reached his hand out to shake. "Sounds good."

"So what now?" Maddy asked.

"I've got someone looking into the phone records to see where Knuckles' call *really* came from. That will tell us something once we get that. I'll call when I get it. By the way, I was surprised Mrozinski didn't order this, so if I were you, I'd suggest it and see what he says. If it proves to be useful, we'll need an official copy anyway because we won't be able to use mine."

Maddy laughed. "All right, Donovan. You got it." Maddy stood and tossed her trash into the can next to her. "You've given me a lot to go over. Now I better go home and do my work."

"Good," Frankie said. "I'll keep busy on my end, and I'll call when I get something."

"I'll do the same," Maddy said. "And tell Fusco, despite what he may think, I only want who did this—who *really* did it, not a scapegoat."

"He'll be glad to hear it, but not surprised."

Maddy turned. "What do you mean by that?"

"Nicky's the one who told me to seek you out. I was hesitant, but he said he trusted you. That he felt you'd be fair."

Maddy smiled. "No shit?"

Frankie nodded. "No shit."

"All right, Donovan, I'll see you later. I gotta go."

Chapter Nineteen

IS JOEY STILL ALIVE?

Frankie's phone rang after he went to bed. He jumped up and grabbed it, looking at the time as he did—11:30. He grabbed the phone, answering in a pissed-off mood. "Who the hell is this?"

"Damn different way of answering the phone."

"Miller? Is this you?"

"Don't you look at Caller ID? Yeah, it's me. Why, were you sleeping?"

"Yeah, I was sleeping. It *is* almost midnight."

"I need you to find something out for me."

"What?" Frankie asked.

"I think Manny is giving me the runaround. He's telling me 'Fat Fingers' Joey is gone, as in left the city. I tend to think he may be gone as in dumped in a swamp somewhere. I need you to find out which it is."

Frankie laughed. "Miller, I may be close to Manny, but I'm not *that* close. He's not gonna tell me if he whacked someone."

"I know that, but you can get an idea. Talk to him and let me know what you think."

"All right, I'll check it out." Frankie looked at the clock again and realized there was plenty of time to call Manny. He went downstairs and made a pot of coffee, then picked up the phone and dialed.

As he thought would happen, Manny answered right away, and he sounded bright and alert. He definitely wasn't asleep.

"Bugs! What the hell are you doing calling this time of night?"

"Come on, Manny. It's the middle of the day for you."

"You got that right. What do you want?"

"I need a favor," Bugs said.

Manny laughed. "I knew that much when the phone rang. So tell me what the favor is."

"Is Joey alive?"

"How the hell should I know? If you're asking, did I kill him, the answer is no."

"But I didn't ask that, Manny. I asked if he was still alive?"

"Let me answer a different way. I presume you're asking for your partner. If I were you, I'd tell her not to bother looking for Joey anymore. I think she'd be wasting her time."

"In other words, he's dead."

"I didn't say that," Manny said.

"But you wouldn't look any further?" Frankie asked.

"No, I wouldn't," Manny said.

"Let's say Joey killed your brother, would you still be looking for him?"

"I doubt it," Manny said. "I'd probably just move on to other things and forget about Joey."

"Okay, Manny. Thanks."

"No problem," Manny said. "How are things going with Nicky?"

"Not good, but I'm working on it."

"Don't hesitate to call," Manny said. "You only owe me one favor right now. Plenty of room for more. I like having people owe me favors, especially cops."

"I'm working on it, Manny. I just need to figure out who hated Nicky so much that they'd kill for it."

"You got a big suspect list, starting with Renzo Ciccarelli."

"Why do you say that?" Frankie asked.

"Because Renzo had a big family. Couple of kids, two brothers, and lots of cousins. Any one of them could be a suspect."

"I doubt they'd even know about it. Most of what happened was kept secret."

Manny laughed. "Secret? You still naïve enough to think you can keep a secret? This town has eight million people, and secrets don't last long."

"What are you talking about?"

"Secrets are bullshit, Bugs. If one person knows, a hundred know. We had a saying growing up that the only person who could keep a secret was a dead man. Hell, even the three monkeys can't keep a secret."

"The three monkeys?"

"Yeah, you know, the ones who can't see, or hear, or talk. Christ, Bugs, don't you know nothin'? I thought the Irish educated their kids."

"Who else would be on this imaginary list of yours?" Frankie asked.

"Bugs, you're getting dangerously close to another favor. I want you to know that."

"Keep going," Frankie said.

"You got Tommy Devin, but he didn't have much in the way of family. Had a brother, but he was older than Tommy. I doubt it would have been him."

"Why do you say that, because he was older?"

"Two reasons. Patrick was never a patient guy, so I don't see him waiting this long. But more importantly, he didn't like Tommy that much. I don't see him risking anything to get even for him."

"Okay, I'll buy that. Who's next?" Frankie asked.

"You got Donnie Amato. He had a kid in his twenties. That's a possibility. And you got Johnny Muck and Tito, but I'd say no to both of them."

"Why's that?"

"Johnny Muck didn't have anybody that I know of, and nobody liked Tito enough to care about him. I can vouch for that. I worked for that son of a bitch for years, and I bet there weren't three days that I liked him."

"So your guess is Renzo or Donnie Amato?"

"Off the cuff, yeah. That's my guess. But you gotta do the leg work on this. Find out where these people were when things went down."

"All right, Manny. I'll take care of that. God forbid I owe you another favor."

"Ain't that the truth. I'll make a corrupt cop outta you yet."

"Yeah, yeah. I hear you. Just keep your ears open for me. And that's *not* a favor."

Manny laughed. "You got it, Bugs. I'll let you know if I hear something."

Frankie disconnected the call and dialed Sherri Miller.

"Hello?"

"Miller, it's Frankie."

"Frankie, so strange to hear from you at this hour. I didn't expect a call back so soon. How are things going? Are you on your way home?"

"No, I'm still down in Wilmington. I was calling regarding your case with "Fat Fingers" Joey."

"What about it?"

"You should probably drop it. Write up what you have about who did it, but leave it open. Just say you can't find the guy."

"Where's this coming from? Did you talk to Manny?" Miller asked.

"Let's just say it's a hunch."

"A hunch? You had a hunch that Joey disappeared?"

"Let's leave it at that, yeah."

"All right, Frankie. I'll go with what you say. By the way, how's Nicky?"

"Not good. Somebody's trying to frame him, and they're doing a damn good job; at least by Wilmington police standards, they are."

"Any leads on who it may be?"

"Nothing yet," Frankie said. "I'm working on it."

"Whatever you do, don't waste any time. Morreau is pissed. I've never seen him this mad."

"Screw him," Frankie said. "He can stay pissed. I don't need him or his job. I've got to help Nicky."

"All right, Donovan. Take it easy. I'll see you when this is over."

"Yeah, see ya, Miller."

Chapter Twenty

THE PHONE REPORT COMES IN

Frankie arrived at the jail ten minutes after visitation was allowed. "Here to see Fusco," he said to the guard.

"Who?"

"Fusco. I know you don't have too many people with that name in here."

The guard escorted Frankie to Nicky's cell and let him in. Frankie waited for him to be out of earshot, then sat at the table, leaned over, and whispered. "I got the call from Doggs. His contact at the phone company came through."

"And?"

"And it's even better than I hoped for. Knuckles placed the call to Viola from his house, which means there'd be no reason for him to say he had ears everywhere."

Nicky lifted his head. "That leaves a few questions. Why'd he make the call? Why'd he do it from his house? And why'd he say he had ears everywhere?"

Frankie nodded. "We need to give all of those some thought. And by the way, you were right about Viola. I met with her last night. I think she's okay."

Nicky smiled. "Good to see my bullshit meter still works."

"Easy going, Nicky. I said I *think* she's okay. That's not a full-blown endorsement."

"I'll go with my gut," Nicky said. "Keep working with her. She'll do okay."

Frankie flipped through a couple pages in his notebook. "Nicky, I can't help but wonder how whoever's doing this is getting his information."

"You mean about the Brooklyn crimes?"

"That, but a lot more too. The big one is how'd he know about Brooklyn. I'm gonna assume that had to come from somebody in New York, but who? And the next is just as important. How'd he know who to target down here? What made him pick Paulie and Freddy?"

"I don't have the answer, Bugs, but it wouldn't take much digging to find out I wasn't on the best terms with them."

"I'll buy that, but what about Knuckles? Why would somebody target him? For all intents and purposes, you and he were friends and on good terms. Who could know he talked to Viola about a lead? And if they did know, why would they target him. If they're after you, you'd think Charlie giving the cops information would be a plus."

"Yeah, but what information could he have been giving them?" Nicky asked. "All he said was he saw me on Union Street, a couple cars behind Freddy. Hell, I would have told them that much; I basically did when I said I went to Casapulla's. The only thing I didn't say was Freddy was a few cars ahead of me, but that was because I didn't know."

"What else do you think it could have been?" Frankie asked.

"That's just it, Bugs. I can't think of anything. As far as I know, there *was* nothing else."

"The timing on all of these was too precise as well, Nicky."

"What do you mean?"

"Paulie was killed right after you left the card game. With no alibi, I might add. Freddy was killed while you were close by, and again, with no alibi. And Knuckles was killed right after he said he was coming in with information, and you with no alibi once more."

Nicky thought for a moment. "What if Knuckles had no other information? What if that's why he was killed, simply to cast suspicion on me and make it seem as if I wanted him dead because he might tell the cops something?"

"Then why did he call to begin with?"

"Suppose he had no choice," Nicky said. "Suppose someone made him."

Frankie laughed. "Who the hell could make Knuckles do something he didn't want to do?"

"Anybody with a gun," Nicky said, "which would explain why Knuckles was killed in his house. Maybe the person targeted him there so he could make the call, then, after the call, he killed Knuckles."

"But why Knuckles?" Frankie asked, then he slapped the table with his palm, as if an idea struck. "The other person on Union Street that night, the one Jimmy said Knuckles waved to."

"Wait a minute," Nicky said. "You didn't tell me anything about that."

"What? I thought I did. Anyway, Jimmy said Charlie saw Freddy go by, then you beeped, then he waved to someone else."

"But Jimmy didn't know who?"

"He said he didn't see him, and he didn't ask Charlie, so no, he didn't know who it was."

"Then that has to be it," Nicky said. "Whoever was in that car has to be the guy. He'd be the only one besides Jimmy who knew Knuckles saw me that night."

Frankie nodded slowly. "And if he was following Freddy, he'd know Freddy was just ahead of you."

"Exactly," Nicky said. "By killing Knuckles, it looks as if I'm killing him to shut him up, prevent him from telling the cops something."

"But that also means he saw Jimmy. Does that mean he's in danger?"

Nicky shook his head. "Not now. I don't think so. He wouldn't kill him while I'm in jail with a solid alibi. Everything so far has been done to pin it on me."

Frankie tapped his pen on the table. "But if you got out of jail, it would be a different thing."

"What are you getting at, Bugs?"

"If we could get Mrozinski to go along with us, we could get a judge to give you bail and let you out so everyone would know."

"No way," Nicky said. "It'd put a crosshairs on Jimmy. I can't risk his life."

"We can watch him," Frankie said.

"I knew a cop a few years back who thought he could keep an eye on a few mobsters. You know where that got him?"

"Screw you, Rat."

"Just saying." Nicky thought for a moment. "But if you substitute a cop decoy for Jimmy, I'd go along with that."

"Son of a bitch! Son of a bitch. You might have it, Nicky. I'll talk to Mrozinski and see if we can put this in motion."

"Don't tell anyone about it, Bugs. Mrozinski and Viola. No one else."

"Hey, I *have* run police operations, you know."

"But have they been successful?" Nicky asked, and laughed.

"Screw you again, Rat. I've got half a mind to let you rot in here."

"I know. I know," Nicky said. "But that's only half a mind. Now go get Mrozinski to buy into this plan and let's get it moving."

———

Frankie left the jail and immediately went to see Mrozinski. He waited a few minutes, then was shown to his office.

"What's on your mind, Donovan?"

Frankie sat in the chair across from the detective. "I've got a proposal you're not going to like, Mrozinski, but I want you to listen to the whole plan before you say anything."

"Start talking. If I like what you have to say, I'll go along with it," Mrozinski said. "Let's hear."

Chapter Twenty-One

THE TRAP

After pressure from Swayzee—not to mention Viola, his own partner—Mrozinski okayed Nicky's bail and said he'd handle the arrangements. That meant Frankie had to set things up with Jimmy the Gem.

He drove to the smoke shop just after lunch. Doggs was out front when Frankie drove up.

"Donovan, what the hell do you want? I'm not comfortable with the damn cops hanging around here like it's a donut shop." Doggs turned his head and mumbled. "That shit will give a respectable place a bad name."

Frankie stifled a laugh, though he did grin. "Jimmy here?"

"In the back, why? What do you want with him?"

"Because I need to talk to him, Doggs. For Christ's sake, you his mother or something?"

Doggs hit the buzzer and let Frankie into the back room. Frankie lit a smoke and sat at the table with the Gem. "Jimmy, hard at work I see."

"Yeah, it's a bitch, but you gotta put the time in," Jimmy said as he placed a red deuce on a black three.

Frankie moved the chair next to him and whispered, "Jimmy, I'm talking low because it's important to keep this quiet."

Jimmy nodded. "It's okay to talk low, but you gotta get above a fuckin' whisper or I can't hear you."

"Where do you live?" Bugs asked in a slightly raised voice.

Jimmy scowled, but he managed to keep his voice lower than normal. "Over on Bancroft Parkway, Bugs. You know where I live. Ain't three blocks from here."

"Jimmy, I've been gone a long time. I didn't know if you were still there."

"Yeah. Same place. Why'd you ask? You wanna go dancing or something?"

"We think you might be in danger, Jimmy, and we want to set a trap."

"In danger? Me? Who the hell wants to hurt me? And why?"

"In danger from the same guy who killed Knuckles," Frankie said. "We think he may target you next."

"Why would he target me? I don't know nothin' about nothin'. And I wouldn't say so if I did."

"Because you probably saw the killer, or at least he *thinks* you saw him."

"Saw who? What the hell are you talking about?"

Frankie took a deep breath. "Remember the night Freddy was killed—when you and Knuckles were leaving here and saw Nicky? The same night you told me Knuckles waved to someone else on Union Street?"

Jimmy nodded. "I remember. So what?"

"We're convinced that whoever Knuckles waved to is the killer. And if he is, he might think you saw him too."

"I didn't see anybody. At least nobody I recognized."

"I know that, but the killer doesn't. If he thinks you recognized him, you're a likely target. We're pretty sure that's what got Charlie killed."

"I thought Charlie had something on Nicky and was gonna tell Mrozinski."

"That's what Mrozinski said, and maybe he really thought that, but I don't buy it, do you? You ever known Charlie to rat on anybody? For *anything*? I think the killer forced him to make that call in order to throw the cops off, then he killed him."

Jimmy nodded. "Sounds more like Charlie. Like I told you, he wouldn't rat on anybody."

"I'm with you on that," Frankie said. "Now back to your situation."

"They're letting Nicky out of jail. Once that's done, the killer is free to kill you because he can do it when Nicky has no alibi."

"What do you want me to do?"

"You got a back door you can sneak out of?"

"Yeah, no problem."

"Okay, the plan is simple. You go home, walk in, and right away go out the back door. We'll have two officers waiting to escort you to a safe house. In the meantime, a decoy will be inside, and we'll have him step onto the porch to distract whoever might be watching. Then he'll be joined by another officer from the back, and they'll wait for the killer to make his move."

"And suppose he doesn't make a move?"

"Then the next morning, the cops will deliver you back into your house the same way, and we repeat the procedure until he does."

"And you feel sure he'll try something?" Jimmy asked.

"Almost positive," Frankie said. "I wouldn't ask you if I wasn't convinced of it."

"What's Nicky think?"

"Nicky wouldn't go along with it unless we used a decoy. He didn't want anything happening to you."

Jimmy laughed. "Good ol' Nicky. He's a great guy."

"Well?" Frankie asked.

"All right," Jimmy said. "When do we start?"

"Tonight," Frankie said.

"Tonight? What were you gonna do if I said no?"

"We weren't going to go through with it, and Nicky would stay in jail."

"You mean Nicky was willing to stay in jail to protect me?"

Frankie nodded. "He insisted you were kept safe."

"Son of a bitch," Jimmy said. "Let's get this prick."

Frankie handed Jimmy a piece of paper and a pen. "Write down your address so I can get the cops positioned. Plan on going home about seven o'clock."

"That's early, Bugs. Way too early."

Frankie thought for a moment. "Okay, how about nine?"

"Better make it eleven. Even that's early, but it's not unheard of."

Frankie smiled. "Okay, eleven it is. And don't worry. We'll have your back."

"I'm not worried, but hey, Bugs. Tell them cops I'll be carrying just in case."

"Will do, Jimmy. Take care."

———

Frankie went back to the station and let Mrozinski know the plan was a go. "It's on for eleven o'clock," Frankie said. "Jimmy said it would look fishy if he went home any earlier."

"He bought into it, then?" Mrozinski asked.

Frankie nodded. "I explained the whole thing, dangers and all. Jimmy said he'd be glad to help."

Mrozinski shook his head. "I don't know why people are so willing to stick their necks out for Fusco."

Frankie scowled. "Because he's a damn nice guy, that's why. Ask your ex-partner—Borelli. He'll tell you."

"What's he going to tell me? That Nicky killed a dozen people."

"Why don't you call him and find out."

"I would, but I've got no way of reaching him," Mrozinski said.

Frankie smiled. "Ask Nicky. He can reach him."

"Fusco can reach him?" Mrozinski asked.

"Maybe Borelli trusts Nicky more than you," Frankie said.

"All right, enough of that, Donovan. If we're getting Fusco out of jail, we need to get busy. I'll get prepared while you notify reporters what's going on."

———

Around three o'clock, Mrozinski walked out of the jail on Twelfth Street with Nicky Fusco beside him. A half dozen reporters swarmed them like kids at a concert.

"We're outside the prison facility in the 1300 block of Twelfth Street witnessing the release of what had been the number-one suspect in the string of killings the city has experienced. Three bodies, two of them brothers, have turned up in recent weeks, and they are said to have striking similarities to a series of murders in Brooklyn years ago, where surprisingly enough, the same person was also a suspect, though no charges were brought against him in those instances."

Mrozinski walked out onto Twelfth Street and headed toward his car. "Detective, what prompted the release of your suspect?"

"No comment," Mrozinski said.

"Do you have someone else? Has Fusco been cleared by evidence? What about the DNA? I thought there was DNA evidence."

"No comment," Mrozinski said again. He opened the back door of the car for Nicky, and then he climbed in the driver's seat and started the engine.

As he drove away, his phone rang. "Yeah, who is it?"

"It's me, Mrozinski. Try looking at Caller ID from now on."

"What do you want, Donovan?"

"I just wanted to tell you that your show looked good. Could've fooled anyone."

"Let's hope it fooled the right person," Mrozinski said, assuming there *is* a right person.

"No doubt there is one, and my guess is he's fooled. Call your men and tell them the game is on. I'll call Jimmy."

"All right, Donovan. I'll keep you posted."

"Good. I'll be with Nicky all night. I intend to stay at his place. Call if you need me."

Frankie had already arrived at Nicky's house when Mrozinski pulled up. He let Nicky out of the back of the car. "Don't go anywhere, Fusco. With any luck, you'll be a free man in a day or so."

"Don't worry, Detective, I know how to play the game. Good hunting. And take care of Jimmy."

Mrozinski drove away with a sour look on his face. He called Preswick for the second time. "Preswick, it's Mrozinski. Make sure you keep your eyes open and call me for anything. I mean *anything*. No matter how late."

———

Nicky gave Angela a big hug, then hugged Rosa and Dante. Lastly, he grabbed hold of Bugs and hugged him. "Thanks for everything, Bugs. You're a friend."

"Nonsense, Nicky. You've done a lot more than this for me.

Now let's get to work and figure this out. We can't leave anything to chance."

"Got anything in mind, Bugs?"

"One thing I thought of since you left. We need to get hold of the medical examiner's reports and see if everything matched up. It might tell us a lot."

"Good idea," Nicky said, and looked at the time. "Maybe you should call him now."

———

Mrozinski's phone rang, and he answered quickly. "Hello?"

"Hello, sweetie. It's just me. Are you on your way home?"

Mrozinski sighed. "Yeah, I'm trying. I should be there in thirty minutes or so. And I'd love it if you had a couple of cold beers waiting for me—hell, make it a six-pack. I need the refreshment."

Mrozinski's phone rang again almost immediately. "Yeah."

"Mrozinski, it's Donovan. Since you're in such a good mood, I have a favor to ask. I need to look at the coroner's reports on all the murders. I could have our lawyer, Swayzee, put in a formal request, but let's not play games. How about just turning them over?"

"Fine, Donovan. Call Maddy and have her get them for you. You're not going to find anything, but have at it."

"Thanks, Mrozinski. I'll call her now."

———

Frankie hung up the phone and called Viola. "Maddy, it's Frankie Donovan. I just spoke to Mrozinski, and he said to call you to get a copy of the medical examiner's reports for the murders."

"For real, Donovan?"

"For real. Call him if you like. He's on his way home."

"All right. Don't take offense that I'm calling. I'm just covering my ass. Assuming your story checks out, stop by in the morning and get the copies. I'll have them ready."

"Okay, thanks, Maddy. I appreciate it."

"Hey, Donovan. How'd you convince Mrozinski to let Nicky go? I know it was your doing."

"It was my charm, Maddy. Nothing else."

"Just call me in the morning, Donovan. I don't have time for your shit tonight."

Chapter Twenty-Two

HOW WERE THEY KILLED?

Frankie pulled in front of the station and walked inside, leaving Nicky in the passenger seat. Mrozinski met Frankie when he opened the door.

"Donovan, what the hell are you doing here? Who's watching—"

"Fusco's in the car, Mrozinski. Calm down."

"Oh shit, I thought—"

"I know what you thought, but I wouldn't do that. I told you I'd watch him, and I will. I came by to pick up the coroner's reports. Remember, I asked about them?"

Mrozinski nodded. "Yeah, I remember. And Maddy asked me about them before making copies." He pointed toward the front. "The desk sergeant has them, and they're already packed neatly in a manilla folder."

"So nothing happened last night?" Frankie asked.

Mrozinski shook his head. "Not a damn thing. My guys said it was as quiet as could be. My other team brought Jimmy back this morning. He showered, changed clothes, and left a few minutes ago. Maybe something will happen tonight."

"When's your team going back?" Frankie asked.

"They're staying at Jimmy's house in case the guy tries to get inside and wait. I figured it's better to be safe."

"Good idea, Mrozinski. And I agree it's always better to be safe. Don't worry. We'll get this guy sooner rather than later. In the meantime, I gotta go. See you later."

Frankie picked up the report from the front desk, then headed out the door. He handed the package to Nicky when he got in the car.

"No sense in giving this to me," Nicky said. "I can't understand what it says."

"I didn't expect you to," Frankie said. "I just gave it to you to hold. I'm going to send the report to Kate and let her look at it. It'll be especially good since she did the original murders in Brooklyn. She'll be able to tell us about any differences."

"Damn, Bugs. Who said you weren't smart?"

"You better watch out, Nicky. I promised Mrozinski I'd be with you night and day until this was over."

"He's afraid I'm going to sneak out and kill someone, huh?"

Frankie laughed. "Something like that, yeah."

"By the way, does Kate know you're sending these files up?"

"Not yet, but she will in a minute." Frankie pulled out his phone. "Hey, Siri, call Kate."

"Kate Donovan."

"Good to see you're answering with the right last name," Frankie said.

"I only married you because of your nice Irish name," Kate said. "Besides, I saw it was you on Caller ID, which might also be why I answered that way. But I'm impressed. What a great detective you are."

Frankie laughed. "I forgot about Caller ID, so you're right, that's not good detective work, is it?"

"How are things down in Delaware?" Kate asked. "Anything new?"

"Not great, but getting better," Frankie said. "Listen, the reason I'm calling—"

"I knew there was a reason you called. If you were a good detective, you'd have pretended you called just to say hello and tell me how much you loved me and missed me. Then you could suddenly remember something to ask me."

"I'll do that next time, Mrs. Donovan. For today, just pretend I did it."

Kate laughed. "What do you need?"

"I'm going to send you the local coroner's report on each of the murders we've had. They appear to have been staged to resemble the Brooklyn murders you worked on a few years ago. I'd love it if you could compare them and tell me what—if anything—is different."

"No problem," Kate said. "Can you send them as PDFs in an email?"

"PDFs would make it easier," Frankie said. "I was dreading having to fax all those pages."

"Send them up, and I'll get right on it. And tell Nicky not to worry."

"Hell, he *never* worries. I think I'm more worried than he is."

"Then tell Angela not to worry."

"Will do," Frankie said. "I'm going to send you the files as soon as we get to Nicky's house. Shouldn't be more than a few minutes."

Frankie's phone rang just as he turned the corner onto Beech Street. It was Mrozinski. "Yeah, Mrozinski, Nicky's right here with me."

"That's not why I called, asshole. I was checking to see if we needed to do anything with Jimmy? Does he know what to do?"

"I'm sure he does, but I'll call him to double-check. It's the same as last night, right?"

"Right, the same routine," Mrozinski said. "Let's hope something happens tonight."

"Fingers are crossed," Frankie said. "Talk to you later."

———

Jimmy hung around the smoke shop until almost 11:00, then he went to his car and drove home. He parked in front of his house and stayed alert as he walked in. Once inside, two of the cops escorted him out the back door and drove him to a safe house while two more cops stayed inside.

"You know this is ridiculous," Jimmy said as he walked to the officer's car. "There's nobody after me. Nothing's going to happen."

"Not for me to decide," one of the cops said. "We're just following orders, and those orders say to take you to a safe house when you get home and bring you back in the morning."

"At least stop and let me get a coffee," Jimmy said.

The driver shook his head. "Not gonna happen. We're not supposed to stop or to tell anyone where we're taking you."

"Christ's sake, I'm bored. Do you guys at least play pinochle?"

"Never learned to play," the cop said.

"How about I teach you? We can play for a dollar a point, and I promise to take it easy on you."

"If you're going to take it easy on us, what's the sense in playing for money?"

"Christ sake, ya gotta play for something."

"No thanks. I think I'll pass."

"How about gin? You play gin, don't you?"

The driver sighed. "We don't play cards, so just relax and be thankful you're alive."

———

Frankie and Nicky sat at the table playing cards—gin and pinochle. His phone rang just before midnight. He saw it was Kate and picked it up quickly. "Everything all right?"

"Of course," Kate said. "I was calling about your reports. You said you wanted them right away."

"I know, but it's pretty late."

Kate laughed. "Mr. Donovan, when was the last time you were in bed before midnight?"

"Okay, point taken. What have you got?"

"What I've got are *almost* identical killings."

"No shit?"

"Note, I said *almost*. There is one significant difference."

"What?" Frankie asked.

"I went through these twice, and in the cases where the victims were beaten, they were shot to death *before* they were beaten. In Brooklyn, they were beaten to death and *then* shot."

"All right, I heard what you said, but I don't see what that gives us," Frankie said.

"Aside from the fact that it shows a difference, it could mean a lot. Maybe the killer is not as confident of being able to beat the victims to death and maintain the upper hand, so he—or she—shoots them first."

"She? You really think a woman could do this?"

"You've been focusing on male relatives of the previous victims. But suppose it's a female. A daughter, wife, sister? It would explain the shooting coming first. And don't think a woman couldn't do any of these, especially when you consider they were shot first."

Frankie found himself nodding. "Damn, Kate, you might have something. You just might have something. Thanks."

"Following the same logic, it could also be a younger male rather than a woman and for the same reason. Maybe one of the victims in Brooklyn had a younger son or brother or whatever. Now they're old enough to take vengeance, but still young enough to not feel confident, so they shoot the victim first."

"You're all right, Mrs. Donovan. Damn good work."

"Always happy to help with the gory details," Kate said.

———

Frankie hung up and poured another glass of wine, then he reached over and refilled Nicky's glass.

"Was that Kate?" Nicky asked.

Frankie nodded. "She finished with the reports and said after examining files that the murders were almost identical."

"Almost?"

"Yeah, she said in Brooklyn the victims were beaten first then shot. Down here, they were shot first, then beaten after they were dead. She said that might indicate a woman or younger person did the killing. I don't know if I buy it, but it introduces doubt."

Nicky sipped his wine. "It's worth thinking about, but I'm with you. I don't know if I buy it."

"Let's hope we don't need to think too hard on it," Frankie said. "Maybe something will come of this trap with Jimmy."

"Bugs, I don't have a problem buying the fact that a younger person could have done this, but I don't know if a younger person would have the street smarts to pull this off. Whoever is doing this, is doing a damn good job, and that shows a degree of street smarts that takes a while to acquire."

Frankie nodded. "I might have to agree with you, Rat. I was only thinking about the physical aspect, but you brought up a good point."

Chapter Twenty-Three

THE TRAP DIDN'T WORK

Mrozinski kicked up his feet and stared. "It's been two days, Donovan, and nothing's happened—nothing."

"We might need to give it more time," Frankie said. "Two days isn't shit in a multiple murder investigation and if you were any kind of detective, you'd know that."

Mrozinski nodded. "I know two days isn't long, but time is something we don't have much of, not on this case. I'm getting a lot of pressure to close it." Mrozinski pointed to a folder on his desk. "I'm running this off the books to keep it quiet, but we're using four officers; that's a lot of manpower, which equals a lot of money."

"Mrozinski, let's at least give it one more night. I can't imagine the killer will let it drag on longer than that."

Mrozinski sighed. "Donovan, I'll go for one more night, but that's it. After that, I've got to pull the plug."

"And if that happens? If you pull the plug? Where does that leave Nicky?" Frankie asked.

"Not much I can do after setting him free. I'm counting on you to stay with him. And I mean *all* the time. Don't let him out of your sight."

"You've got a deal," Frankie said. "But maybe the killer will try something tonight with Jimmy. Not that I want him to, but if it helps close the case, I'll take it."

"Yeah, maybe. I'm with you though, Donovan. I need these murders solved, and any way we can get that done is fine with me. By the way, what happened with the coroner's reports?"

"Oh shit! I forgot to tell you. Kate said there was a major difference in how the victims were killed. The ones in Brooklyn were beaten to death first, and the ones here were shot to death, *then* beaten. I don't know if that qualifies as *major,* but it seems significant."

Mrozinski nodded. "That qualifies as a major difference as far as I'm concerned. I need to find out why good old Dr. Frederick didn't catch it. Thanks, Donovan. That helps."

"It should do more than help," Frankie said. "You need to recalibrate your thinking. Nicky didn't do these crimes, and you know it."

"Maybe that information should do more than help in your mind, but it doesn't register the same in mine. All this does is make me wonder why Fred missed that detail, and it introduces a possibility for another way the crimes were committed. But Fusco could still be doing these killings, just staging them to look different."

"I know you don't believe that shit, Mrozinski. You're smarter than that. Why would he want to stage killings and make it look as though he did them?"

Mrozinski shrugged. "I don't know, Donovan, but who else would do it?"

"It's obvious. Someone who knew about the crimes in Brooklyn and who *thinks* Nicky did them. This person is obviously holding a grudge, and now he wants to make it look like Nicky is doing these killings as well."

"I don't know. I'd like to believe you, but . . ."

"But you don't. Is that what you're saying?"

"In a nutshell, yes," Mrozinski said.

"All right, forget about that for a minute and tell me how this is going down tonight."

"Same as before. I've got four officers. Two will go with Jimmy after he gets home. They'll leave through the back door, then they'll call me, and I'll tell them where to take him. It's a different place every night, and I'm the only one who knows where that place is."

"That's good," Frankie said.

"The other two officers will stay in Jimmy's house and wait to see if the alleged killer shows up."

"You think you ought to have someone keeping watch outside?" Frankie asked.

"What for? If he goes into Jimmy's house, we have two officers waiting. Besides, Jimmy's not there, so the only ones risking anything are the officers inside his house."

Frankie nodded. "I guess so. All right, let's see if he shows."

———

Bugs stayed up for hours playing cards with Nicky. "I guess nothing happened, Rat, otherwise Mrozinski would have called."

"I didn't expect anything to happen," Nicky said.

"Why the hell not?" Bugs asked. "The trap was planned well and set to precision."

"I know that," Nicky said. "But something hasn't rung right with this since the beginning. The killer has been ahead of us the whole time, and he shouldn't be. We've got to figure out how."

"That's what we're trying to do, Rat, but whoever is doing this is doing a pretty good job. It's not so easy to figure it out."

"I know that, Bugs, but I'm counting on you to do just that. I have confidence in you."

"I'm glad you have confidence because I'm beginning to question it," Bugs said. "I've been racking my brains, and I haven't come up with anything."

Nicky laughed. "You can question your confidence all you want as long as you deliver in the end. You won't leave me hanging. I know that."

Nicky tapped Bugs on the arm. "You hear that?" he asked, pointing upstairs.

"You mean the creaking?"

"That's exactly what I mean. It's Angie pacing. She's so worried she can't sleep. I've got to find this guy for her more than anything, Bugs. Her and the kids. There's no way I'm letting them put me away for something I didn't do. If I have to take the family and go on the run, I will."

"Nicky, stop talking nonsense. You—"

Nicky nodded. "I know what you were going to say, and yes, I could do that. I not only could do it, I could make it work. I've got plenty of fake IDs for me, and I know where to get them for Angie and the kids."

"Don't worry. We won't let it get that far. We'll get whoever's doing this, Rat. I'm going to figure out how this guy stays ahead of us if it's the last thing I do."

Nicky drew a card and was positioning it in his hand when he stopped and stared. "Bugs, you remember when we were kids and Sally's brother Pete got busted for everything he did?"

Bugs thought for a moment, then lit up. "Christ, yeah. Why didn't I think of that? It was her younger brother who was listening to everything the older brother planned. Through the heating duct, wasn't it?"

"Exactly. Now imagine we have something similar happening."

"You mean somebody listening?"

"Something like that."

"But who? And where?" Bugs asked.

"The only place that makes sense is the smoke shop. That's

where I was playing cards. And it's where Knuckles saw me behind Freddy on Union Street."

Bugs thought out loud. "If he's listening in on the smoke-shop conversations, he'd have a heads-up on what's going on?"

"Exactly," Nicky said. "He'd have known when I left the poker game. He'd have known about Knuckles seeing Freddy. All of it." Nicky set his cards on the table and stared. "And he'd have known about the trap with the Gem, which is probably why he didn't bite."

"Son of a bitch," Bugs said. "I think you might have something, Nicky."

"Run it by Mrozinski," Nicky said. "Even Polacks have to listen to reason."

"Maybe so, but there's no way I'm gonna bring it up. He'd never buy it if he thinks it came from you. I'm going to have to figure out another way to make him see it."

"What?"

"I don't know yet, but I'll think of something."

"Whatever you do, do it fast. I'm tired of pretending to lose to you at cards."

"You son of a bitch," Bugs said. "And here I thought I was finally beating you fair and square."

"I take back what I said earlier. Maybe you *are* slipping."

"I don't slip when it counts, Nicky."

"I know. Now let's figure out how to get Mrozinski to realize the killer may have infiltrated the smoke shop. Maybe he's got a listening device planted."

"Leave that to me," Bugs said. "I'll get him to come to that conclusion and have him think it's his own idea."

"If you weren't dealing with a Polack, I'd say that's a neat trick, but considering . . ."

"Nicky, you're an asshole," Bugs said, and discarded a nine of hearts.

Nicky smiled as he picked up the card. He rearranged the cards in his hand, then laid them down. "Gin," he said. "And yes, I know I'm an asshole, but I'm an asshole who knows how to play gin."

Frankie tossed a ten-dollar bill on the table. "You're gonna have a lot of time to get better if I can't figure this out quickly."

Nicky picked up the ten and smiled. "I'm not worried, Bugs. You'll find the prick."

WHO WAS WITH FAT FINGERS JOEY?

Sherri and Jack walked out of the station. Sherri wore a frown like she hadn't gotten any presents for her birthday.

"What's the matter?" Jack asked. "You seem down."

"I'm down because we apparently lost Joey, our prime suspect, and we have no clue where his partner-in-crime is. We don't even have a clue where to look for him."

"How about we canvass the neighborhood again?"

"We've done that twice," Sherri said. "As expected, we got next to nothing. The only person who's been a help is Manny, and I'm betting he's also the one who made Joey disappear."

"You mean—"

"Exactly," Sherri said. "I don't like to think about it, but I can't help but wonder. And to make matters worse, I'll probably have to go back to Manny to get information on Joey's partner."

"So we're going to Manny's house again?"

Sherri lowered her head and thought. "I don't know. Maybe," she said. Then an idea struck her. "Maybe Bobby Whiskers knows who Joey ran with."

"Bobby Whiskers? Who the hell is he?"

Sherri smiled as she turned over the engine. "One of Manny's men, and Manny gave us the okay for Bobby to talk to us. Maybe he hasn't taken that back." Sherri looked over her shoulder, then put the car in gear and headed out.

"So this is one of Manny's men we're going to see?" Jack asked.

"Bobby 'Whiskers' DeNuzzio," Sherri said. "He's a bagman who works for Manny. He knew Joey, so he might know who ran with him."

Twenty minutes later, Miller spotted Whiskers sitting outside a coffee shop. She pulled to the curb and got out. "Bobby, remember me?"

Whiskers looked over, squinted, then smiled. "Sure, I remember you. You were here with Irish Donovan."

Sherri smiled back at him. "You've got a good memory, Bobby, but I guess that comes in handy for what you do."

"You got that right. So what's up? What can I help you with?"

"We know Joey is gone, but we still haven't found his running partner. You got any ideas there?"

"If you mean who he is, I'd say Teddy McNulty. He and Joey loved knocking over joints together. I just can't believe either one of 'em was so stupid as to hit Manny."

Sherri scribbled in her notebook. "You know where we might find Teddy?"

"That's a little tougher. He could be out at his mother's place on the island, but my guess would be his cousin's place in Queens. I doubt he'd bring his mom in on this. She'd be tougher on him than Manny."

"This cousin in Queens—you know where he lives?"

"I don't have an address, but it's a guy with the same last name, and I think the first name's Sean. Sean McNulty. I can't swear to it, but I think he's in the Belle Harbor section of Queens."

"Any names to check with in Belle Harbor?" Sherri asked.

"Let me think," Whiskers said. He gulped the rest of his coffee, took a bite from his bagel, then nodded. "Yeah, try Roddy McNulty. He owns a bar in Belle Harbor. I think it's called McNulty's. He'll know. All the Irishmen go there for a drink, and all the Irish drink, so he's bound to show up sooner or later, and probably sooner."

Miller set a five-dollar bill on the table. "Here, Whiskers, get yourself another coffee. And thanks."

Sherri got back in the car. "Buckle up, Jack."

"Where we going?"

"Queens," she said. "Whiskers pulled through. We're looking for a guy named Teddy McNulty, and according to Whiskers, we'll find him by talking to the folks at McNulty's bar in Belle Harbor."

M iller drove to Queens and before long found McNulty's bar. She parked, then she and Jack walked inside.

A few patrons occupied seats at the bar, and the bartender—who she pegged as the owner—stood rigidly and wore a deep frown.

"You cops?"

Sherri smiled. "We are. How'd you know? Good guess or experience?"

"You learn quickly in this neck of the woods, or you don't stay in business long. I can always tell a cop. What are you here for?"

Sherri showed her badge. "Looking for a guy named Teddy McNulty. Seen him around?"

Roddy turned away, filling a mug with beer, which he handed to one of the people on the barstools. "I don't know anybody by that name."

"Really?" Miller asked. "That's funny because I heard you knew him well. In fact, I heard he frequented this place quite often."

"Maybe we should just park ourselves here until he shows," Jack said.

Sherri moved to the closest table, pulled a chair out, and sat. "I think you might be right, Jack. Then we'll get Bernstein and Johnson to take over when we leave."

Jack sat in a chair next to Miller. "Yeah, between the four of us, we could cover this place from morning till night."

Roddy came out from behind the bar. "All right, what do you assholes want?"

Miller looked up. "Besides a cold beer, I need to know where to find McNulty."

"I can handle the beer, but I don't know where McNulty is or where he's going to be."

"I was afraid of that, Jack. Guess we'll have to hang around like I said."

Roddy slapped a towel against the bar top and cursed. "It's like I said, I don't know where he is."

"I believe you," Miller said. She turned to her partner. "Don't we, Jack?"

Jack ate a few peanuts and nodded. "Sure do. Why would he lie?" Jack turned to Sherri. "You hungry? I'm thinking burger and fries since we're gonna be here a while. Might as well eat."

"All right, listen," Roddy said, "I don't know his address, but if you come by tonight after nine, I'm sure you'll find him deep in the cups."

"That's all I needed," Sherri said. "I don't even need the beer, but I'll be glad to pay for it." She set a ten-dollar bill on the table. "In fact, I'll pay for two, but don't tell McNulty we'll be here."

Roddy scooped up the ten and walked away mumbling, "Cops."

Sherri and Jack returned that night and waited until eleven o'clock, but McNulty never showed.

"Somehow I smell your friend Manny's hand in this," Jack said.

"I don't know how," Miller said. "He didn't know we were coming here. What I smell is Roddy's interference, and the *lack* of Manny's hand. But when he hears about it, he won't be too happy."

Jack looked over to Miller. "How's he going to hear about it? He won't know."

"Don't be too sure about that," Sherri said. "Manny's got ears everywhere. Anyone might tell him." She gulped down the rest of her beer and set the mug on the table. "Anyway, let's go. I'm sure McNulty isn't showing tonight."

The next morning Miller and Jack showed up at Manny's house while he was eating breakfast. Giorgio answered the door, then hollered to Manny. "Hey, boss, it's that dame who partners with Bugs."

"Let them in, Giorgio. What the hell did you do with your manners?"

Sherri and Jack walked into the kitchen. Manny stood and hugged her. "*Principessa, buon giorno.*"

"And good morning to you, Manny. Now, I have a favor to ask."

"Ask away. In the meantime, I'll put on some espresso." He turned and looked at Jack. "You liked my espresso, right?"

Jack nodded. "Yes, sir. It was delicious."

Manny laughed, causing his belly to roll. "Giorgio, you hear that? He called me *sir*. That might be the first time in my life anybody's called me *sir*."

"Now that you've had your laugh, Manny. I need to know if you have any idea where I can find Joey's partner. He was supposed to be at a certain bar last night, but he never showed."

Manny brought a cup of espresso to the table and set it in front of Miller. "I thought Whiskers gave you that information."

Miller let silence fill the gap in their conversation. "He did, Manny, and we went looking for him, like I said, but he wasn't there. Don't take this wrong, but I'd really like it if I could find this guy alive, especially after losing Joey."

Manny's belly rolled as he laughed. "You got it Miller." He pinched her cheeks, then said, "You know, if you keep this up, I might end up liking you more than Bugs. If that happens, you'll force me to come up with a nickname for you."

"I appreciate that, Manny, but you're avoiding my question."

"Damned if I'm not. All right, go back to McNulty's, and I'll bet you find McNulty alive and well. But you gotta promise me he'll pay for what he did. And I don't mean a stint in some prison with golf courses; I want him to do hard time."

"By that I presume you mean do time in a joint where you have friends that can keep an eye on him."

Manny slapped Giorgio on the side of the head. "Damn, but I like this kid."

Miller smiled and sipped her espresso. "All right, Manny. I can't promise it, but I'll do my best to see he gets the hard time. I can't guarantee it, but I'll try."

"Good," Manny said. "And one more thing, Miller. I'd give it till tomorrow night. I have a feeling he'll be there then."

"A feeling?" Jack said.

Sherri tapped Jack's arm and started for the door. "Yeah, Jack, a feeling. Manny's got good intuition."

As Sherri and Jack exited, Manny and Giorgio laughed. "Good intuition. You hear that, Giorgio?"

———

Roddy put two mugs on the counter and called to the guys who ordered it. "Fresh and cold," he said.

While he filled another person's shot glass, two men walked in and sat at the end of the bar.

Roddy walked over. "What'll it be?"

"Information," the bigger man said.

"What kind of information?" Roddy asked.

"*Good* information," the shorter one said.

Roddy sighed and shook his head. "Hey, bud, order something or leave. I'm gonna get busy in here any minute, and I'll need those chairs."

The taller of the two opened his jacket, revealing the handle of a gun. "Manny said to tell you that two people are gonna be here to scoop up Teddy McNulty. You're not only going to keep your nose out of it, you're going to make sure no one lets McNulty know it's going to happen. And it'll be your job to make sure no one interferes."

"But they were cops," Roddy said.

"Never noticed," the tall one said. He turned to the man with him. "Did you?"

The short guy shook his head. "Not me. But if I owned a bar, I'd sure as hell be more eager to please Manny than some loser who's going to either be locked up or dead any day."

The taller guy nodded, then stood. He threw a hundred-dollar bill on the counter before leaving. "Think hard, Roddy, 'cause me and my friends ride by here late at night sometimes. We patrol the area because there have been so many fires in the neighborhood."

The shorter guy pointed a finger at Roddy. "I'd think *real* hard if I were you."

Roddy gulped. "You got it," he said. "Tell Manny, I'm pretty sure he'll be here tomorrow night."

The tall guy smiled. "I'd make *real* sure he was, Roddy."

———

Sherri and Jack went back to McNulty's the next night, and around nine o'clock, a man fitting McNulty's description walked in and ordered a beer.

Roddy filled a mug and set it in front of him, then spoke loudly. "Here you go, Teddy. Good seeing you again."

Miller tapped Meyers on the shoulder and gestured to the guy sitting at the bar. "That's gotta be him," she whispered, then she and Meyers cuffed him before he took his second sip. "You're under arrest for murder."

"That's bullshit," Teddy said.

"Bullshit or not, you're under arrest," Sherri said.

"You've got nothing on me. This won't stick for long."

"After you confess, it will," Sherri said.

"Confess? You're nuts. I ain't confessing to nothing."

"Would you rather I turn you over to Manny?" she asked.

Teddy shut up after that.

"Let's go," Sherri said. "If you talk and tell us everything honestly, I'll treat you fair. If not, you'll suffer the same fate as Joey."

She didn't know what happened to Joey, but she figured Teddy would assume the worst. And he did. She could barely stop him from talking all the way to the station.

"You're going to have to repeat all this on tape once we get to the station," she said.

"Don't worry," Teddy said. "I'll tell you what you need. Just make sure to keep me safe."

"You've got a deal," Sherri said, and she turned to the back seat of the car. "Just make sure you don't forget between now and the time we get to the station, or I'll revoke the deal. Remember, I can say I acted on illegally obtained information which would set you free. And if that happens, I'll make sure Manny knows about it."

She tapped her pocket. "I've got his phone number right here, and I know where he lives."

"I got a good memory, lady. I won't forget."

Sherri pulled away from the traffic signal and hit the gas. "That's good, Teddy. Just what I wanted to hear."

Despite Sherri advising him twice to wait for his lawyer, Teddy talked all the way to the station, blabbing to Sherri and Jack about the crimes he committed with Joey and others. He didn't stop there, though, he told her about other crimes as well.

"You know you're gonna have to repeat this in front of a camera when we get to the station," Sherri said. "I've already told you that."

"I know. I'm just practicing. I want to make sure I get it right."

"In that case, keep talking," Sherri said as she elbowed Jack.

Chapter Twenty-Five

WHO KNEW ABOUT THE TRAP?

After three days of setting the bait with Jimmy, the killer still hadn't shown. Frankie and Mrozinski sat down to figure out why. "Who knew about the trap?" Frankie asked.

"Nobody," Mrozinski said, then held up his hands. "Let me correct that. You, me, Jimmy the Gem, and the cops assigned to the case knew. Other than that, nobody. Not Maddy, my boss, or his boss. Not even the judge who oversaw Nicky's proceedings."

"You trust the cops?" Frankie asked. "You sure they're clean?"

"Absolutely. And none of them knew more than necessary. They didn't even know who they were guarding. Nobody knew it was the Gem, and they didn't know where they were taking him until he got home. When he walked in, one of them called me to get the site and the location."

"How about Viola?" Frankie asked. "She knew about Charlie."

"Yeah, she knew about Charlie because she's the one he called, but she didn't know anything about this operation. Like I said, not even the judge or my boss knew."

"Maybe it was one of the cops you had guarding him," Frankie said.

Mrozinski shook his head. "I doubt it. These were old-timers, and besides, I used different people every night, and they never knew what they were in for or who they were guarding until they got there. Same with the ones who took him to the safe house. They didn't know where it was until they were on the way and called me. And even then, they didn't know who they had in the car."

Mrozinski offered Frankie a bottle of water. "Besides, I checked the phone logs every day to see who they called. A couple of them called home, but nobody called anyone suspicious. I even checked the outgoing calls from their houses afterward, in case they routed calls that way. Nothing suspicious there either."

Frankie rested his chin on the palm of his right hand. "So how the hell did the killer know it was a trap?"

"Who said he knew?" Mrozinski asked.

"Don't give me that shit, Mrozinski. You know as well as I do that somebody else is staging these murders. No way it's Nicky."

"Maybe Jimmy leaked it."

"Why would he leak it?" Frankie asked. "I told him not to tell anyone; besides, it's his life that's in danger if the killer finds out."

"Maybe he told someone he thought was okay, and it turns out he wasn't," Mrozinski said.

Frankie got a light in his eyes. This was the opportunity to introduce Nicky's theory. "I think you hit on it, Mrozinski. Maybe he told someone without knowing it."

"What's that supposed to mean?" Mrozinski asked.

"Suppose there's a bug—you know, a listening device—in the smoke shop. It would explain how the killer knew when Nicky left the night Paulie died. And it would explain him knowing about the trap, not to mention being on the inside track regarding Knuckles."

"No way Doggs is gonna let his place be bugged. I'd bet he has it swept regularly," Mrozinski said.

Frankie stood and headed for the door. "I know he did in the old days, but I'm guessing he's slacked off. I say we find out, Detective. Let's pay Doggs a visit."

"Just call him," Mrozinski said.

Frankie shook his head. "If there's a bug, there's no way of knowing *what* is bugged or where. It could be Doggs's phone or somewhere close to where he's talking."

Mrozinski grabbed his jacket and walked to join Frankie. "All right, let's get moving. I need to solve this case one way or another."

Frankie pulled up outside the smoke shop. "Wait here, Mrozinski. I'll get Doggs and bring him out."

A few minutes later Frankie and Doggs exited the shop and walked to the car.

"You want to tell me what the fuck this is about, Donovan? I'm a busy man."

Frankie got close to Doggs and spoke in a whisper. "Doggs, we think somebody may be bugging your place."

Doggs twisted his face into a scowl. "Bugging *me*? You're crazy. Who the hell would want to bug me?"

"Hear me out, Doggs," Frankie said. "We had a trap set for whoever is doing these killings, and it should have worked, but it didn't. We're pretty damn sure of the people involved, which leaves your shop as the likely leak."

"Donovan, you—"

"Listen up, Doggs," Frankie said. "It would also explain how Knuckles got killed, and how the killer knew what time Nicky left the card game."

Doggs looked quizzically at the detectives. "What do you mean about Charlie?"

Mrozinski stepped forward. "Charlie called my office and said he had information regarding Nicky following Freddy home the night he was killed. The next day, Charlie was dead. When we looked into it, Jimmy said Charlie had seen someone driving down Union Street the night before, somebody he knew."

"That doesn't make any fuckin' sense. If Charlie knew him, the Gem would too."

"Exactly, but Jimmy said he didn't see the guy. Charlie did and waved to him."

Doggs shook his head. "There's no way it's anybody from here."

"I agree that it's not likely to be anyone who hangs out here, but suppose it's someone who works here or used to work here, or even someone who did work on your place, like electric work or sheetrock work. Didn't you have some remodeling done last year?"

Doggs nodded. "I did," he said, "But I don't know—"

"Do you still sweep the place for bugs?"

Doggs shook his head. "I stopped a while ago. There was no need."

"Then do me a favor and let Mrozinski's men sweep the place to see if they find anything. If they do, we're going to leave it in place because we might want to use it to set a trap."

"Shit, be my guest," Doggs said. "I got nothing against having a clean house. But if I catch you puttin' anything *in* here, I'll kick your fuckin' ass."

Frankie laughed. "No need to worry, Doggs. We don't have a warrant, and no one is out to bust you, anyway."

"You swear?" Doggs asked.

"I swear on my mother's eyes," Frankie said.

Doggs nodded. "All right, then. Go ahead and sweep it."

Mrozinski pulled out his phone and walked a few feet away. "I just ordered the sweep. They should be here this afternoon."

"Tell them to come dressed as electricians or plumbers in case anyone's watching," Doggs said. "If we're going to do this, let's do it right."

———

The sweep of the smoke shop finished around four o'clock. The men who'd done it asked Doggs to step outside where they filled him in on the results. "You've got two bugs: one in the air-conditioning duct and one in the ceiling light above the card table. Both are remotely monitored, so we can't tell who's listening, but *somebody* is definitely listening."

"Son of a bitch!" Doggs said. "And you left them in there?"

"I was told not to touch a thing, so I left them where they were, which means if I were you, I'd watch what you say."

"All right," Doggs said. "Thanks. And tell Mrozinski I said thanks."

"Will do," the officer said.

———

Nicky got up from eating to answer the doorbell. *Who the hell could this be?*

When he opened the door, Doggs pushed his way in. "Christ's sake, Fusco. Invite somebody in, why don't you?"

"Given time, I would have, Doggs. But some people have no patience. Besides, I'm a little shocked. You've never been here. How'd you even know where I live?"

"I know where everybody lives," Doggs said. "Donovan here?"

Frankie stepped into the living room, wiping his mouth with a napkin. "I'm here, Doggs. What's up?"

Doggs walked over and whispered, "They found a bug. Actually, they found two bugs."

Frankie laughed. "Who the hell are you telling, Doggs. I was there. Remember?"

"Maybe I was telling Nicky, you Irish prick."

"Doggs, why are you whispering? It's just us here," Nicky said.

Frankie laughed. "I think he's embarrassed they found bugs in his shop. It's a mortal sin for that to happen."

Doggs turned to Frankie. "You're damn right it is. I've run a respectable place for all these years, and now I find out somebody's got it bugged. If word gets out—"

"Don't worry, Doggs. Nobody's going to find out. I'll make sure to tell Mrozinski too."

"I'm here to get confirmation that nobody's gonna use anything on those bugs against me or my people."

"They won't."

"I need your word," Doggs said. "And I need you to get Mrozinski's word."

Frankie smiled and patted Doggs on the shoulder. "Don't worry, Doggs. You're good. Nobody's interested in what goes on in the back room, anyway. How do you think you've lasted so long without a raid? No one cares, that's how."

Nicky offered Doggs a glass of wine. "Any idea of who planted the bugs, Doggs?"

"If I did, I'd kill the son of a bitch. When I find out, I may still kill him."

"You left the bugs intact, right?" Frankie asked.

Doggs nodded. "Yeah, we left them there. I don't like it, but I went along. You guys better decide quickly if you're gonna use them. I ain't leaving them there for long."

"I'll make sure Mrozinski knows," Frankie said. "Now back to what Nicky asked. Who could have done this?"

"Hell, I don't know. No way it was any of the regulars."

"Who else could have done it?" Frankie asked.

"Fu— Shit, I don't know. Could've been a worker. We've had plenty of repairmen in there in the last year or so. Could've been somebody who worked for me. I've had a couple of them as well."

"You have any A/C men or electricians in there?" Frankie asked.

"No, but I've had painters, drywall men, and plumbers. Any one of them would have had plenty of time to place a bug."

"How about workers," Nicky asked.

"What about 'em? I've had more than a few."

"Can't be that many. Who was there the longest? Any of them strangers? I'm not interested in workers who were recommended from people you knew. I want the ones you stumbled upon or who came to you out of the blue."

Doggs shook his head. "I can't think of anybody. If I do, I'll let you know. In the meantime, work on gettin' those damn bugs out of my shop."

"Will do," Frankie said. "And, Doggs, kudos on controlling your language. I didn't hear a single 'f' word."

Doggs laughed. "You almost did. And next time, you will, especially if those bugs aren't gone."

Nicky patted his back. "Okay, Doggs, thanks."

Angela walked in after Doggs left. "What was he doing here?"

"Trying to help," Nicky said. "We found bugs planted in his shop and think whoever planted them may be the one doing this."

"Dear God, I hope so," Angela said.

Nicky sat in his favorite chair. "Hey, babe, would you mind asking Rosa to pour a glass of wine for Bugs and me? In fact, ask her to just bring the bottle. I'm sure we'll finish it."

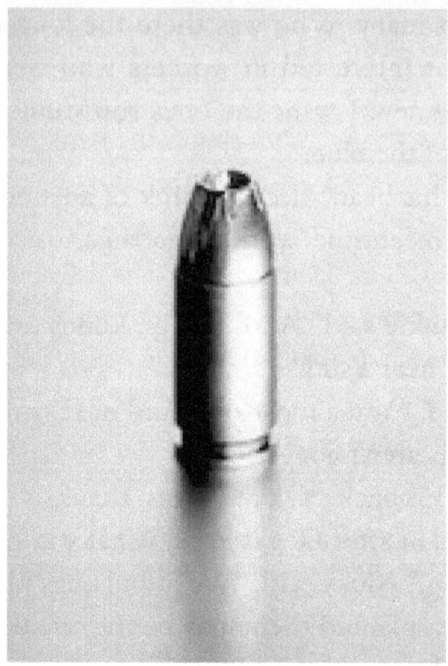

I turned to Bugs after Angela left. "Any plans, Bugs? Who do you think it could be?"

"I have no idea on that, but I think we should look at it from another angle, one we should have explored long ago."

"I'm open to any ideas. What do you have in mind?"

"The list of who planted the bug could be long, even if we eliminate the regulars, but the list of who might hold a grudge against you, and who also knew about the murders in Brooklyn will be much shorter."

"Yeah, but whoever did this, got it wrong. Remember, the victims down here were killed first."

"Exactly, and that makes the list even shorter. If it came from the department in Brooklyn, they would have known the victims up there were beaten first, then killed. That eliminates any department ties."

"Unless they were purposely trying to throw us off," I said.

"I don't think anyone would do that. If somebody goes to the trouble to create murders resembling the ones in Brooklyn, I think they'd do it *exactly*, not mess up on something so important."

"All right," I said. "I'll buy that, so who does that leave us?"

"I'd start with all the victims of the murders in Brooklyn; they'd have the most logical reason to do something like this."

"So you're talking Ciccarelli, Amato, Devin, Tortella, Muck, and Martelli."

"They're the ones," Frankie said. "I thought about this earlier and even asked Manny about it, but then something happened, and I put it on the back burner."

"Guess it's time we got it back up front," I said.

"Guess so. Anyway, Manny said if it were him, he'd start with Renzo and Donnie. Both of them had family that might fit the retribution angle."

"How about Nino?"

"Nino had no family alive, and Tommy Devin only had an older brother. Muck had nobody that we know of, and according to Manny, nobody would have cared about Tito."

"Any ideas on how we check this out?" I asked.

Bugs nodded. "I can call Manny and have him check on Renzo's family. I know he's close to them. And I can get Miller to check on the others."

"Sounds like a good start," I said. "Let's get it moving."

Bugs got his phone out, but I stopped him from calling. "Bugs, before we do this, are you sure about the cop angle. You don't think it could be any of them?"

Bugs nodded. "Pretty sure, Rat. Lou's dead, Morreau never knew the full details, Miller wasn't around then, and no one else I can think of knew you were suspected of being involved. The only other one I can think of is Tony's family, but I ruled them out based on us knowing them for so long. And I ruled Paulie out completely. He has a lot of family, but nothing happened to Paulie. He's alive and well in Texas."

I thought for a moment, running images of Tony's brothers

through my head. "I agree. I don't think it would be any of them. None of them were very close with Tony, anyway."

"All right. I'll make the call then," Bugs said. "Be sure of this, Rat, 'cause I'm about to sell my soul to Manny. He's not quite the devil, but he can be close."

"Bugs, I don't want you to do this just for me. You can't owe Manny favors and still work as a cop."

Bugs laughed. "Bullshit. You sold your soul to the real devil when you put yourself in debt to Dominic. Owing Manny is nothing by comparison."

"You know we're leaving out a lot of possibilities. It could be any of Manny's men or people they told."

"But they don't have a good motive," Bugs said. "I'm comfortable with what I'm doing, Rat. Relax."

"But your job—"

"If it becomes too much, I'll quit. We can live off Kate's salary with ease. Besides, I wouldn't mind raising Alex as a stay-at-home dad."

I laughed. "I can see it now—Mama Bugs."

"Screw you, Rat. Now let me get this done."

Chapter Twenty-Six

WHO PLANTED THE BUGS?

Frankie stopped by the smoke shop on his way to see Mrozinski. He walked inside and asked Doggs to meet him on the sidewalk.

"Yeah, Bugs, what the fuck's up?"

"I dropped by to see if you thought any more about who might have planted the listening devices."

"Christ's sake, Donovan. It's only been a day. I got a life, you know."

"From what I can see, that life's about over, Doggs. I came by to make sure I got hold of you before you cashed in."

Doggs laughed. "You fuckin' prick. All right, I'll give it some more thought. Call me later or stop by tomorrow. But don't count me out yet, Bugs. You're no picture of health yourself, and I'll still bet five-to-one that I'll be here to piss on your grave."

Bugs laughed and slapped him on the back. "I believe that, Doggs. Take your time thinking on it."

Bugs hadn't been gone twenty minutes when his phone rang. "Donovan, it's Doggs."

"Yeah, Doggs, what's up?"

"I thought of two guys who could have done it. One of them I doubt; I'm pretty sure about him; he was a local guy, and I knew his father."

"Who was he?"

"You probably don't know him, but he was a good guy. Name's DeCicco. Lived up on North DuPont."

"*You* trust him though?" Bugs asked.

"I do," Doggs said, "but the other one was a younger guy who was recommended by one of the Whale's cousins. I didn't know him personally, so he's suspect."

"Would the Whale have done that?" Bugs asked.

Doggs scowled. "Hell no, you fuckin' idiot. But the Whale trusted his cousin like he's supposed to. Who knows if his cousin should be trusted, is all I'm saying?"

"Where's the guy from?"

"Got no idea. Whale's cousin was from Philly, but I don't know where the kid was from. I gave him a job dealing at the card games but only twice a week."

"When was this?"

"I hired him last summer, and he left about three months ago. Said he had something better lined up. Now that you mention it, he was a tight-lipped mother fucker. Never said shit about his family. That's not like an Italian."

"You sure he was Italian?"

"Christ's sake, Donovan, I told you the Whale's cousin recommended him. He wasn't no fuckin' Polack."

"You remember his name?"

"I don't. I can picture him—tall, dark hair, good-looking—but I don't remember the name. I've probably got it somewhere, though. I'll look through the files. If I find it, I'll get it to you. But it may take me a couple days."

"All right, think on it, Doggs, and let me know if you get anything that might help. We need to find this guy, and quickly."

"Like I said, Donovan, I'll think on it and check the files."

"Do that, Doggs, and I'll owe you. Better yet, Nicky will owe you. I'm sure you'd rather have that."

"That ain't no shit. Now work on gettin' your shit outta here before somebody thinks I'm legit."

Bugs laughed. "You got it, Doggs. See you later."

————

Instead of going to see Mrozinski, Bugs went back to Nicky's house and filled him in on what Doggs said.

"Has to be the guy," Nicky said. "It's too much of a coincidence for it not to be."

"I don't know about *has* to be, but I'd bet ten dollars to a donut it's him. Now all we gotta do is find him and prove it."

"I'm sure he's hanging out somewhere, drinking a brew and waiting to kill someone else," Nicky said.

Bugs snapped his fingers. "And if that's the case, we should set another trap. But this time, nobody but us knows."

"I like the trap idea," Nicky said. "But it's going to have to be more than just us in on it. At the very least, we're going to have to have Mrozinski. And probably Doggs, assuming you're using the bug in his shop."

"Yeah, I guess you're right," Frankie said.

"And whoever we're using for bait," Nicky said. "But it can't be Jimmy again. This guy wouldn't fall for that."

"All right, let me think. We'll come up with something."

"Maybe we should ask Doggs," Nicky said. "If anybody would know, it'd be him; besides, he's got to know about the deal, anyway."

"All right, that's what we'll plan on. I'll tell Mrozinski when we get back, and in the meantime, you tell Doggs. Once we get all the players, we'll set it up."

"You think it should be tonight?" Nicky asked.

"Definitely," Bugs said. "We could do it tomorrow night, but I'd rather get it over with."

"One more thing," Nicky said. "If Kate's still got the crime scene reports, see if she can look at the DNA of the suspects."

"In what way?" Frankie asked.

"These are violent crimes," Nicky said, "which means that the killer likely left his DNA at all the scenes."

"Yeah but—"

"Hang on, Bugs. I know he put other people's DNA there also, including mine. But I'd bet that the only ones with DNA at *all* the scenes are his and mine. Find out whose DNA that is, and we've got our killer."

Frankie thought for a moment, then nodded. "Damn, Rat, I think you might have something. I'll call Kate right away."

Chapter Twenty-Seven

ANOTHER TRAP

Frankie took his time eating breakfast despite Nicky rushing him the whole time. "C'mon, Bugs. Christ, it's like you've never eaten before. Drink your damn coffee and get out of here."

He gulped down the last few sips of coffee, grabbed his files, and headed for the door. "I'm leaving, prick. Satisfied?"

"I'll be satisfied when you make some headway, you lousy Irish cop. And don't forget, I'm heading over to the smoke shop, so I'll see you there."

Bugs laughed as he rushed out the door, then he got in his car and drove to the police station to see Mrozinski. Once at the station, he sat down with the detective.

He plopped his feet on Mrozinski's desk and smiled. "That rotten coffee of yours get any better since the last time I was here?"

Mrozinski laughed. "Not likely, Donovan. At least not to your liking."

"I figured as much, but I'll take some, anyway."

"I don't remember offering you any, though I *will* get you some." Mrozinski pressed the intercom button on his phone. "Nina, would you please get Detective Donovan a cup of coffee and bring it in here?"

Mrozinski turned back to face Frankie. "I know you didn't come for the coffee, so what do you want?"

"Got an idea for trapping this guy."

"You mean this phantom killer?"

Frankie sat up and leaned toward Mrozinski. "No, asshole. I mean the *real* killer."

"We already tried a trap, and it didn't work."

"That doesn't mean we quit trying," Frankie said. "We just need to get smarter."

Mrozinski leaned back and folded his hands behind his head. "Let's hear it."

"We know Doggs has a bug planted in his back room, so we get somebody to tell Doggs something confidential about the killer. Something like—he knows a way to identify him—and then he asks Doggs whether he should go to you with it."

Mrozinski unfolded his hands and leaned forward. "Go on."

"Doggs tells him you're out of town but will be back in a day or so. That way, the killer has to act quickly or risk being exposed."

"*If* he believes the guy has something on him."

"Exactly," Bugs said. "We've got to come up with something good."

Mrozinski smiled. "All right, Donovan. I like it. I don't know if it'll work, but I think it's worth a shot."

"A shot may be all we need," Frankie said. "I talked to Doggs for a long time. He said there were only two guys he could think of who might have planted the listening devices. I say we set the trap to catch whoever it is."

"I'll ask it again," Mrozinski said. "What makes you think this trap will work when the last one didn't."

Frankie shook his head. "Mrozinski, is it in your DNA, or do you try to be stupid? The last time we didn't know we had a listening device in the smoke shop; this time we do. That evens up the odds some."

Mrozinski stood and put his phone in one of his front pockets. "All right, Donovan, let's go. But if this one doesn't work, Fusco's in trouble."

I parked across the street from the smoke shop and got Doggs to meet me outside.

Doggs came out a moment later, cursing and mumbling. He flipped a cigarette butt to the curb. "Go over this with me again, Fusco. I need to know what kind of shit you're getting me into."

I took a deep breath and explained. "We know—or at least we think we know—that somebody is listening in on the conversations in your back room. Furthermore, we think whoever's doing this is the guy who killed the Campisi brothers and Knuckles."

Doggs pulled out another smoke and lit it while I continued talking.

"We need somebody who'd be willing to be bait and trap this guy."

"Trap him how?" Doggs asked. "What's he gonna have to do?"

"We'll get him to tell you he has information, and he's gonna give it to Mrozinski. He'll tell you this in the smoke shop close to the listening devices so the killer hears him. Then we'll set up at his house for the trap."

Doggs shook his head. "I don't like it, and I don't know if it'll work, but we can run it by Sonny Bruno. For the right amount of money, Sonny will do anything."

I liked the sound of what Doggs said, but I didn't want to put anyone in harm's way. "You think he'll go for it? It's a risky proposition. I don't know Sonny that well. I've seen him around, but we're not friends."

"Christ, Fusco, I just told you. For the right amount of money, he'll do anything."

"How about a deuce?" I asked.

Doggs laughed. "Throw him a deuce, and he'll jump at the chance. He'd kill his sister for a deuce. And you got nothin' to worry about with Sonny. He's a good guy. Not too smart, but loyal. You can count on him to come through for you."

"How do I get in touch with him?"

"I'll call him. Don't worry."

"Just give me his number," I said. "I can call."

"I said *I'll* call him. After I talk to Sonny, I'll call *you*," Doggs said.

I recognized the stubbornness in Doggs's voice. Once he made his mind up, it was hard as hell to change it. "Deal," I said. "I'll be waiting."

———

"No need to wait. Step away and gimme a minute; I'll call him." Doggs headed for the door, then turned around, cursing. "Forgot about them fuckin' bugs." He turned back around, opened the door, and tossed a set of keys to the guy behind the counter. "Sally, watch the place while I step down the block. I'll only be a minute."

Doggs walked halfway down the block and dialed Sonny's number, filling him in on the plan. "We'll have a dialogue for you to follow by the time you get here."

On his way back to me, Doggs nodded. "It's a go," he said.

After getting the okay from Doggs, I called Bugs and told him things were in motion, and that I'd give him Sonny's address later. I also reminded him to tell no one other than Mrozinski.

Bugs must have his time driving to the card shop, knowing Sonny wouldn't be there for a while. He showed up forty minutes later, but it was an hour after that before Sonny arrived.

Sonny met me and Bugs outside—where I gave him his instructions on what to do and say—then I went inside and motioned for Doggs to see me in the back. Bugs stayed outside, watching the front.

While Bugs waited for them to finish, he stepped away from Mrozinski and dialed Miller's number. "Hey, Miller. I need a favor."

"Anything, Frankie. Just tell me."

"I need you to check the whereabouts of a couple people for the past few weeks."

"Whereabouts meaning what? You want to know if they left the neighborhood? Left the city? The state? How close does it have to be?" Sherri asked.

"No need for the nitty-gritty. Just find out if they were in the city or not. And I don't care if they were missing for an hour or so; I'm interested in any gaps that extend for more than four or five hours."

"That's doable. Who you got? Want to text me the names?"

"I don't have all the first names, but I've got the surnames, and they're all in Brooklyn."

"You've got my number. Send 'em up."

"I'll do it in a minute. I'm just getting to Nicky's house."

"Tell the Rat I said hi," Sherri said.

While Frankie waited for Nicky and Sonny, he sent a text of the people he wanted checked to Miller. The list included Devin, Amato, and Martelli. He figured he'd have Manny check out

Ciccarelli and Mucchiato, and he'd check on Paulie and the Sannullos himself.

"Who are you texting?" Mrozinski asked.

"Brooklyn business," Frankie said. "I'm almost done."

Nicky waited outside for Sonny. When he showed, he went over everything, then they went to the back room of the card shop.

After a few minutes, Sonny pulled Doggs aside and whispered, but he made sure he was close to the bug planted in the lamp. "Doggs, I'm in a jam," Sonny said.

"What the fuck you telling me for? Do I look like a priest?"

"I'm serious, Doggs. I saw Charlie the night before he died, and he told me he saw somebody following Freddy Campisi down Union Street."

"No shit," Doggs said. "It was Fusco. Everybody knows that by now."

"I know he saw Fusco. But what everybody don't know is he saw somebody else too."

"Who?" Doggs asked. "Who was it?"

"I'm not saying," Doggs. "Look what happened to Charlie. I'm worried."

"Stop being a pussy. If you're pissin' your pants, go see Mrozinski. He's scraping dirt to get information on this case."

"You think I should?"

"Absolutely. Go see him and tell him what you know and make

sure to say you want protection. Tell him if you don't get protection, the deal's off."

"All right. I'll go see him now."

Doggs shook his head. "Won't do you any good. I know for a fact he's on the other side of town right now—damn near to Chester—and I heard he's heading downstate early. If I were you, I'd drop by tomorrow after lunch, maybe late afternoon. And make sure you talk to nobody but Mrozinski. I mean *nobody*."

"All right, Doggs. Will do."

Sonny turned to leave, and Doggs grabbed his shirt sleeve. "Hey, Sonny, Fusco's over at the card table. If I were you, I'd tell him about it too. In fact, you might want to tell him before you see Mrozinski in case he wants you to say something different. I have no idea what role Fusco played in this, but I'd fill him in."

"Why say that? Why would he want me to say something different?"

"How the fuck do I know? But I'd do it to be safe. You know how Fusco can be. As much as the guy pisses me off, I wouldn't want to be on his bad side."

"You got that right. I'll tell him now."

Sonny walked to where Nicky was sitting. "Hey, Nicky, got a minute?"

"What's up?"

Sonny glanced left to right as if someone might be watching. "I got some information you might want to hear about. It has to do with the night Freddy was killed."

"What kind of information?" Nicky asked.

"Never mind what kind. Just come by my house tonight, and I'll fill you in. But it has to be tonight. I'm going to see Mrozinski tomorrow."

"Sonny, this is serious shit. Don't be fuckin' with me on this."

"I'm not fuckin' with you. It's like I said."

"It better be, that's all I know. Now give me your address."

"Yeah, okay. I'm down on Broom Street, close to the old hospital. You been there before. Remember? We played cards one night. Come by around seven or eight."

Nicky nodded. "You're right. I do remember. Had a good game. All right, see you around seven or so," Nicky said.

"Yeah, okay. See you then," Sonny said.

Nicky left a few minutes later. He nodded to Bugs to let him know it was a go, then he got in the car and drove away.

Frankie grabbed Mrozinski by the elbow and tugged him toward the car. "It's a go," he said. "We're on for tonight."

"That's all we came for?" Mrozinski asked? "We didn't do anything."

Frankie laughed. "You should be used to that, Mrozinski. I thought you'd enjoy it."

"Screw you," Mrozinski said. "Just take me back to the station. I've got police work to do."

Frankie dropped Mrozinski off after leaving the smoke shop, then he drove back to Nicky's house and walked in. "Rat? Rat, you home?"

Nicky bounded down the steps. "Right here. What's up?"

"While you were at the shop, I talked to Miller. She's gonna check on some names; in fact, I'm sending them to her now: Devin, Amato, and Martelli. Manny will do Nino's and Muck's family, and we'll check on Paulie and Tony's family."

"That should cover it," Nicky said. "Now I guess, we wait for answers."

"Shouldn't be long," Frankie said. "Miller will do her job quickly, and we can always count on Manny. He can be a dick, but he gets things done."

"For a price," Nicky said.

"Yeah, for a price, but not as expensive a price as Dominic charges."

"Ain't that the truth," Nicky said.

"Guess it's time to pay the piper," Frankie said, and dialed the phone.

"Yeah, Bugs, what do you need?" Manny asked.

"I hate to say it but a favor."

"Damn, you know I love hearing that," Manny said. "You're getting deep into the favor department. What's up?"

"I need to know where the Ciccarellis have been for the past few weeks, and if they've been missing for five hours or more on the following dates." Bugs then read him the dates of the murders of the Campisi brothers and Charlie Knuckles.

"You need all the Ciccarellis?"

"Focus on the younger males, but . . . oh, what the hell, do all of them."

"You got it. I'll have your info in a couple of days."

"Oh, and Manny, check on any relatives of Johnny Muck too."

"You got it. I'll call, but I told you, I don't think he had any relatives."

Bugs hung up, leaned back, and sipped the wine Nicky had handed him. "There. That's done with."

"What did it cost?" Nicky asked.

"I don't know, and I don't want to know," Frankie said. "I guess I'll find out when Manny calls in the debt."

"Let's hope it's not too expensive," Nicky said.

Frankie sighed. "Let's hope so."

"Aside from waiting for Manny, what do you have in mind?"

"You feel like a cheesesteak? I thought we'd take a ride to Casapulla's and chew on this."

"I'm always up for a cheesesteak, Bugs. You know that."

"Get dressed to go. We'll eat, then come back here and figure it all out."

"That quick, huh?" Nicky asked.

"If we're lucky," Bugs said.

. . .

After eating the cheesesteaks, Bugs and Nicky returned and opened a new bottle of wine. "Can't think very well without this," Nicky said.

Bugs smiled. "I'm not arguing."

"So where do we start, Einstein?"

"We're relying on Doggs, so keep that in mind. He might be giving us good information, and he might be protecting somebody else. It's anybody's guess."

"I'm with you on that," Nicky said. "You can never tell where you stand with Doggs, or who's standing in front of you."

"We've got two possibilities from Doggs—if he's not holding out, that is."

"Who are they?" Nicky asked. "You didn't tell me about this."

"One's a guy named DeCicco from up on DuPont. You know him?"

Nicky nodded. "I know the family. If it's the same DeCicco, I'd say he's probably good. What about the other one?"

"He said the other one was a young card dealer that one of Whale's cousins recommended."

Nicky scrunched his eyes. "I'd feel better if it had been a recommendation from the Whale. His cousin I don't know about. I can ask Johnny, though. See if he knows him."

"Doggs said the cousin was from Philly. That's all I know. If you need more, I'll see if I can find out."

"No problem," Nicky said, and picked up the phone. "Johnny! It's Nicky.

"Yeah, it has been a long time.

"Hey, I got a question. Doggs said one of your cousins from up in Philly recommended someone to deal for him about a year ago. You know who it might have been?"

Frankie leaned over as if he wanted to hear, so Nicky put it on speaker.

"Damned if I know, Nicky. We got a shitload of cousins in

Philly, and it could have been any one of them. He give you a name?"

Nicky looked to Bugs, but Bugs shook his head. "No names, Johnny. But don't worry about it. If I get anything else, I'll call."

"Okay, do that. But make sure to get a name. I got at least fifty cousins up there."

Nicky laughed. "Will do, Johnny. Thanks."

Nicky hung up and looked over at Bugs. "So much for that. Guess we'll have to tackle this a different way."

"Maybe Sherri will turn something up. If not, Manny will."

"Hate to say it, Bugs, but I'm betting on Manny. Nothing against Sherri, but Manny's got the connections."

"Don't I know it," Bugs said. He stood and took his empty glass and set it in the sink. "It's time for me to hit the sack, anyway. I'm tired."

"Still the same old pussy, huh?" Nicky laughed when he said it, and so did Bugs as he walked up the stairs.

Chapter Twenty-Eight

A LONG NIGHT

Mrozinski shifted his weight and rested his shoulder against the car door. "I'd kill for a cup of coffee right now," he said.

"I would too," Frankie said. "But there's no way we can risk it."

"I don't know, Donovan. Fusco left the house hours ago and nothing's happened. Haven't heard a peep from inside."

"The TV is still on," Frankie said. "I can see the light flickering through the window."

"Donovan, call Fusco and see if Sonny said anything to him before he left the house."

Frankie called Nicky, who picked up quickly. "Hey, Rat. Did Sonny say anything to you before you left? Or do you know if he had anything planned?"

"No idea, Bugs. He knew the plan, so I assume he was just gonna take it easy the rest of the night. I told him you and Mrozinski would be standing guard outside. You *are* still there, right?"

"Yeah, we're here. In fact, against my better judgment,

Mrozinski stationed two guys to watch the back door as well. One of them is his cousin though, so he swears we can trust him. Either way, the house is covered. Nobody's getting in there without us spotting him."

"Okay, good. Listen, unless you got something else for me, I'm going to hit the sack."

"Go on, prick. I'll just spend my night stuck in a car with this Polack asshole."

Nicky laughed. "I was going to say it could be worse, but I don't think it can."

"Just remember this, you prick. You'll get yours." Frankie hung up and turned to Mrozinski. "Nicky's home for the night."

"That's where I should be," Mrozinski said. "Instead—"

"Hey, Mrozinski. Imagine what *I* feel like being stuck with you."

"Donovan, how'd you get hooked up with Fusco to begin with?"

"We grew up together. Nicky's been my best friend since we were five or six. For a while, I counted Tony Sannullo right there with him, but Tony turned bad."

"What happened?" Mrozinski asked.

"Drugs," Frankie said. "Made him a different person."

Mrozinski nodded. "I've seen it happen to a lot of people. Is he still messed up?"

"He's dead. He was one of the guys who got killed a few years back in Brooklyn."

"You mean when Fusco—"

"I told you before, Fusco didn't do it. Get that out of your thick Polack head."

"Screw you, you potato-picking mick."

"Just watch the door, Mrozinski. I'm going to shut my eyes. If I'm lucky, I'll catch a nap."

"I think we should go in to check on Sonny," Mrozinski said.

"Go ahead—if you want to blow the operation, that is. If not, be patient and watch the house. Morning will come soon enough."

"All right, I'll stay here, but I'm waking you in two hours, then it'll be my turn to nap."

"Fair enough," Frankie said. "See ya in two."

Mrozinski and Donovan took turns napping the rest of the night. When morning came, still nothing had happened. Frankie woke Mrozinski by tapping him on the shoulder.

"What do you think, Mrozinski? No sign of Sonny yet. Should we go in or wait for him to leave?"

Mrozinski checked the time on his phone. "It's still early. Let's give him another hour. If he doesn't come out, we'll go in."

"Sounds good," Frankie said. He leaned his head against the cushioned part of the door's interior. "Wake me when you're ready."

Mrozinski checked the time on his phone, made sure his gun was situated right, then he woke Frankie. "Let's go, Donovan. It's been an hour, and there hasn't been a peep from inside. I say we go in."

Frankie stretched and yawned. "Why don't you get your guys from out back to go in the back way, and we'll take the front."

Mrozinski nodded. "All right. I like that." He called one of the officers out back. "Nathan, check on Sonny but do it quietly. We'll stay out front while you do."

"Got it," Nathan said. "I'll call back shortly."

Five minutes later, Mrozinski's phone rang. "Hello?"

"Boss, he's dead. Blood's everywhere."

"What? Shit, I'm coming in. Don't touch anything."

"What's wrong?" Frankie asked.

Mrozinski was halfway to the front door. "He's dead, Donovan. The son of a bitch is dead."

Frankie ran to the house. "We were here all night. How'd this happen?"

"Because we let him in," Mrozinski said. "That's how."

"Bullshit," Frankie said. "There's no way Nicky did this; besides, he knew we were watching."

Mrozinski ran up the steps and went inside. "Nathan, where's the body?"

"Upstairs, sir, near the bedroom. It's not a pretty sight."

"Check the—"

"We've already searched the house, sir. Nothing here."

"All right, call Fred. Tell him it's an emergency and see how fast he can get here with a full crew."

"Yes, sir," Nathan said. "Right away."

Fred got there in less than an hour accompanied by a full crew of technicians. "What've we got, Mrozinski?"

"Looks like the same as before, but that's why you're here, doc —to confirm or deny."

"And I suppose you want it yesterday?" Fred asked.

"Of course," Mrozinski said. "And I really *do* need this one yesterday."

While Fred and his crew analyzed and processed the scene, Mrozinski and Frankie talked.

"You can't really think Nicky had anything to do with this?" Frankie asked.

"Whether I think it or not makes no difference," Mrozinski said. "You were with me. Sonny went in; a short while later, Nicky went in; no one else went in or came out, and this morning we find Sonny dead. Give me a logical answer other than Nicky did it, and I'll listen."

Frankie gritted his teeth and clenched his fist, but in the end, he had no answer. "I don't know what the answer is, but it's something. I'll find it."

"You do that, Donovan. In the meantime, ride with me to Fusco's house. I don't want to get shot."

"The guy who worked for Doggs had to have done it," Frankie said.

"I'm listening," Mrozinski said. "But I still don't hear how he could have done it. For Christ's sake, Donovan, we were there watching. We watched all night."

"I know," Frankie said. "There's an explanation. I just don't have it yet."

"Well, you better get it quickly, because without an explanation, your friend Nicky is going to jail, and this time, he's staying there."

Chapter Twenty-Nine

YOU'RE UNDER ARREST AGAIN

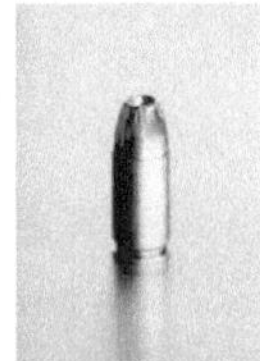

I woke to the sound of the doorbell ringing non-stop. I jumped out of bed, looked at the time—5:30—threw on some pants, and ran down the stairs.

When I opened the door, Bugs and Mrozinski stood before me. "What the hell's up?" I asked.

"Sonny's dead," Bugs said.

"What? How? I thought you were watching him."

"We were," Mrozinski said. "The last activity we saw was you leaving his house."

I held up my hands. "Whoa! I don't think I like where you're going with this. Sonny was alive and breathing fine when I left him. In fact, he had just poured himself a glass of wine."

"Well now, he's deader than duck shit," Mrozinski said. "Beaten like a squashed watermelon and shot in the head and chest."

"And I guess you think it was me," I said.

"Give me an explanation otherwise. I saw Sonny go into the house. I saw you go into the house a little later. Then I saw you exit an hour afterward. No one else went in or out of the house. This morning when we checked, Sonny was dead." Mrozinski stepped a little closer. "What would you think, Fusco?"

I looked to Bugs, who only shrugged.

"I was with him all night, Nicky. It's like he said. I don't have an explanation, but that's how it went down."

"I didn't do this, Bugs."

"I know you didn't," Bugs said.

Mrozinski held out a pair of handcuffs. I looked at Bugs, then him. "We need cuffs, Mrozinski?"

Mrozinski paused as if he were thinking. "You can wait till you get in the car if you give me your word you won't try anything."

"You've got it," I said. "One more thing, Mrozinski. I need to talk to Angie first."

"As long as you do it where I can see you," he said.

I walked to the bottom of the stairs and called up to Angie. "Hey, babe, can you come down here a minute, please?"

Angela walked down the steps carrying a laundry basket filled with clothes. She looked suspiciously at Mrozinski, then to me. "Nicky, what's going on? What's he doing here?"

I took the basket from her hands and set it on the floor. "There have been some developments, and I'm going to have to go with Detective Mrozinski for a while."

Her eyes widened. "Go where? Why?"

I grabbed her shoulders and hugged her. "Don't worry about why or where; Bugs will explain later. But I need you to do something."

"What?"

"I want you to go with Bugs to New York. You can stay with Kate and Alex."

"I won't do it; besides, we haven't even asked Kate."

Frankie stepped close. "It'll be no problem, Angela. I'll tell Kate as soon as we leave. She and Alex will love it."

"I don't know, Nicky. Why do I have to go?"

I squeezed her tightly and kissed her, then I whispered in her ear. "Someone is going to a lot of trouble to frame me. If they're willing to kill people, they won't think twice about hurting you or the kids. I can't do my job if that's on my mind."

"Your job? This isn't your job," Angela said. "You're an estimator. Let the police do their work."

I laughed. "If I let the police do their work, I'll be in prison before the week's out—convicted of murder."

"You can't believe that, Nicky."

I held Angela by the shoulders and kissed her again. "Angela, I not only believe it, I'm fully convinced of it. If I'm going to get out of this mess, I have to do it myself, or with Bugs's help."

Tears filled Angela's eyes. "I can't go through you being in prison again. I can't."

I pulled her close. "That's why you need to do as I say. But don't worry, you won't have to. Bugs and I will figure out who's doing this."

"We can't all stay at Frankie's house."

"You heard Bugs. He said Kate would be thrilled to have you and so would Alex."

"I vote yes," Rosa said as she entered the room.

Angela spun to face her. "Rosa, were you listening?"

I looked at Rosa. "What the hell are you doing home? I thought you were in school."

"I only had half a day, Dad, so I took off the whole day. Remember? I told you yesterday."

Rosa turned to her mother. "As to your question—it was hard *not* to listen; besides, it's my life too, isn't it? I say we stay with Aunt Kate and Alex."

I smiled. "It's settled then. Pack some things and listen to Bugs. He'll get you to the train station tomorrow."

"The train station?" Angela seemed surprised. "I can drive."

"I know you can drive," I said, "but I'd feel better if you took the train; besides, Dante's never ridden a train. He'll love it."

Angela wiped her eyes and smiled. "You always know what to say to get your way. You know I'm a sucker for Dante."

"You're sure not a sucker for me," Rosa said.

I laughed and turned to Bugs. "Will you stay here and talk to Angie?"

"Of course," he said. "And don't worry about anything. I'll figure this out."

"And somebody needs to take care of Sonny's family," I said.

"Don't worry," Frankie said. "I'll talk to Doggs."

I kissed the girls goodbye, then walked out with Mrozinski.

Mrozinski got behind the wheel and waited for me to slide into the passenger seat. "Fusco, if I were you, I'd worry more about myself than Sonny's family. You're in a shitload of trouble."

I smiled. "That's the difference between us, Mrozinski. I feel sorry for Sonny's family, and I have faith that Bugs will figure this out."

Mrozinski shook his head. "He better be damn good at figuring because I don't see any answers."

Mrozinski cursed as he turned the corner onto Clayton Street. "Fusco, you know I didn't want to do this, but the circumstances leave me no choice."

"You were outside his house all night?" I asked.

"From before you went in until Donovan and I found his body. I had guys out back also, and they said nobody entered or exited. And before you ask, yes, they did check the house beforehand. They did a thorough search of all floors and even the attic."

"And I was the only one you saw come in or go out the front?"

"You got it. We even marked the times you arrived and left."

"Then there has to be another way to get in. Did you check the basement? The roof?"

"How the hell is anyone getting in the basement? The only windows are in the front, by the porch, and in the back next to the stoop. I didn't see anyone go in the front and my men didn't see anyone go in the back."

"What about the roof?"

"The roof? How the hell is anyone getting in from the roof? Can't be done."

"Give me some time. I'll think of something."

"You'll have plenty of time, Fusco, and I'll make sure you're not bothered by noisy cellmates."

"I ought to kick your ass, Mrozinski."

He laughed. "You might find it hard with those cuffs on."

I reached over and laid the cuffs on Mrozinski's lap. "You mean these?"

Shocked, Mrozinski hit the brakes and reached for his gun only to find my hand on it. "Relax, Mrozinski. If I wanted to, I could have kicked your ass long ago and taken your gun for grins. I just wanted to show you that I'm going with you because I'm innocent, not because you think you have me subdued."

Mrozinski pushed my hand away. "You're an asshole, Fusco. Try that shit again, and I'll—"

"No matter how you finish that sentence, Mrozinski, it's bullshit. If I try that shit again, it will end the same way. Just drive and then focus on doing your job. Figure out how somebody got past you and Bugs and killed Sonny 'cause sure as shit, someone did."

"I'll give it thought," Mrozinski said, "but I can't see how anyone could have done it."

"There's the difference between you and a good cop. A good cop would figure it out despite it looking impossible."

Mrozinski turned his head and stared. "All right, Fusco. I'll give it a shot. Between Donovan and me, we should be able to find something."

We drove the rest of the way to the station in silence, then Mrozinski took me inside and put me in a cell. "Don't forget about me, Mrozinski."

"I won't. I'll get with Donovan as soon as I finish the paperwork."

Chapter Thirty

A LONG WALK HOME

Angela sat on the sofa, hands folded in her lap. "Sit, Frankie, and tell me what's going on. When we were growing up, I always counted on you for the truth. Don't let me down now."

Frankie reached behind him and closed the door. "He, uh—"

Dante tugged at Angela's skirt and climbed up on her. "Rosa, come get your brother, please? I need to talk to Uncle Frankie."

She turned back to Frankie and stared. "Don't hold back. I know something's wrong or Mrozinski wouldn't have taken him. What happened?"

"Maybe you should get a drink."

"Frankie, it's way too early for a drink. Just tell me."

Frankie leaned forward in the chair, elbows on his knees. "We set a trap for whoever's doing these killings last night, and Sonny—the bait—got killed."

"Sonny's the guy you used in the trap?"

Frankie nodded. "That's what I meant by 'the bait.' "

"And I suppose whatever really happened, it looks as if Nicky is the one who killed him?"

Frankie nodded again, then explained the situation in detail.

"What do we do, Frankie? We can't leave him in jail. He has a family to take care of and a business to run."

"I know that," Bugs said. "I also know that 'don't worry' doesn't help, but *don't worry*. I'll figure something out."

Angela stifled tears. "And while you're figuring it out, who's going to run the business? Who's going to feed the family? Nicky does okay, but he puts most of the money back into the business. We don't have the savings to tide us over."

Frankie walked over and hugged her. "Don't worry, Angela. I'll get it taken care of."

Angela almost laughed. "There's that 'don't worry' again. You've said it so many times, it makes me think I *should* worry."

Frankie and Angela finished off a bottle of Chianti, then Angela went to bed. "Please help, Frankie. I don't know what to do."

Frankie got up early and left the house to see Nicky, but before he did, he called Manny.

"Yo, Bugs. What the hell? You keeping my hours now?"

"Manny, the Rat's in a jam, and I need some help."

Manny's fist must have slammed on the table or the counter. "Goddamn, but I'm on a roll. What's up, Bugs? What do you need?"

"We set a trap for the killer down here, but he outsmarted us and got the bait we used. Worse than that, he made it look as if Nicky did it. Now Nicky's back in jail."

"Shit, don't worry about it, Bugs. You'll get him out."

"I'm not worried about that, but—"

"But what?" Manny asked.

"It's gonna put him in a jam as far as money goes. Can you spot me a few grand? You know I'm good for it."

Manny laughed. "Shit, is that all? How much you need? Ten large? Twenty?"

The weight of the world went off Frankie's shoulders. "I think ten will do, Manny. And thanks. I can't tell you what this means."

"Who's your local guy down there?" Manny asked.

"My what?"

"You know, your local guy. Who would you go to if you needed to place a big bet, or if you needed something done?"

"Guy named Doggs Caputo. He has a smoke shop on Union Street."

"That's all I need. See him after noon, and he'll straighten you out. And tell Nicky not to worry. No favors owed."

Bugs smiled. "Manny, you're the best."

"I been telling you that for a long time, Donovan. Maybe now you'll believe me."

Frankie did some chores that had accumulated, stopped for coffee, visited his sisters, then went to see Doggs. He walked in and got buzzed into the back room.

"Doggs, I—"

Doggs nodded and walked toward a small room in the back of the shop. He opened a safe and pulled out a wad of bills, which he stuffed into a paper bag and handed to Frankie. "I already got the call, Donovan. You could have asked me, you know. Didn't have to go out of town. Now I look small time, like I couldn't handle it."

"Sorry, Doggs, but I didn't know if you'd want to do that. I know Manny, so I asked him."

Doggs mumbled, then handed Frankie the cash. "Just take the fuckin' money."

Frankie took the bag without looking inside. "Thanks, Doggs. This means a lot."

"Yeah, yeah, just get the fuck out of here. And don't forget to put in a good word for me to Manny. You can't have too many friends."

Frankie smiled. "You got it, Doggs. Thanks again." Frankie walked outside and got into his car, then he drove to see Nicky.

He pulled to the curb in front of the jail and went inside. "Here to see Fusco," he said.

The guard looked as if he was going to say something, but

Frankie held up his badge. "Any problems, call Mrozinski. He'll vouch for me."

"I'll need to check the bag," the guard said.

Frankie handed him the bag and was about to offer an explanation when the guard gave it back to him. He called someone on the intercom, then another officer showed up to escort Frankie to Nicky's cell.

"Bugs, what the hell are you doing here?"

"Wanted to drop by and tell you there's no need to worry about anything. I called Johnny Moresco and asked him to handle things at the office, and Manny graciously sent you this." Bugs pulled the bag of cash from inside his jacket and showed it to Nicky.

Nicky's eyes went wide. "What the hell? Must be fifteen or twenty grand in there."

"I haven't added it up, but I asked for ten," Bugs said, then he grabbed the bag from Nicky and began counting. "Shit, Rat, you're right, there's twenty-five large here."

"Son of a bitch! What's that gonna cost?" Nicky asked.

Frankie shook his head. "Manny said no favors. Said it's on him."

Nicky smiled. "That's nice, but Manny never does things without expecting favors. He may not ask for favors, but he'll let you know you owe him, nonetheless."

Frankie laughed. "Yeah, he probably will. Anyway, we've got time to worry about that later. For now, let's figure out how to get you out of here."

———

Rosa rushed down the hall toward her next class, the last of the day. As she turned the corner, Cindy grabbed her by the elbow and pulled her to the side. "What's going on with your dad? I heard he was arrested."

Rosa shook her head. "It's nothing. A mistake. My dad didn't do anything."

"That's not what I heard."

"Cindy, you know my dad. Do you think he killed four people?" When Cindy didn't answer, Rosa said, "Well, do you?"

Cindy shook her head. "No, it's just—"

"Just what? You can't believe that shit."

"I don't, but Emily said he was arrested."

"A lot of people get arrested, Cindy. Being arrested doesn't mean you're guilty."

"All right. Forget I said anything. I'll see you after school."

"Don't bother," Rosa said. "I'm *walking* home. I need some private time."

"Suit yourself, but if you want a ride, meet me at my car in the parking lot."

"I don't *want* one and I don't *need* one," Rosa said, and headed off to class.

When the bell rang, Rosa walked out the front door and headed south on DuPont Street. As she crossed Seventh Street, a man leaning against a parked car addressed her. "You Nicky Fusco's daughter?"

Rosa sighed. "Yes. Why?"

He grabbed her arm and yanked her toward him, pulling a knife while he did. "You're coming with me, bitch."

Rosa tried pulling away. "Let me go, you freak."

The man put the knife to her throat and pressed. "Shut up and get in the car."

———

Three young black men, sitting on the front steps of a house across the street, got up and walked over. "You all right?" one of them asked Rosa.

"No, I'm not!" she screamed.

The larger of the black men glared at the man holding Rosa. "Maybe you should let her go."

"Mind your own business," the man said. "This is my daughter."

The black man shook his head. "I don't think so. I heard you ask if she was Nicky Fusco's daughter."

The man pulled aside his jacket to reveal a gun in his waistband. "I said mind your own business."

All three black men pulled their jackets aside. Each one of them had a gun in their waistband. The one who'd been speaking drew his and pointed it at the man. "My name's Bmore, and like I said, let the girl go."

The man holding Rosa hesitated, and then Bmore cocked the trigger and aimed the gun at his head. "You're *gonna* let her go, and it don't much matter to me whether you're alive or dead when you do."

The man stared momentarily, then pulled the knife away from Rosa and put it away. He then backed slowly to his car door, opened it, and got behind the wheel. "I won't forget this," he said, and drove off.

"Oh my God, thank you," Rosa said. "I was scared."

Bmore put the gun away and motioned for Rosa to follow him. "C'mon, we'll give you a ride home."

"You don't need to," Rosa said.

"I know we don't need to," Bmore said, "but we're doing it. Monroe would have our asses if something happened to the Rat's daughter."

Rosa followed him to a new Audi parked across the street and got in the back seat. "I live down—"

"We know where you live," he said. "Don't worry, you'll be safe at home in a few minutes."

Bmore drove her home and parked next to the house. "Your dad home?"

Rosa shook her head. "He's in jail."

"What?" He opened the car door and turned to the other two men. "Frisco, Marlo, let's go. We can't let her sit by herself."

"What the fuck you mean? I got to be somewhere," Marlo said.

"The only place you got to be is inside watching this girl. Now get your ass in there."

Bmore, Frisco, and Marlo watched TV for a while, then Rosa got up and went to the kitchen. "If I'm going to be stuck here, I might as well cook something. You guys hungry?"

"What you got in mind?" Bmore asked.

"You like spaghetti and meatballs? I've got plenty left over from the other night."

"Kick my ass if I don't," Bmore said.

"Then somebody get out here and help me heat it up, and someone else open a bottle of wine," Rosa said.

"I can handle the wine," Frisco said.

"I don't know," Marlo said. "This wine's bound to have a cork."

————

"This shit's good," Frisco said. "Ain't had nothin' this good since Mrs. Robino's."

"Shit, Frisco. You ain't been there in twenty years. How the hell you even remember?" Marlo asked.

The front door opened and Angie and Dante entered. Angie stared, confused. "Rosa?"

Rosa smiled, got up, and walked to her mother. "This is Bmore, Frisco, and Marlo. Some man was bothering me, and they helped."

Angie looked to her quickly. "Bothering you how?"

Rosa shrugged. "He was just talking inappropriately and—"

Bmore stood. "Not quite true, Mrs. Rat. The man was trying to kidnap her. He had a gun."

Shock registered on Angie's face. "What? Kidnap you?"

"Yes, ma'am," Bmore said. "And I'm sure he meant harm to her. We heard she was the Rat's daughter, so we intervened."

————

ngela walked over and hugged Bmore. "Thank you. Thank you so much."

Angela brought another bottle of wine and set it on the table. "I think you'll find this much tastier," she said. "Now please excuse me. I need to make a call."

Angela called Frankie, speaking calmly when he answered. "Frankie, this is Angela. A man tried to kidnap Rosa. He held a knife on her and tried forcing her into a car."

"What? Who? Is she all right?"

"Yes, she's fine," Angela said. "Thanks to three young black men who came to her rescue. I'm not certain, but it sounds as if they're some of Monroe's men."

"Did she get a good look at the guy?"

"She said he was medium height and build and slightly balding. No facial hair."

"I'm guessing it's the guy we're after," Frankie said. "What about the men who helped her? They still there?"

"They're eating dinner right now."

"Good, keep them around until I get there. It won't be long."

———

rankie made a turn and headed to see Nicky. He'd want to know what was going on.

"Bugs, what's up? What are you doing back here?"

"Somebody tried to kidnap Rosa."

Nicky grabbed hold of the bars. "What? Is she all right? What happened?"

"Take it easy, Rat. That's why I came here. Apparently some guy —probably the killer—approached her on the street and tried forcing her into his car with a knife. Three of Monroe's men stopped him."

"Son of a bitch," Nicky said. "You need to get home with Angie and Rosa."

Frankie held up his hands. "Easy, Nicky. Monroe's guys are still with them, and they're going to stay until I get there."

"The hell with that. Ask them to stay afterward, too. In fact, Bugs, I need a favor. I need you to get them out of town as soon as possible, but not to your house."

"I was thinking the same thing, but where should I take them?"

"I want you to take them to Manny's. Tell him I'll owe him two for this."

"Nicky, there's no need—"

"That's what I want, Bugs. They need to be kept safe, and nobody can keep them safer than Manny."

"I can't argue that, Rat, so consider it done. I'll drive them up there today."

"See if Monroe's men will go with you. Tell them I'll pay for it. And consider taking the train. With that many people, you'll need two cars. The train would be more convenient, not to mention it would be easier to guard them."

"Agreed. Maybe we'll pull a trick or two on the way."

"Like what?"

"I haven't figured it out yet, but I will. Don't worry. I'll take care of them."

"And you're going to have to call Manny. I can't do it from here."

"No problem," Frankie said. "He's going to love racking up all these favors."

"All right, Bugs. Now get out of here. I don't want Angie sitting home by herself."

Frankie turned to leave, but Nicky called him. "And, Bugs, see if you can nail down a description of the guy. Between Rosa and Monroe's men, we should be able to."

"All right, got it. Anything else?"

"Yeah," Nicky said. "Ask Monroe to come see me. I gotta get out of here."

———

F rankie crushed his cigarette on the sidewalk and walked into Nicky's house. He hugged Angela and Rosa and patted Dante on the head. "Everybody okay?"

"Thanks to them, I am," Rosa said as she gestured to the sofa and chair where Monroe's men sat. "This is Bmore, Frisco, and Marlo. They stopped that man from grabbing me."

Frankie nodded. "I thank you, and I know Nicky thanks you. I just came from seeing him."

Frisco smiled and nudged Marlo's arm.

"He asked if you'd do him a favor. He wants me to take his family to New York, and he said he'd owe you one if you could help protect them."

"I got nothin' better to do," Bmore said. "Count me in."

Frisco and Marlo nodded. "Me too," they both said. "When we goin'?"

"We'll leave in a couple of hours," Frankie said. "And we're taking the train, so no need for cars."

"Where you taking 'em?" Bmore asked. "I know a place we could go."

"That's all right. I appreciate it, but we've got a place."

"Where? You got a safe place?"

Frankie looked at Bmore. "You heard of Manny Rosso?"

Bmore raised his eyebrows. "*The* Manny Rosso? The one over in Brooklyn?"

Frankie nodded. "That's him."

"Shit. Forget what I suggested. Ain't nobody gonna mess with Manny's place."

Rosa smiled. "We're going to stay with Manny?"

Frankie nodded again. "Pack your things. Enough for at least a few days."

Bmore stood. "We're gonna do the same if it's all right with you. Pick us up at Seventh and DuPont on your way to the station."

"That'll be fine," Frankie said. "We shouldn't be more than an hour."

F rankie picked up Monroe's men where they said, but he used two cabs to do it. The cabs took him to the train station where he got tickets for New York. "We'll try to get the last car," Frankie said. "It'll be easier to spot a problem that way."

"By the way," Frankie said. "Can any of you draw?"

"Frisco can," Bmore said. "He can draw like a mother fu—" He looked at Angela and gulped. "Like a son of a bitch."

Frankie couldn't help but smile. "Good, see if you can come up with a likeness of the guy who tried taking Rosa. I know Nicky will want to have it. Work with Rosa on it if you need to."

"I know what he looks like," Marlo said. "Like he was my brother."

Frisco punched his arm. "You don't have no brother."

Marlo appeared to be insulted. "I said *like* he was my brother, asshole."

Chapter Thirty-One

MANNY'S HOTEL

Frankie and Marlo got on the train with Angela, Rosa, and Dante, boarding the last car on the train for New York. Bmore and Frisco boarded behind them and took seats near the rear.

Just before departure, Bmore approached Frankie and tapped him on the shoulder. "You can catch a snooze if you need to. Me and my boys will keep an eye on things; besides, we're still working on that description."

Frankie shook his head. "Thanks anyway, Bmore, but we won't be here long enough to matter."

Bmore tilted his head to the side. "What you talking about? It's a good two-hour trip."

"It is," Frankie said. "But we're not going that far. We're gonna get off in Princeton and rent a couple of cars so we can drive the rest of the way."

"Princeton? What for?"

"Mix things up. If he found out where we were headed, he could be waiting at the station in New York, but he'd never suspect we'd get off in Princeton, and he'd have no idea where we're going once we get to New York."

Bmore nodded. "Shit, I like that. Damned if I don't." Bmore returned to his seat and filled Frisco in on the plan.

Frisco listened to Bmore, then leaned his head back on the seat. "How long we got?"

"About an hour," Bmore said. "It's not very far."

Bmore and Frisco played cards during the ride to Princeton, and Frankie called Kate to chat and catch her up on what was going on.

"Frankie, your boss has called every day since you've been gone. He sounds upset."

"Did you tell him I was away on personal business?"

"I did, but he keeps asking where, and he wants to know why you're not answering your cell phone. What should I tell him?"

"Tell him you're pissed as well. Tell him you haven't talked to me either, and you've left half a dozen messages."

"Frankie, I can't say that; besides, there's no way he'd believe me. I don't like lying to him."

"All right, for Christ's sake. I'll call him and get it straightened out."

"I'd appreciate it if you did. You know I don't like this kind of thing."

"No worries. Let me go so I can get this done."

"All right, let me know once you've talked. Love you."

"Love you too, babe. See you soon. And tell Ace I said I love him too. Tell him I said I'm gonna kick his ass in some Ninja Gaiden when I get back."

"Isn't that game about as old as you?"

"This is a new version. Good God, get up to speed."

Kate sighed. "I'll tell him, but I'd rather you did homework with him."

"That's not nearly as much fun," Frankie said.

"Goodbye, Mr. Donovan. Be safe. Oh, and by the way—that DNA evidence you requested—I finished it. Nicky's DNA was at every scene, Mrozinski's was at two of the scenes, there was miscellaneous DNA at each of the other scenes, but one more person's DNA matched all the scenes, and only one. It's not in the records though, so I'm no help on who the person is."

"Shit, that's good, Kate. If you think of anything else, let me know. We'll do the same. In the meantime, I better call the boss."

Angela leaned toward Frankie as he disconnected the call. "Frankie, don't get yourself in trouble over this. I'm sure Monroe's men can take care of us."

Frankie smiled. "Angela, I promised Nicky I'd look out for you guys. If anything happened to any of you . . ."

Angela nodded and straightened. "All right, Frankie. I understand. He was the same way when you got hurt in New York. Nothing I said would keep him home."

"Don't worry, Angela. It'll all be over soon."

"I hope so, Frankie. I get tired of the worry. I just want a normal life."

The train made its Princeton stop and Frankie and the rest of them got off. He rented two cars for the rest of the trip, putting Bmore and Frisco in one, and he and Marlo in the other with Angela, Rosa, and Dante.

Bmore leaned his head out the car window. "Don't go speeding. I don't like to drive fast."

Frankie didn't know if he was joking, but he made note of the request just in case. Afterword, he drove the short distance to the turnpike, and then went north toward New York.

An hour and a half later, Frankie veered onto the Verrazano-Narrows Bridge leading to Brooklyn.

"Are we close to where you live, Uncle Frankie?" Rosa asked.

"Not far. I'm only a few miles from the other side of the bridge, in Brooklyn."

"Are we going to see Alex and Kate?"

"Good question, Rosa, and I don't know the answer. I guess it depends on how things go once we get to Manny's. I need to see my boss too so I can get things straightened out."

"Yes, you do," Angela said.

Frankie shook his head. "Angela, you're starting to sound like Kate."

"And you haven't been married long enough to be talking like that."

Frankie laughed. "Yes, ma'am. I know when to quit arguing."

"I wish you'd teach it to Nicky."

Frankie smiled as he switched lanes. "Angela, I'm going to drop by the station like I said. It won't take long. While I'm in there, I want you and the kids to wait in the lobby. I'll tell the desk sergeant to keep an eye on you."

"What about Bmore?" Rosa asked.

"I'm sure they'll be more comfortable keeping watch from outside the station."

"Got that shit right," Marlo said.

Frankie exited the bridge and drove to the cop station. With the precautions he'd taken, he hadn't expected any trouble, but he looked continually in the rearview mirror for tails, and he also checked with Bmore. Even if he missed someone following him, going to the cop station should throw them off—at least momentarily.

As planned, he parked and took Angela and the family inside the station. He asked Bmore and his men to keep watch from the street.

Frankie approached the desk sergeant. "Where's Bud?" he asked.

"Took off for the day. You need something, Donovan?"

"Yeah. I got a lady and her two kids who need a place to sit for a few minutes. And I need someone to keep an eye on them too. I gotta go upstairs and see Morreau, but I won't be long."

"Not a problem. Bring her over here, and I'll get it taken care of." He turned to his right and hollered. "Hey, Mush. Take this lady to an empty office and keep an eye on her."

"For how long?" Mush asked.

"Till I tell you not to," the desk sergeant said and shook his head.

Once Mush took Angela and the kids, Frankie went upstairs and into Morreau's office. He wore a smile as he walked in and plopped into a chair across from the lieutenant's desk. "What's up, Lieu?"

Morreau leaned back in his chair and stared. " 'What's up, Lieu?' That's all you've got to say?" The lieutenant bit the inside of his lip, then ground his teeth. "I've called you twenty times. I've left ten messages. I've called your wife, your partner, and anyone else I could think of. Shit, I even texted you, and you know I despise texting. And after all that, I didn't get so much as a go to hell, lieutenant."

"Sorry, Lieu. I had a family emergency."

"That's bullshit, Donovan. I forgot to mention I called your mother. She hasn't heard a peep from you."

Frankie's smile disappeared. "Okay, Lieu, the truth is I've been helping a friend. My oldest friend got in a jam, and he needed my help."

"Your oldest friend? This wouldn't be the guy you once suspected of murdering five people, would it?"

After a moment of silence, Frankie nodded. "It might be, Lieu, but remember that guy was only a suspect. He didn't do it."

"So says the lead inspector."

Frankie narrowed his eyes. "Yeah, Lieu. So he says."

"Well, I was pissed off, Donovan, but now that you're back, I might forgive you."

Frankie stood and placed his palms on Morreau's desk. "That's the thing, Lieu. I'm not back. Not yet. I've still got a few things to do."

"Bullshit! You're back or you're gone."

"Just like that? What happened to personal leave and a boss's understanding?"

"You've had your personal leave, and no one ever promised you an understanding boss, just a boss. So either be here tomorrow morning to start the day or be here to turn in your badge."

"Don't threaten me, Lieu. I don't do well with threats."

"And you should know by now that I don't make threats, Donovan. I meant what I said. Every word of it."

Frankie took off his badge and laid it on Morreau's desk. He placed his gun alongside it. "Here you go, Lieu. Have a good life." He turned and started to leave.

"Donovan, what the hell do you think you're doing? Are you serious? Do you know what you're doing? Really know?"

"I'm not an idiot. I know *exactly* what I'm doing. I'm helping a friend, a man I've been friends with all my life, and I'm not about to desert him now because you're having an ego problem."

"Ego problem? What's that supposed to mean?"

"Just what I said. You're pissed because I didn't get your blessing, so you're acting like a little kid."

"Get out of here, Donovan. Think about what I said. Take the whole damn night if you need to. I'll give you one last chance to make a sane decision. If you show up tomorrow morning, we'll forget this happened."

Frankie laughed. "Lieu, there's no need to wait till tomorrow. You've got my decision, and you've got my badge and gun to go with it. Tell Miller and Carol I'll give them a call. See ya, Lieu."

"You can't be serious, Donovan."

Frankie walked out the door. "See ya."

He went downstairs and got Angela and the kids, then he left. Bmore and Marlo sat on a bench under an elm tree. Frisco paced the sidewalk. "Hey, Bmore. Wake up. It's time to go."

Bmore stood and tossed the car keys to Marlo. "You drive. Frisco can ride with the cop."

Frisco shot him the finger, but then he followed Frankie to his car. "Where we going now?"

"Going to Manny's house," Frankie said.

"How'd it go?" Angela asked.

"Fine," Frankie said.

"Fine as in . . .?"

"Fine."

"Frankie, what happened? I know you went there to talk to your boss. What did he say?"

Frankie looked over his shoulder to Rosa. "Is she always like this?"

Rosa laughed. "I'm afraid so, Uncle Frankie. You're better off just answering her, or she won't stop hounding you."

"Rosa!"

"I quit, Angela," Frankie said.

"What?"

"I said, 'I quit' as in I stopped working there."

"What do you mean? You can't quit."

"Angela, I don't want to go through this with you. I'm going to have more than enough of that when I talk to Kate, so let's leave it at 'I quit' and move on."

"But, Frankie—"

"Mom, that's enough. It's not your business. Uncle Frankie asked us to leave it alone, so let's do that."

"Fine," Angela said, and folded her arms across her chest.

Twenty minutes later, Frankie turned onto the street where Manny lived. He found a parking space half a block away and pulled to the curb. Bmore pulled alongside him. "I don't see nowhere to park."

"You'll probably find a spot on the next street over. Check it out, and we'll wait for you here."

Ten minutes later, Bmore and Marlo walked up the street to where Frankie stood. "Now what?"

"Now we go see Manny," Frankie said.

Halfway down the block, at a nondescript house, Frankie walked up the sidewalk and onto the front porch. He knocked on the door and waited.

A moment later, the door opened and a large, barrel-chested man with an even larger stomach grabbed hold of Frankie and hugged him. "Bugs! What the hell brings you to Manny's hotel?"

"Like I told you on the phone. Nicky's got trouble, and I need to make sure his wife and kids are safe while this is going on."

Manny gestured toward Bmore and his men. "And who are these guys?"

Frankie pointed them out and introduced them. "This is Bmore, Frisco, and Marlo. They work for one of Nicky's best friends, and they came along to help."

Manny stepped aside and held the door open. "We won't need their help, Bugs, but it's always welcome. In the meantime, come on in. I'll put some espresso on."

Bmore whispered in Frankie's ear. "Us too?"

Manny laughed. "Yeah, you too. Don't think I'm prejudiced just because I'm a fat dago living in Brooklyn. Hell, I even let Bugs's Irish ass in here. As long as you like espresso, you're welcome in my house."

Everyone settled into seats in the kitchen while Manny made espresso. "Won't be long," he said. "Hey, Rosa, grab the biscotti from the counter and get some plates if you don't mind. Gotta have biscotti with espresso."

"Yes, sir, Mr. Rosso."

Giorgio turned his head and spit out his coffee, laughing uncontrollably. He stood up and got a towel to clean up the floor. "Sorry, but that's only the second time I heard anyone call Manny *sir*."

Frankie stifled a laugh. "Rosa, he's right. Manny's been called a lot of things, but *sir* isn't one of them."

Manny brought a few cups of espresso to the table. "Rosa, pay no attention to these buffoons. You can call me *sir* or anything else you want."

Rosa smiled. "Thanks, Manny."

Manny set the last cups on the table, then joined his guests. "Okay, here's how it's gonna be. Giorgio is in charge of operations. Angela, you and Rosa and the kid go nowhere without asking him first." He looked to Angela with a question written on his face.

She nodded, then Manny turned to Rosa, and she nodded as well.

"Okay, that's settled. Giorgio, you know how the deal works. Nicky's family is under the tightest protection. Got it?"

"Understood, boss."

"Bmore, you and your men are welcome to stay here, but if you choose to go elsewhere, you need to be here by eight in the morning. Got it?"

Bmore nodded. "Got it."

A broad smile covered Manny's face. "Damn, now that the tough part is taken care of, let's enjoy the espresso and some biscotti. Rosa, would you please pass me a couple biscotti?"

She smiled and handed him the plate. "Of course, *sir*."

Manny laughed and blew her a kiss. "Damn, I like this girl."

SOME THINGS HAVE TO BE DONE

Frankie came down the steps like a kid rushing to go play. He opened the front door and hollered, "See ya later, Manny."

Manny poked his head out of the kitchen. "Where the hell you goin' at this time of day?"

"I need to see Kate. If she finds out I was in town and didn't let her know, I'm a dead man."

"You mean you haven't told her you're in town yet?"

"On my way to do it now."

"You better lie to her and tell her you just got in. If she finds out you got here yesterday, you're in a shitload of trouble."

"Manny, you guys have been lying to your wives for decades."

"Hey, Donovan. I know that, but Italian women expect to be lied to. Irish women think you'll tell the truth. The difference is in the expectation."

"Don't I know it," Frankie said, and laughed. "Anyway, gotta go, Manny. See ya later."

Frankie drove to Kate's work and walked inside. Kate was busy in the lab, and when she came out, she almost bumped into him. "Frankie, my God, what are you doing here?"

He kissed her cheek and smiled. "I had to bring Angela and the kids up to keep them safe. They're staying at Manny's."

"Angela? Why didn't you bring them to our house? We could have made room."

"Room's not the issue. This killer already tried to kidnap Rosa. God knows what he'd have tried next."

"What about Nicky?"

"He's in jail again. The detective down there isn't too smart, and despite conflicting evidence, he is convinced Nicky's involved. He's never heard of common sense either."

"What are you going to do? You can't investigate down there; you have no jurisdiction."

Frankie nodded. "It's making it difficult. I'm going to have to try to persuade Mrozinski to see things my way to get this resolved."

Kate smiled as she washed her hands. "I hope you're not relying on your Irish charm because that doesn't work."

"Huh. It worked on you."

"You only think it did." Kate dried her hands with a towel and moved to a corpse. "You got time for lunch?"

"Not really," Frankie said. "I have to see Miller, and I have to strategize with Manny on some leads we're looking into. But you could stop by tonight for dinner."

"No thanks," Kate said. "Nothing against Manny, but I don't think Alex needs to be exposed to that element at his age."

"You're probably right—as usual—so let me get busy and try to get this over with." Frankie leaned over and kissed her. "See you when I'm done."

———

Rosa wiped the remnants of a night's sleep from her eyes as she entered the kitchen. "Good morning, Manny."

Manny stood quickly and hugged her. "Rosa! *buon giorno, principessa.* You want some coffee or espresso?"

She nodded. "Thanks, Manny. I'd love some." She sat at the table across from him and said, "And a biscotto if you have one."

"You got it," Manny said as he boiled water. "Where's your mother?"

"She was getting Dante ready when I came down. She'll be here in a minute."

"Already here," Angela said as she entered with Dante.

Manny kissed her cheek. "*Buon giorno*, Angela." He then picked up Dante and hugged him. "*Anche tu, principesso.*"

Angela leaned down and spoke to Dante. "Mr. Rosso said 'Good morning' to me, then he said 'and you too, little prince.' " She stood and took a seat next to Rosa. "We haven't been teaching him Italian, Manny."

Manny nodded. "Should've known. Not many people learn the mother tongue anymore. Anyway, here's your espresso," he said, and handed a cup to Angela. "Want a biscotto?"

Angela shook her head. "What have you got planned for today?"

"You tell me. I got Giorgio and four of his men, and we've got Bmore and his two guys. There are enough men to protect you from a small army, so you can go wherever you want."

"Central Park!" Rosa said.

"Central Park? What the hell you want to go there for? Go to Prospect Park; there's a lot more to do. A lot less crowded too."

"Where's Frankie?" Angela asked.

"He went to see Kate. He left early, so he'll be back soon."

———

Frankie drove toward Brooklyn Heights and called Miller on the way. "Miller, where are you?"

"Not far from the station, why?"

"I'm in town and wanted to get an update on the names you were looking into. You get any info yet?"

"Some, but not all. Meet me in my office, and I'll fill you in."

"Probably not a good place to meet," Frankie said. "I turned in my badge yesterday."

"What the hell? Turned in your badge? Are you nuts?"

"I didn't intend to, but Morreau was an ass."

"Damn. Have you told Kate?"

"Not yet, so don't say anything if you talk to her. I'll tell her tonight. Maybe tomorrow."

"Chicken-shit is what you are, Donovan. You need to tell her. If she hears it from someone else, you're really in trouble."

"Yeah, I know. All right, I'll call her now. But we still need to meet."

"How about that coffee shop we liked in Brooklyn Heights?"

"That'll work. I'll be there in twenty minutes," Frankie said. "That is, if Kate doesn't shoot me."

"Through the phone?" Miller asked.

"You never know," Frankie said. "See you soon."

He dialed Kate as he turned the corner to go to the coffee shop.

"Frankie, what a surprise. Are you calling to tell me you quit your job?"

"What? How'd you find out? Did Miller call you?"

"No, it wasn't Miller, but now I've found out that she knows too. Was I the *last* person you were going to tell?"

"No. I mean. Hell no. I was going to tell you this morning, but I didn't want to ruin your day, so I planned on telling you tonight at Manny's."

"But I told you I wasn't going to Manny's."

"I know. That put a damper on my plans, which is why I called you now."

"Well, it sounds like it's too late to worry about anything. Financially, we can manage off what I make. You'll have to deal with it mentally. And since I know you're dying with curiosity—it was Morreau who told me about you quitting."

"That son of a bitch."

"Are you dropping by to say hello to Alex?"

"Of course. I'll be there for dinner. I'm not going to eat at Manny's without you guys."

"Alex will be ecstatic. How about seven?"

"I'll be there. Love you."

Frankie pulled into a parking spot reserved for the coffee shop and sat in the car waiting for Sherri Miller to arrive. Five minutes later, she pulled in across the street and got out of her car. Frankie opened the door to go greet her. "Miller, good to see you."

Sherri picked up her pace as she crossed the street, hugging Frankie when they met. "Good to see you too, Donovan. How've you been? And what happened with the Lieu?"

Frankie shook his head. "Nothing. He insisted I report for work tomorrow. The only option was to turn in my badge, so I turned it in; Nicky still needs help. You gotta do what you gotta do."

"Speaking of which, I checked on Martelli and Amato. I'm still waiting on some information on Devin's older brother, but I haven't found anything on Amato or Martelli. And from what little I know, I doubt if the Devin connection will turn up anything either."

"And you're confident about this? You trust the sources?"

Sherri nodded. "I confirmed everybody's whereabouts with neighbors and employers, and nothing seemed fishy. If any of them did it, it was the middle of the night, and they'd have had to work with a damn tight timeline. Besides, from what you told me, none of the murders happened after midnight."

"Thanks, Miller. That helps." Frankie headed toward the coffee shop. "Come on, let me buy you a cup."

Sherri fell in step alongside Donovan. "So give me the scoop on why you're up here."

"Whoever is doing these killings tried kidnapping Nicky's daughter."

Sherri whistled, a long monotone sound. "I don't like kidnappers, but I hope you find this guy before Nicky does. Nobody deserves what fate that would be."

Frankie nodded. "I hear you, Miller. I'm trying to put this to bed as much for the guy who tried kidnapping Rosa as I am for Nicky. There'd be no stopping him if anything happened to her."

"So why are you up here loafing? Get back down there and solve this thing. Or do I have to handle the tough cases for you?"

"Don't worry. I'm leaving shortly. I've just got to make sure things are set up here."

"All right, Donovan, keep in touch. And say hi to Manny. He came through for me on that murder."

"So I heard," Frankie said. "And don't think you owe him for it. He might try to make you feel that way but don't let him."

Miller laughed. "Got you, Donovan. Now get out of here."

Chapter Thirty-Three

WE'VE GOT TO FIND THE KILLER

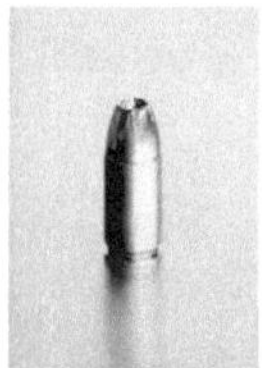

The door opened and Mrozinski walked in. He came up to the cell, unlocked it, and stepped inside. "Nicky, how are you?"

I didn't get up, just stayed on the bed, hands under my pillow. "Suddenly you're interested in my health, Mrozinski? What's going on?"

"Nothing going on. I just wanted to check on you. I told you I'd try to help, and I will, but I need to know everything you know."

I laughed, and I sat up to respond this time. "Mrozinski, you're so full of shit you don't even know it. You didn't expect to come in here playing nice guy and hope to get something out of me, did you? That wouldn't work with a newbie."

I pointed my finger at him. "If you hope to catch this killer, you're going to have to let me go because you're not going to catch him yourself."

"You think not?"

"That's right, Mrozinski. I think not. You're too stupid to catch him. If you want the killer, you'll have to get me out of here. The other option would be to let Maddy run the investigation. She seemed like she was sharp. Where's she been, anyway? I haven't seen her."

"Not that it's any of your business, but she had to go out of town for a funeral. I expect her back soon."

A guard poked his head through the door and hollered in. "Visitor for Fusco."

Mrozinski glared, but then he stood and left the cell just as the guard escorted Monroe in. "Fifteen minutes," he said.

I stood up and hugged Monroe. "What the hell are you doing here?"

"Bmore called me from New York. Seems like your buddy enlisted the aid of a few of my men to take your family to safety."

I sat on the edge of the bed and indicated that Monroe should too. "Yeah, your boys stopped the killer from kidnapping my daughter. Tell them I owe them."

"They were glad to help out. Shit, they're freaking out just being up there with Manny. I'm sure they don't mind. Besides, I told them they owe you for being so stupid as to not cap the guy when they had him."

I laughed. "Now that the bullshit is over with, tell me what you're doing here."

"Need to figure out how to get you out of here and find the real killer before this asshole detective gets lucky and finds a way to pin it on you."

"I got you there, Monroe. Fact is, he may have already gotten lucky. We set a trap using Sonny Bruno, a guy from the smoke shop. We had cops out front and in back. I went inside and talked to the guy, and after I left, someone killed Sonny."

"Who?"

"That's the whole point—who?" I stood and paced. "Frankie and Mrozinski were out front and two cops out back. They swear no one went in or out after me, but in the morning, the guy was dead. Shot and beaten."

"Shit," Monroe said. "Sounds easy to me. All we got to do is figure out how the guy got in. If he didn't come in the front or back, he had to do it some other way."

"How?" I asked. "You know those houses on Broom Street. Not many ways in or out."

"If you didn't kill him, there's got to be a way, Rat. Get me in there, and I'll find it."

"Fat chance of getting you in there," I said.

Monroe leaned back and thought for a moment, then he spoke. "How about that cop you helped? You know, the one I worked with you on up in Hockessin."

I turned to look at him. "You mean Borelli? The one whose kid we rescued?"

Monroe nodded. "That'd be the one. I bet he could get me in there to check it out."

"He probably could Monroe, but I have no idea where he is. He's in hiding. Probably in some a shitty little town in the Midwest. I can't risk bringing him out. You never know who's watching."

"Why don't you let him decide that," Monroe said. "You *did* save his kid. I'm guessing he'd do anything to return the favor. And remember, you gave me his number."

I thought about what Monroe said as I paced. I could just wait for Bugs to get back, but then again, I didn't know when that would be, and it was more important for him to be with Angie and the kids.

I looked at Monroe and nodded. "All right. Give him a call, but take all the precautions and tell him not to take any chances. And tell him if he thinks he can convince Mrozinski over the phone, he should do it that way."

Monroe smiled. "You got it, Rat. I'll have DuPree call him this afternoon. If this Borelli is any kind of man, he'll be here by tomorrow."

I lowered my head. "Maybe so, Monroe. Maybe so."

Monroe got up to leave, but I grabbed his arm and whispered. "One more thing, if you don't mind."

"Anything, Rat."

I gestured to my new cellmate, sitting near the back. "He's been trying to give me a hard time since he got here. I don't want to hurt him because it will put him in the hospital and earn me more time besides. Can you talk to him?"

Monroe glanced over my shoulder. "Shit, no problem. Give me a minute," he said, and walked up to the guy.

"What's up, bro?" Monroe slapped his hand and bumped fists.

The man stood. "Monroe, I didn't think you'd remember me. It's been a while."

"Shit, I don't forget people. Johnson, isn't it? Pete Johnson."

Johnson laughed, obviously pleased that Monroe remembered him. He then gestured in Nicky's direction. "You know that cracker?"

Monroe nodded.

"You done your business with him, 'cause I'm about to go fuck him up. He won't give up the bottom bunk, and I want it."

Now it was Monroe's turn to laugh. "Yeah, I know him? You don't? Shit, bro, I took you for smarter than that."

Johnson lost his smile. "What do you mean? What are you laughing about?"

"I'm laughing 'cause your cellmate is none other than Nicky 'The Rat' Fusco, and he's the meanest mother fucker I know. Maybe the meanest I've ever known."

Johnson's eyes opened wide. "You mean the 'Rat' from Brooklyn?"

Monroe nodded. "And Hockessin, and California. And he's in here now 'cause they think he killed those four people recently. When I was in prison with him, he killed two of the meanest white dudes in there."

Monroe whispered to Johnson, "A couple years back, I saw him take care of eleven guys at a house in Hockessin in one night. And this wasn't a goddamn college frat party. This was a Mexican drug-dealer stash house."

Johnson's jaw dropped. "No shit?"

Monroe started to walk away and Johnson called him back. "You said you saw him kill those two dudes in prison. What did he kill them with?"

Monroe said, "A bar of soap."

Johnson looked at him like he was crazy "A bar of soap?"

Monroe smiled. "Yeah, think about that for a minute." He stared at Johnson and said, "It's none of my business, but—"

"No need to say more," Johnson said. "Bottom bunks don't mean *that* much."

"I agree," Monroe said. "Now I gotta go. Me and Rat got some strategizing to do."

"Okay, Monroe. See ya."

Monroe smiled as he approached. "Taken care of, Rat. He won't be causing trouble any more."

"Now let's get down to business and get you outta here, Rat."

"It doesn't matter if I'm out," I said. "I'll be back in jail before you can blink if we don't get the real killer."

"I'm here to help," Monroe said.

"There's nothing for you to do, Monroe. I'll get out of this."

"I know you'll get out of it eventually, but I also know that every day behind bars is a day of torture."

"You got that. So what bright ideas have you got. And they can't include a breakout. I've still got to live in this town."

"Tell me what happened and don't leave anything out," Monroe said. "How is it they came to bust you for this? And what makes the cops think you did it?"

I sighed. "It started with Knuckles being killed. Mrozinski was convinced Charlie had something on me and was about to spill the beans."

"Shit, we know that ain't right," Monroe said. "Knuckles wouldn't give it up under torture. Everybody's heard how Knuckles witnessed his cousin murdered and wouldn't identify the guy. I think he waited three years to get the guy, but get him he did. That's some cold shit there."

"I know," I said. "Anyway, we set a trap for the killer. We used 'Crooked Nose' Sonny down on Broom Street."

Monroe smiled. "I know him. Bad gambler."

Nicky smiled. "That's Sonny. Anyway, I was with him early in the night, then left. After that, it's like I said. Bugs watched the house with Mrozinski and two of his cops. According to them, no one went in or out after me, but in the morning, Sonny was dead."

"And then?"

"And then, I was arrested for Sonny's murder."

"What do we need to do?" Monroe asked.

"We need to find this guy, and then we need to prove he did it. It's not going to be easy. He seems to have his shit together. At least some of it."

"Sounds like I need to prove the killer could have gotten into the house without Mrozinski seeing him."

I smiled. "Yeah, Monroe. If you can do that, it would be great."

"I can do that. You figure out who the guy is, and I'll show he could have done it. How's that, Rat?"

I bumped fists with Monroe. "Sounds good. I'll work on my end, and you do your part. Let's see who finishes first."

Chapter Thirty-Four

A CALL TO BUGS

Angela walked down the street, Dante by her side and Giorgio and two of his men in front of them with Bmore and Frisco behind them. Marlo was across the street.

Angela's phone rang. "Hello?"

"Angela, it's Brenda Connor."

"Brenda, how are you? How are the kids?"

"The kids are fine, Angela, but I'm in the hospital."

"What? What's the matter?"

"I don't know. They say I've got a problem with my kidneys, and it looks as if I'll be here a few days or more, and that's if I'm lucky."

"What can I do, Brenda? Just name it."

Brenda's voice seemed to relax. "I knew I could count on you, Angela. I don't have anyone to look after the kids. If you—"

"Say no more, Brenda. Where are they now?"

"They're with my sister, but she can't keep them after tonight because she's going out-of-town."

"Your sister lives on Maple Street, right?"

"Yeah, two houses north of Broom on the east side."

"Think no more about it. I'm out of town now, but I'll pick them up tonight and take care of them for as long as you need."

"Thank you, Angela. I knew I could count on you."

———

Frankie answered his phone as he rounded the corner by Prospect Park. "Donovan."

"Bugs, it's me. How is everybody?"

"Everybody's fine, Rat. But you know that. We're at Manny's for God's sake."

"Bugs, Monroe's working on getting me out of here, but he may need some real detective help. Not that I don't trust Monroe, but I think you could do better."

"Thanks for the vote of confidence, Rat, but what am I supposed to do better than Monroe?"

"Monroe's looking into how the killer could have gotten into Sonny's house without going in the front or back doors. Besides that, I think Borelli might be coming into town to try to persuade Mrozinski to let me out again on bail."

"So you want me to come back and work with Monroe?"

"And Borelli. Between the three of you, I might get out of here before Christmas."

"All right, I'll leave in an hour or two."

"Great, but leave Angela and the kids with Manny. I need them safe."

"Will do. See you soon."

Frankie drove back to Manny's and went upstairs to pack. He hadn't brought much, but he might as well take back what he *did* bring.

———

Angela had gone outside with Giorgio and Bmore beside her. While she spoke to her friend, Frankie came outside. She disconnected the call, pointed to the bag he carried, and raised her brows. "Where are you going?"

He leaned in to kiss her cheek. "I wasn't going to leave without saying goodbye."

"Goodbye? Where are you going? Is something wrong?"

"Not at all. I just talked to Nicky, and he said things are heating up. Monroe needs help investigating some things, so I'm going back to work with him."

"Good. I'm going with you."

"No way, Angie. Nicky was specific. I'm supposed to leave you here with Manny. Things may be getting better, but this guy is a long way from being caught."

"No matter what's happening, I need to go home. One of my friends is in the hospital, and her family needs to be taken care of. I promised her I'd do it."

Frankie shook his head. "Nicky said—"

Angela stepped forward, close to Frankie. "I don't care what my husband said; I'm going. The kids can stay here, but I'm going back with you. If you say no, I'll take a flight or ride the train myself."

Frankie started to say something several times, but in the end, he sat down and set his bag on the porch. "Get your stuff. We need to go."

Angela raced in, packed her bag, then said goodbye to the kids. "Rosa, I have to go home for a few days. While I'm gone, I want you to listen to—"

Rosa laughed. "To Manny? Bmore? Giorgio? Not many exemplary role models, Mom."

Angela kissed her on the cheek, bent down and kissed Dante, then said. "I've got to hurry. Just do what I said and listen to what Mr. Rosso tells you."

She walked to Manny and gave him a hug. "Manny, I hate to do this to you, but I've got to go, and I can't take the kids with me. I—"

Manny patted her back. "Hey, Angie, you do what you need to. Don't worry about me and the kids. We'll be fine, and I'll make sure they're safe. More importantly, I'll make sure they have fun. I'll even give them a proper education and teach them some Italian."

"Thanks, Manny. Bye." Angela rushed out the front door and got into Frankie's car. "Ready," she said.

"I still don't like it," Frankie said.

"You don't have to like it, Frankie. Now let's get a move on it. By the way, are you flying or taking the train?"

"Train. It'll be easier to get someone to pick us up from the station than the airport."

The train pulled into the Wilmington station at 4:06 pm. Frankie had called ahead and arranged for DuPree to pick them up and then drop them off at Nicky's house. "Angela, he'll take you wherever you need to go, so take him up on it. I don't want you driving yourself."

Angela sighed. "All right, Frankie. No need to keep saying it. All I need is for him to drive me to pick up Brenda's kids, then we can be dropped off at my house."

"After I check it out."

She sighed again. "Yes, Frankie. *After* you check it out."

DuPree dropped Frankie off to pick up his car, then took Angela where she needed to go. In the interim, Frankie checked out Nicky's house to make sure all was okay. He then went to the jail to visit Nicky.

"Bugs! Good to see you. How are Angie and the kids?"

"The kids are fine, Rat. But Angie came home with me. She said she had to take care of somebody's kids. A friend of hers is in the hospital or something."

"What? You left the kids up there?"

Bugs nodded. "Up there. Yeah. Under Manny's protection, who also has three of Monroe's men. I don't think they'd be any safer at an army base."

"What about Angie?"

"That's a different story, Rat, but it's also all on you. You know damn right well what Angie's like. Once she sets her mind to something, no one's going to change it."

I knew Bugs was right, but him being right didn't stop me from worrying. If the killer tried getting Rosa, he might try getting Angie too. "Bugs, I have to get out of here. I can't leave Angie out there unprotected."

"I know you want out, Rat, but do you have any idea how we might accomplish that?"

"Yeah, I do. Monroe's getting Borelli, and hopefully, he'll persuade Mrozinski to let him investigate the crime scene. Maybe he'll find something."

"Not to sound like a pessimist, Rat, but I heard a lot of *ifs* and *maybes* in there."

I nodded. "I know. I know. Also, Mrozinski told me Maddy's coming back, so maybe you can work with her on stirring some things up."

"More *maybes*, Rat."

"That's all the hell I've got, Bugs. You have anything better?"

"Not yet, but I'm working on it. Frisco, one of Monroe's men, is supposedly getting me a sketch of what the guy looks like."

"Based on what?" I asked.

"Based on Frisco seeing him when he tried to snatch Rosa. He said he got a good look, and he thought he could make a good sketch."

The first bit of promise filled me with hope. "I like the sound of that, Bugs. If we get a good likeness, we can nail this bastard."

"*If* we get a good likeness," Bugs said.

"Where's your optimism, Bugs? I'm betting he'll come through for us, and once he does, it's only a matter of time."

"By the way, Kate said did the DNA workup you asked for."

"And?"

"And she said there is a John Doe whose DNA was at all of the crime scenes, and yours was the only other one like that."

"Good, we need to find out who the hell that is."

Chapter Thirty-Five

ACTIVATE BORELLI

Monroe sipped on a beer while waiting for DuPree to show. Five minutes later, he walked in.

"S'up, Monroe?"

Monroe glanced at the time on his phone, then stared at DuPree. "You're late, that's what," he said.

DuPree took a seat in a chair opposite Monroe. "Sorry, but—"

"DuPree, I don't give a shit *why* you're late. Being late says it all."

DuPree sat up straight. "You got it, boss. Won't happen again."

Monroe scoffed. "I doubt that. Anyway, I need you to make a call."

DuPree scrunched his eyebrows. "Make a call? What the hell are you talking about? Why can't you do it yourself?"

"I *could* do it myself, but obviously there are reasons why I don't want to, so stop being a fucking idiot and do as I say."

DuPree gulped. "Okay, what do you need me to do?"

"That's better," Monroe said, and handed DuPree a burner phone and a piece of paper. "You need to use this phone, and you're to call the number on the top of the paper I gave you."

"And say what?"

Monroe reached over and smacked the side of his head. "I'm getting to that, asshole."

He pointed to the paper. "What you need to say is written on the paper. Follow the dialogue. It will only take a moment."

DuPree looked at the paper, then back to Monroe. "Not to be nosy, but why is it you can't do this?"

"Because we like to follow a set of rules for safety," Monroe said. "The more removed a person is from someone of interest, the better off we are, and the less chance the call can be connected. This way, if I'm ever asked under oath, I can swear that I never called him."

DuPree nodded. "I don't know what the hell you mean, but all right. When you want me to do this?"

"Right now," Monroe said, "while I'm listening."

DuPree read through the lines several times, then sat even straighter in the chair and dialed the phone.

"Hello?"

"Mr. Whoever-the-hell you are, this is a friend who is a friend of someone who was once your friend long ago. He helped you once, and now he's in trouble."

"What? Who the hell is this?"

DuPree looked to Monroe and shrugged, not knowing what to say.

Monroe cursed and grabbed the phone from DuPree. "Fuck swearing under oath," Monroe said. "I should've done this from the beginning."

"This is a friend of a friend who once helped your son."

"Oh shit. Okay, what do you need?"

"As my associate said, your friend is in trouble, and we thought you might be able to persuade a certain Polish detective of the right thing to do."

"Goddamn, that stupid son of . . . all right, I'll be there. It's going to take me a while, but I'll leave right away."

"Good. Now, one last thing. I'm tossing this burner now. I suggest you do the same."

———

Jimmy Borelli hung up the phone and made a call to the airlines. He pulled out a fake identity, one of a number he had, and used it to make flight reservations to JFK Airport on the earliest possible flight.

Once on the ground in New York, he rented a car and headed toward Brooklyn where he rented a motel room, then stopped at a bodega he'd been given the name of and purchased another burner phone. Afterward, he drove to Newark, NJ, and used a second identity to rent another car, which he used to drive to Wilmington.

Borelli thought about all that Nicky had taught him since he helped him disappear so long ago. It seemed like decades. The best thing Nicky had ever told him was to use some of the money he had to buy several good identities with established histories attached to them. "They'll be your best friend" Nicky had said.

And he was right, Borelli thought as he pulled in to get gas. He filled the tank, paid cash for the gas, then continued on his way to Wilmington. When he finished business in his hometown, he'd drive back to New York, check out of the motel, and take a flight to his new hometown using the same identity he flew to New York with.

Borelli's first stop was to see Nicky to let him know he was in town to help, then he went to see Mrozinski, but he went to his house, not the station.

Mrozinski answered the door, shocked to see his old partner. "Jimmy! What in God's name are you doing here?"

"I came to talk to you about Nicky."

"What? Fusco? How did you know?"

"I have ways," Borelli said. "Now tell me what's going on."

Mrozinski invited him inside, where they both sat down in the living room, and he filled him in on what had happened.

Borelli shook his head. "No way Nicky did those killings. Trust me on this. There's no way it's him. Get your head out of your ass and look at the evidence."

"How can you say that?" Mrozinski asked. "You haven't been working this case."

"I can say that because you always made up your mind who did the crime, then you looked at the evidence to see how it fit your theory. It needs to be the other way around, Ed. I told you that for years."

"I'm working this by the book," Mrozinski said.

"It doesn't matter how you're looking at it or how you're working it. Nicky didn't do it," Borelli said. "I saw what he did when he saved my boy. He risked *everything* for my boy with nothing to expect in return. And he *saved* him, Ed. He brought my boy back safe, and he did it by himself. Little Jimmy is alive because Fusco risked his life for him."

"So you're telling me that Fusco is the one who killed all those drug dealers up in Hockessin?"

Borelli was silent for a long time. "I can't say he did. I don't know who did that, but I know he brought my boy back to me. I'm asking you to let it go, Ed. Look the other way."

"Even if he committed murder?"

"I don't think he did."

Mrozinski downed his last sip of water. "Think all you want, Jimmy, but there's nothing to talk about. I'm just doing my job."

"If Nicky's in jail, there's definitely something to talk about— like you've got the wrong man arrested."

Mrozinski stood and walked toward the door. "Okay. I guess we'll see," he said. "Talk to you soon, Jimmy."

"Let's make it *real* soon. How about tomorrow morning at Nicky's house? I want Donovan to be there too."

"Name the time."

"Nine o'clock. You remember where he lives?"

Mrozinski smirked. "I arrested him there."

Frankie answered the door, smiled, and welcomed Borelli inside. "Have a seat, Jimmy. You're worst half is already here."

He then turned and said to Mrozinski. "Look who the cat dragged in."

Mrozinski frowned. "I never did ask you, Jimmy. How'd he get your number?"

Borelli shook his head. "I already told you; he didn't call me, but I got word. I said it last night, and I'll say it again—get your head out of your ass."

"How did you hear? You've been sitting on your ass in Podunk, Iowa, or someplace like that. If Fusco didn't call, who did? Did you get a sob story from Donovan?"

"No, you stupid Polack. This is the first time I've talked to Frankie in years, and even if I had spoken to him, I wouldn't tell you."

Jimmy sat in the stiff-backed chair near the steps. "Like I've said several times now—I heard. Leave it at that. But I know Fusco, and there's no way he committed these crimes. First, he had no reason to, and second, he wouldn't be so dumb as to kill people using the same method that he was suspected of in Brooklyn."

"And you're sure of that?" Mrozinski asked. "It could be the perfect distraction, making us think exactly what you're thinking now—that he wouldn't kill that way."

"All right, *Detective*," Borelli said. "Tell me what Nicky has to gain from killing any of these men."

Mrozinski smiled. "He hated the Campisi brothers. Everyone knows that."

Borelli laughed. "Ed, *everyone* hated the Campisi brothers. Hell, the rest of their family hated them. But let's give you the benefit of the doubt with them. How about Knuckles?"

"Knuckles was going to meet my partner and tell her he saw Nicky following Campisi."

"We don't know that," Frankie said. "All we know is Charlie called her, but it could have been while a gun was pointed at him."

"Is that right, Ed? You didn't verify the call as legit?"

"There was no need to. Charlie knew Nicky and saw him all the time. He'd know if anything fishy was going on."

"What he's not telling you," Frankie said, "is that we found two bugs in Doggs's shop, and they were planted to make the most out of almost any conversation."

Jimmy looked at Mrozinski. "You find out who planted them?"

Mrozinski shook his head. "Not yet."

Borelli accepted a glass of coffee from Frankie and took a sip. "So you got a guy who has never squealed in his life, and he's offering to give up a long-time friend, and you found bugs in the smoke shop. What else?"

"He's the one who placed the call to Maddie."

"What did he tell your partner?" Borelli asked. "Exactly."

Mrozinski sighed. "He said he'd meet her at the Columbus Inn at seven, and he'd be at a table near the back."

"And that's it? Nothing else?"

Mrozinski pulled a notepad from his inside pocket and flipped through it. "He said he couldn't wait to sink his teeth into one of those luscious steaks."

Jimmy smiled, as did Frankie. "And that's why you're not first-grade yet. You need to know your neighborhood. You solve *any* cases since I've been gone?"

"Screw you, Jimmy. I solved the biggest one we've had in years—the abduction of seven girls."

"From what I hear, Nicky did most of the work on that one. You didn't do much more than welcome those girls home."

"So what the hell did you mean about knowing the neighborhood?"

"I meant that everyone who knew Knuckles knew that he was fond of the Columbus Inn, but he didn't like steak. He'd have never ordered steak."

Frankie laughed. "Jimmy's right. The closest Knuckles ever got to a steak was a cheesesteak—those he loved."

Mrozinski appeared confused. "What are you saying?"

Jimmy leaned forward. "I'm saying Knuckles probably said that about the steaks hoping someone would pick up on it as a clue. He was more than likely staring down the barrel of a gun like Donovan said."

Mrozinski sighed. "All right, what do you want?"

"I want to see the latest crime scene," Jimmy said. "Get me an okay to go inside and check it out. Maybe even spring for a few resources for prints or other evidence."

Mrozinski didn't answer for a moment, then said, "I can make it happen, but you'll need to have a department representative with you."

"Who?"

"Maddy should be back later today. I can get her to go with you."

"That'll work," Borelli said. "You can have her call—"

Frankie grabbed his cell phone and faced Mrozinski. "I'll call you with a number for her to use. Jimmy shouldn't be using his phone, so we'll stop and get a clean one from Doggs."

"What do you mean a 'clean' one?" Jimmy asked.

"Doggs has people buy burners from all over the country and ship them to him. That way, there's no record of purchase from any of his phones."

Borelli shook his head. "You heard the man, Ed. We'll call you later."

Chapter Thirty-Six

MONROE TURNS DETECTIVE

Frankie picked up two burners from Doggs. He handed one to Borelli and slipped one in his pocket. "Use that while you're in town, and I'll give you the other one when you leave to go home."

Borelli shot a questioning look at Frankie. "You guys are a little paranoid, aren't you?"

"It pays off in the long run. Just do it, and you're likely to remain safe. So will your family."

"All right. Now what?"

"I've already called Mrozinski and given him that number. Maddy should call you soon."

Frankie handed him a slip of paper. "I wrote Monroe's number down so you can call him to help you check the place out. Once Maddy has a time to meet you, let Monroe know."

"I don't need help."

"I know Monroe's not the kind of person you want to be dealing with, but he's a good friend of Nicky's, and he'd do anything to help. Besides, he's got a good criminal mind and sometimes it helps to look at things from that perspective."

Borelli folded the paper and stuffed it into his shirt pocket. "I'll call him as soon as I hear from Maddy."

Borelli didn't have long to wait. His phone rang as Frankie drove down Union Street just before the Elsmere bridge.

"Hello?"

"This is Maddy Viola. I was told to call this number."

"Good to hear from you, Maddy. This is the former partner of your current partner."

Maddy laughed. "I heard you were in town; Ed filled me in. We might as well get right to it. Want to meet in about an hour?"

"How about two? I think I'm just about to sink my teeth into a nice fat cheesesteak from Casapulla's."

"Two, it is. I wouldn't dare interrupt that."

Borelli pulled open the slip of paper Frankie had given him and dialed Monroe's number. "Monroe, this is a friend of Nicky's. Can you meet me at Sonny's house in two hours? I've arranged for us to get inside."

"I'll be there, my man."

———

onroe waited in his car until he saw Donovan pull to the curb, then he got out and walked across the street. "About time. You law enforcement types are always late. It's no wonder you don't catch anybody."

Borelli opened the car door and got out just as Maddy pulled alongside him.

"I'm leaving right now," Frankie hollered. "You can use my spot."

Frankie pulled out, then Maddy parked and joined Monroe and Borelli.

"I feel out of place," Monroe said.

Maddy stared a moment until recognition set in. "Monroe, right?"

When he nodded, she continued. "I'm sure I don't like it any more than you do, but we're all here for a good reason—to find the real killer. Let's focus on that."

Maddy cut the crime-scene tape blocking the front door, then she led the way inside.

She crossed the foyer and started up the steps, holding onto the rail. "I wasn't here that night, but I've read the case files a dozen times, and I've spoken to everyone who was here, including Detective Donovan."

"I heard the body was found upstairs," Borelli said.

"Yeah, just around the landing. I figured we'd start there, and if you want to see anything else, we'll look at that later."

A small—3'-by-3' landing sat at the top of the stairs, and to the left, next to six feet of waist-high railing, more crime-scene tape marked the spot where the body was found.

"This is it?" Monroe asked.

"Right here," Maddy said. "It was the same as the other scenes: shot in the head and heart, beaten badly with a blunt object, and a variety of DNA both *under* and *over* the pooled blood."

Monroe nodded. "So it effectively eliminates all the DNA evidence, including any that the killer may have accidentally left."

"Exactly," Maddy said.

Monroe stuck his head into the bathroom door, but there wasn't much to see: a toilet, sink, tub, and clothes hamper. "Not much of a bathroom," he said.

Maddy shook her head. "Wouldn't work in my house. I know that."

Borelli stepped into the bedroom situated at the end of the hall, Monroe following. A double-bed sat in the middle of the room, and a small chest of drawers on the far wall underneath of two windows.

Monroe walked over, opened a window, and looked outside. "These were locked?" he asked Maddy.

"Yeah, I should have mentioned it earlier. All windows were locked—upstairs and downstairs."

Borelli and Monroe checked out the other two bedrooms and were about to go downstairs when Monroe stopped. "Hear that? What was it?"

"I didn't hear anything," Borelli said.

"I did," Maddy said. "It sounded like a bird."

"Exactly," Monroe said, and he turned and went back into the third bedroom. "I think it was in here."

As Monroe opened the door to re-enter, a small bird flew out and down to the first floor.

"Just a bird," Maddy said.

"Yeah, just a bird, but how did it get in here?" Borelli asked.

"My question exactly," Monroe said, and went into bedroom two. He found nothing that would explain how the bird got in there, so he continued to the bathroom.

Borelli followed him in and immediately said, "The skylight."

"What?" Monroe asked.

Borelli gestured to a chain hanging from the ceiling in the shape of a long, thin oval, and he pointed above. "The skylight. I'd bet all the money I don't have, the killer got in this way."

Monroe looked up. The skylight was cracked open enough to have allowed the bird to slip in. "That explains the bird, but a man couldn't get in."

"This chain cranks it open. When it's fully open, it's big enough for a man to fit through."

Monroe reached for the chain, but Borelli grabbed his arm. "Don't touch the chain. We'll have it dusted for prints. I doubt if we'll find anything, but you never know."

Monroe stared. "I wouldn't swear to it, but it doesn't look like this chain would support a grown man."

"Maybe he used a rope," Maddy said. "I bet there's something on the roof he could have attached a rope to and then used it to climb down and back up."

Monroe led the way down the stairs. He paused in the foyer and turned to Borelli and Maddy. "How about you two stay and do what you do best. I'm going to get a ladder to get on that roof and see what's up there. I won't be long."

"Can you call someone to bring it?" Maddy asked.

Monroe smiled. "Shit, I didn't think of that. I'm a stupid ass." He pulled out his phone and dialed. "DuPree, how about gettin' Wilson's truck and his big ladder and bring it down to me on Broom Street?

"Yeah, right now. Go down Maple and take a left on Broom. You'll see my car."

Monroe rejoined the conversation. "What's going on? I miss anything?"

"We were just saying that if someone came in through the skylight, they would have probably come in before Sonny got here so he didn't hear them."

"If he did that, he'd have been here a long time waiting for Nicky to leave," Monroe said.

Maddy snapped her fingers. "And if he were here a long time, that means he had to park himself. I'm guessing he would have used someplace comfortable and out of sight."

"Like one of the spare bedrooms," Borelli said.

Maddy was already on the phone. "I need a CSU on Broom Street at the site where Sonny Bruno was killed." She cursed and shook her head. "I can't wait till tomorrow. I need it now. Check with Mrozinski if you need to."

"Good call, Viola. If the killer used one of those beds to wait, he probably left DNA there, and I doubt he could have cleaned it all up. I doubt even more that he bothered to contaminate the beds with other DNA afterward."

"I agree," Maddy said. "Maybe we'll get lucky."

A horn beeped outside. "Might be DuPree," Monroe said, and he went out front.

DuPree was parked a few doors down, standing outside the truck and looking around.

"Yo, DuPree," Monroe said, and waved his hand. "Bring that

ladder up here."

DuPree carried the ladder to Sonny's house and then helped Monroe put the ladder against the house so they had access to the roof.

"Hold the ladder steady while I go up," Monroe said.

Monroe stepped from the ladder onto the roof, treading carefully on the shingles as he did. He got to the ridge and looked on the backside, spotting the skylight sticking above the roof. He made his way to it cautiously and looked inside. He almost touched it, but then reminded himself that the cops might want to dust it for prints.

As he was about to leave, he noticed sunlight glaring off something that protruded from the roof. He balanced himself, then slowly walked over.

In front of him sat what looked like a one-inch eye hook. *Could have hooked a rope on that.*

Monroe finished searching the roof, then went back down. He helped DuPree put the ladder back, then got with Borelli and Maddy. "Found an eye hook attached to the roof. It could easily have been used to hook a rope to."

"Did you—"

Monroe shook his head. "If you're asking if I touched anything. No, I didn't."

"Good. We *could* get lucky between the bedrooms and the roof."

"I'm going out back and then out front to check on basement access. Just in case."

"Good idea," Borelli said. "I'll join you in a minute."

"Borelli, if you can catch a ride with Monroe, I'll wait for CSU."

Monroe and Borelli finished checking front and back, then they got in the car and drove off. "Where to?" Monroe said.

"Take me to see Mrozinski," Borelli said. "I want him to hear it from me that *anyone* could have done this; it didn't have to be Nicky."

Borelli and Monroe walked into Mrozinski's office and sat in the available chairs.

Mrozinski looked up over the paperwork he worked on. "What's up, Jimmy? I guess you're going to tell me you got it solved already."

Borelli smiled. "Maybe."

Mrozinski made a sour face. "Maybe my ass," he said, then gestured to Monroe. "And what the hell is he doing here? Should be in cuffs."

Monroe held out his hands. "If you got the evidence, slap 'em on," he said. "If not . . ."

"Spit it out, Jimmy. Got anything or not?"

"We've got a plausible way someone else could have done the crime and they could have done it without you seeing them."

"Bullshit. How?"

"The skylight," Monroe said.

"What?"

"We were examining the scene and heard a bird in the upstairs bedroom. It made us wonder how it got there, and after checking it out, we found the skylight open. With further checking on the roof, we found a one-inch eye hook screwed into the roof. It could have easily been used to hook a rope to and allow someone to go down."

Mrozinski scoffed. "I don't buy it."

"You don't buy it?" Monroe asked. "Or you don't want to?"

"I don't buy it, and luckily I don't have to. There's no way you can prove anyone did this."

Borelli leaned toward Mrozinski and whispered. "And there's no way you can prove someone didn't. A bigger problem is you can't prove Nicky killed Sonny either, especially with this new possibility."

"We'll see," Mrozinski said.

"We will," Jimmy said. "And we're going to see fast. I'm calling your favorite lawyer as soon as we leave here: Braden Shapiro."

"Nicky's already got a lawyer."

"But it's not Shapiro," Borelli said.

Mrozinski frowned. "You're a dick, Borelli. And to think I used to look up to you."

"That's when you were smart, but don't worry, there's still time."

Borelli and Monroe walked out and climbed into the car. "I guess back to Fusco's house," Borelli said.

"Detective, what was all that shit with us having to prove stuff. I thought people were innocent until the cops proved otherwise."

"It's supposed to work that way, Monroe, but it doesn't always happen. We need something else."

"Like an eyewitness you mean?" Monroe asked.

"An eyewitness would be good, Monroe. You got one?"

He smiled. "I just might. Give me a little time."

Chapter Thirty-Seven

MONROE HAS A WITNESS

In the morning Monroe called his crew to a meeting at his house. "I know everybody's wondering why I called you here on a Monday, so I'm gonna tell you. About a week ago, a guy named 'Crooked Nose' Sonny was killed in his house on Broom Street. What I need to know is who saw someone leave his house the next morning and at what time. I *know* someone left, and I'm pretty damn sure they left by way of the roof, so somebody needs to step forward and say so."

Monroe set a slip of paper on the table. "Here's the address in case you forgot it. Think hard and find me a name. I expect to have it before day's end."

That afternoon, Monroe walked into the police station with Jesse Wirth. "I need to see Officer Mrozinski," he said.

A few minutes later, Mrozinski turned the corner wearing a puzzled look. "You wanted to see me?"

"I did," Monroe said. "My cousin, Jess, told me he had information on that killing on Broom Street."

"You mean Sonny Bruno, the man found in his house?"

"Yeah, him. How many killings you got on Broom?"

Mrozinski narrowed his eyes, giving a skeptical look. "Let's go to my office to talk."

Mrozinski stared at Jesse. "And you're sure you saw someone at Sonny's house?"

"Sure as shit," Jesse said. "I was sittin' on my buddy's porch when I heard a noise. I looked over, and some white dude was creepin' across the rooftop. Not a doubt in my mind."

"You know it's a crime to lie about this?"

Jesse cocked his head and looked from Monroe to Mrozinski. "Now why the hell would I lie about seeing a man on a roof? What the hell is wrong with you people?"

"I needed to check," Mrozinski said. "This is serious business. A man was killed that night."

"Seems to me like this might be the man you're lookin' for. Why the hell else would a man be creepin' across the roof at that time of the morning?"

"What time did you say it was?"

"I can't be positive. I got to the house about seven in the morning and sat there reading the paper for a while before I heard the noise. If I had to guess, I'd say it was eight or even as late as nine."

"You can't narrow it down more than that?"

Jesse lowered his head and shook it. "What'd I just say? If I could've narrowed it down, don't you think I would have? Damn, but you make it hard for a man to be helpful. Ain't no wonder nobody wants to help the cops."

He turned to Monroe. "I told you I didn't want to come here. Look at the mess you got me in now."

Mrozinski finished typing his report, then handed the paper to Jesse. "I need you to sign this, then you can go, but I may need you for testimony at some date."

Jesse snatched the paper from Mrozinski's hand and set it down to sign, mumbling all the time. "Didn't want to come in here to begin with."

Half an hour later, Monroe and Jesse walked out of the station. Monroe was all smiles.

"Is that it?" Jesse asked.

"Not quite," Monroe said. "I want you to tell the same story to another man and make sure it's the *exact* same story."

Monroe called Frankie's cell as he pulled away from the curb. "Donovan, this is Monroe. I've got a witness who saw someone leave Sonny's house after Nicky did."

"What?"

"Yeah, I ain't no lawyer, but it would seem to clear Nicky. At least to me, it would."

After meeting with Frankie, Monroe went on his way, and Frankie went to see Mrozinski.

He stood in front of Mrozinski's desk, all smiles. "Monroe's witness raises reasonable doubt."

Mrozinski slapped his desk. "What the hell? Is he telling everybody?"

"Why wouldn't he be?"

"Whoever that witness saw coming from the house could have entered moments before or hours before."

Frankie smiled. "The witness said he was sitting on his friend's porch for at least an hour, like he does two mornings a week. Either the killer went into Sonny's house when we were there, or he was in the house all along."

Frankie let it sink in a moment. "Are you saying we missed seeing the man enter the house? Us *and* your officers out back?"

"We didn't miss him," Mrozinski said.

"Then he was there all along," Frankie said.

"I didn't say that either."

"Mrozinski, it's one or the other. If we missed him entering the house, then you have to wonder why he didn't call the cops right away when he saw the body. And if he was there all along, you have

to wonder why he didn't call the cops when Sonny was killed—
unless he was the one who killed him. Either way you look at it,
Nicky didn't do it. You need to let him loose."

"This isn't a traffic ticket Fusco's in for, Donovan. It's murder."

"I know what you're holding him for," Frankie said. "I'm not a
lawyer, but I'd bet the one Jimmy knows is a good one. I only know
one thing; Nicky's getting out of here with or without a lawyer. The
difference being without a lawyer, no one will know what a shitty
detective you are. With a lawyer, I'll make sure you're a laugh-
ingstock."

Mrozinski sighed. "All right, Donovan. You win. I hope you
know what the hell you're doing. If I let him out of here and we get
one more killing . . ."

"If you get one more killing, you'll have to do some real detective work and find out who did it because it isn't going to be
Nicky."

"Son of a bitch," Mrozinski said. "Wait here."

It took almost an hour, but Mrozinski returned with Nicky
alongside him.

The smile on my face broadened when I saw Frankie. "Bugs, I should have known you'd come through."

Mrozinski stared. "Nicky, I'm going out on a limb here. You've got to help me out. I can't have any more bodies; that means we either have to catch this guy, or you're going to have to go back in until we do."

"What about if you don't catch him?" I asked.

"You need to pray that we do. If not, it may be bad for you."

"What do you want me to do?" I asked.

"Nothing. And I mean nothing. Don't look for him. Don't ask questions. Let me and Viola and Borelli do the work. We'll get the guy."

"You're sure about that? You haven't done much yet."

"Screw you, Fusco. You're lucky I'm going this far for you. If it weren't for Donovan and Borelli, I wouldn't have done it."

Bugs tugged on my arm. "Come on, Rat. We need to get out of here."

"Thanks again, Bugs."

"Don't thank me," he said. "It was Monroe's doing."

"Monroe?"

"Yeah, he found a witness who saw another man exiting Sonny's house after you did."

"I'll be damned," I said. "He must have been hiding because I didn't see him."

Frankie drove back to my house, and we went inside and made coffee. "I need some good stuff. The shit they fed me in jail was horrendous."

"Don't I know it," Bugs said. "I've had it before."

Twenty minutes later, while strategizing with Bugs, the doorbell rang. I stood, then laughed when Monroe entered the house. "Monroe, my man. I owe you."

"You don't owe me shit, Rat. All I did was convince a concerned citizen to come forward and tell what he knew."

"The question is, did you *convince* him or *persuade* him?"

"Shit, Rat. He don't know the difference, and if push comes to shove, I don't know if I do. The bottom line is he'll testify."

"And he's not going to break under pressure?" I asked.

"That man's mother is my second cousin. He'll swear to God that a UFO landed on the front yard and a little green man went into that house—*if* I tell him to."

I clasped Monroe's hand. "Like I said, I owe you one."

"You don't owe me shit," Monroe said. "After all you did to help me when those pricks took my little cuz. Shit, I still owe you a couple. Consider this one of them."

"All this is good," Frankie said. "But we still need to find out who's doing this, and why? Surprise witnesses aren't going to cut it next time."

Chapter Thirty-Eight

FRANKIE GETS A TEXT

Frankie's phone beeped, signaling he got a text. He pulled out the phone, looked at the text, and smiled, then showed it to Nicky. "Here's our guy," he said. "Courtesy of Frisco."

Monroe grabbed the phone from Nicky and stared. "Yea, that's Frisco all right. That son of a bitch can draw."

"That's the picture of the guy who tried to nab Rosa?" Nicky asked.

"That's him," Frankie said. "Bmore said they'd have taken him if they knew who he was."

Frankie looked at Nicky. "You know him?"

Nicky shook his head. "Never saw him, but I bet Doggs can tell us who he is.—"

Bugs nodded. "And that's just where I'm taking it. If this is the guy we think, he almost surely worked at the smoke shop, which means Doggs will know him."

Frankie headed for the door. "See you guys later. I'm going to the smoke shop."

"Tell Doggs I said hi," Nicky said.

———

Frankie walked into the smoke shop and said, "I need to see Doggs."

The man behind the counter started to protest, but Frankie flashed his badge, and the guy stopped and shrugged. After that, he stepped to the other side of the counter and buzzed Frankie into the back room.

Frankie walked straight to where the listening devices had been planted and removed both of them.

"What the fuck's goin' on?" Doggs asked. "We done with them?"

"We're done with them, Doggs, but *you're* not done. I need you to look at a picture, and I need a name."

Frankie showed Doggs the picture on the phone. "You know this guy, Doggs?"

Doggs grabbed the phone and held it under the light. He stared for a minute, then moved under a brighter light where he twisted it several ways. "That's him, Bugs. That's the guy. And now that I've seen his face, I remember his name—Danny. Danny D'Agostino. I remember because of the supermarket chain in New York. I always liked D'Agostino's; they had good lunchmeat and fresh bread. At least they did when I was up there."

"Hey, Doggs, I can get fresh bread here; you know where this guy lives?"

Doggs shook his head. "I'll check, but I doubt it. I don't keep records like that."

"Don't you have records of who worked here?"

Doggs looked at Bugs as if he were crazy. "I don't report income from gambling, so how am I going to report expenses of hiring people to help with the gambling?" Doggs shook his head. "Fuck me twice, Donovan. No wonder you're a cop. You're too stupid to be anything else."

"Come on, Doggs. You gotta know something. I need help on this."

Doggs got a bottle of water from the fridge and sat on one of the stools. "Give me a minute to think."

Bugs picked up a pool cue and shot a few balls on the main table. "Philly, I know. And thinking about it, I have to say South Philly."

"Why do you say South Philly?"

"I remember because we talked about Pat's Steaks and the Italian market. Of course, he could've been lying."

"What's your gut tell you?" Bugs asked.

Doggs shrugged. "If I had to guess, I'd say he lived there. He knew too much about the area. Knew a lot of people too. If he didn't live there, he visited somebody a lot."

"And that's all you can think of?" Bugs asked.

"That's it for now," Doggs said. "If I get anything else, I'll call you."

"All right, Doggs, thanks."

"Hey, Donovan. I hope you get this guy. I don't like people using my place of business to plant listening devices."

Frankie waited for a break in traffic, took a deep breath, then hit the gas. Once he got situated in the southbound lane, he took out his phone and dialed. It was answered right away.

"Manny."

"Manny, it's Bugs Donovan."

The sound of laughter came through the phone. "My favorite detective. What's up? How are things in piss-antville?"

"Manny, I'm pretty sure piss-antville not only isn't a place; it's not a word."

"Doesn't matter. You know what I mean."

"Hey, Manny. I want to thank you for helping Miller out on her investigation," Frankie said.

"No sweat. She's a good kid," Manny said. "In case she didn't tell you, she got her man. Locked up McNulty the other day. I think she's happy with herself."

"She should be. That's her first murder case by herself. Just a shame she couldn't have gotten Fat Fingers Joey."

"Yeah, but people need to know there are repercussions to things you do wrong. You know how that works, Bugs."

Frankie shook his head, though no one could see. "Yeah, Manny. I know how that is."

"All that's good, Bugs, but that's not why you're calling. You already thanked me for that. So what do you want?"

Frankie made the turn and slowed down a bit. "Hey, Manny. You get anything yet on those names?"

"Bugs, I told you I'd call. You're an impatient sort, you know that?"

"I'm impatient for a reason. I had to get my own people to put a name to this guy."

"So you got it. Good. Now do something with it. Just out of curiosity, was it one of Renzo's relatives?"

"No, why? You got something on one of them?"

"I might, but what difference does it make? I thought you had your guy."

Bugs made a quick turn onto Sycamore Street. "I probably do, but we're not sure. Keep an eye on Renzo's kin while I check this out."

"Yeah, all right. Will do."

"And, Manny, maybe you can still help out. I need a favor."

"A favor! Son of a bitch, I love favors. What do you need?"

"I need a heads-up on a guy from Philadelphia."

"Who's the guy?"

"The name Danny D'Agostino mean anything to you? He worked in Atlantic City as a dealer, then got a job with Doggs Caputo down in Wilmington for a while."

"Hang on, Bugs. I know that name."

"Which name? Caputo or D'Agostino? From where?" Bugs asked.

"The D'Agostino guy, but hang on. I'm thinkin'. It's on the tip of my tongue."

"How did you know him? A relative? A friend?"

"Christ's sake, Bugs. I said 'hang on.'"

Frankie stayed silent, biting his lip. Finally, Manny said, "I got it. He was Johnny Muck's nephew."

"What! Are you shitting me?" Frankie asked.

"Not a bit. I remember Muck talking about his family in Philly —South Philly. He always referred to them as the D'Agostinos. Hell, I forgot he even had family."

"This is great, Manny. I owe you big time."

"Hey, Bugs. You already owed me big time. This just adds to the debt. But hey, you know, if you ask me, these D'Agostinos might be more than what they seem."

"What do you mean?"

"I don't know. It was the way Muck talked about 'em. It was almost like they were closer. And he called him his nephew, but as far as I knew, Muck didn't have no sisters or brothers."

"What are you saying, Manny?"

"I don't know, Bugs. Maybe Johnny had a real family and stashed them down in Philly to keep 'em safe. Who knows? He was a strange guy."

"Son of a bitch," Frankie said. "Manny, any way you can get me an address?"

"And the debt grows," Manny said, and laughed. "Don't worry, Bugs. Let me make a few calls, and I'll get back to you. Maybe later today."

"All right, Manny. Thanks.

A few moments later, Bugs pulled to the curb outside Nicky's house. He got out and rushed to go inside.

"Rat, you're not going to believe it."

"What?"

"First, I went to the smoke shop and Doggs instantly recognized him as a guy named Danny D'Agostino, from Philly."

Nicky shook his head. "Still don't know him."

"I ain't never heard of him either," Monroe said. "But I didn't expect to, him being Italian and from Philly to boot. Maybe if he was a brother, I'd know him, but not this."

"Yeah, I got you, Monroe. I didn't know him either. So on the way back from the smoke shop, I decided to call Manny to see if he knew him."

"And?" Nicky asked.

"And he's Johnny Muck's nephew at the least, and possibly his son."

"What! Muck doesn't have any kids. In fact, I don't think he had any brothers or sisters."

Bugs nodded. "I know. That's what Manny said. But he also said Muck used to talk about a nephew in Philly—even though he said he had no siblings—and Manny got the feeling that the nephew was more than a nephew."

"Son of a bitch," Nicky said. "Son of a bitch. If that's the case, we've got to find him fast. He's got plenty of reason to hate me for what happened to Muck, and he probably has plenty of skill if he learned from Muck, which I'm sure he did."

Nicky looked up at Bugs. "You get an address?"

"No address, but Manny said South Philly, and Doggs said he felt sure it was within walking distance of Pat's."

"Close enough," Nicky said.

"We'll go tomorrow morning if you're up to it."

Bugs sat down and kicked his feet up. "I'm always up for a Philly trip. The cheesesteaks aren't as good as Casapulla's, but they're good."

"You need help, Rat?" Monroe asked.

"We should be fine tomorrow, Monroe. I'll call you though if we do."

Chapter Thirty-Nine

INFORMATION ON DANNY

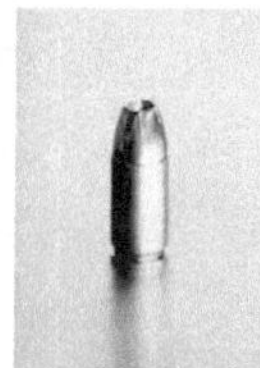

"Hurry the hell up, Bugs. Coffee's on, and the eggs are done."

Bugs damn near ran down the stairs and into the kitchen. "Don't even think about eating my eggs," he said. "Or drinking my coffee."

"I wouldn't dare," Nicky said. "Your coffee's too weak, and your eggs are too runny. I don't like my eggs *peeping* or *clucking* at me, or making any noises at me. And I don't like coffee you can see through. Now you know you have nothing to fear regarding me stealing your food."

Bugs slurped his coffee while placing his egg on a piece of toast. "If I remember, Pat's is by the market, isn't it?"

"It is," I said. "Why? You need to pick something up?"

"I was thinking of getting a big wedge or even a log of nice, sharp provolone."

"If that's what you're thinking, I'll even take you there. I could go for some provolone. Some salami too."

"All right," Bugs said. "Enough talk about food already. It's making me hungry, and I haven't even finished breakfast."

I set his plate and coffee cup on the counter. "After you eat a couple of steaks, you won't be so hungry."

"Damn, I forgot about them. And you're right, I am getting a couple—one from Pat's and one from Gino's."

I laughed. "Didn't I know it? C'mon, let's go."

"Nicky, before we go I think we should stop and see Doggs again. If nothing else, for confirmation on a few things."

"We've got time. Let's do it," I said, and drove up Clayton, then turned left on Fourth and left on Union. There was a space in front of the shop, so I pulled in.

Frankie went inside and found Doggs.

"Donovan, what the hell do you want?

"We're heading up to Philly, and I wanted to check on everything before we went."

Doggs crushed his cigarette butt in the ashtray and turned back to Bugs. "In other words, you want to see if I held anything back. Well, I didn't, smart ass. I told you all I knew. I'm sure as hell not gonna protect a dirty son of a bitch who bugged my shop."

"All right, Doggs. Just checking. You think he lives by the market?"

Doggs nodded. "Can't be far from there. If you have trouble finding him, let me know and I'll put in a call to Skinny Mick. He'll find him."

"Skinny Mick?" Bugs asked.

"Yeah, some guy I know in Philly. He's half Irish like you, but don't let that fool you. He's a good guy."

"Screw you, Doggs, but thanks. I appreciate it."

"Anytime, Donovan. I owe you for getting those bugs out of my place."

"All right, Doggs. We're outta here."

"A little early to be going, isn't it?"

"Maybe for people who sleep in, but it's damn near the middle of the day for me," Bugs said.

"Get the hell out of here," Doggs said. "I hope you find this prick."

After driving a few miles, I said, "Hey, Bugs, call Doggs. I want to ask a few things myself."

Doggs answered right away. "What the fuck you want now, Donovan?"

"Nicky wants you. I'm giving the phone to him."

"Doggs, are you positive this guy lived by Pat's?"

"No, I'm not *positive*, but he said he used to walk to Pat's or Gino's and get steak sandwiches all the time. So wherever he lived, it was within walking distance. And if it's within walking distance, the neighbors are gonna know him. Whether they talk to you is another thing, but they'll know him. Why are you askin'? I already told this to Donovan."

"Just checking, Doggs. Just checking."

We got to Pat's around mid-morning. Some kids were shooting hoops in the courts beside it, so we went over to talk to them.

"Anybody seen Danny around?" Frankie asked.

"Danny who?" a kid asked. He seemed to be the designated spokesperson for the group.

"D'Agostino," Frankie said. "Danny D'Agostino."

"Who wants to know?"

"I do," Frankie said. "There's a twenty in it if you show me where he lives."

"Stuff the twenty up your ass," he said. "I don't know anybody named D'Agostino."

"Would you know him if it was a fifty?" Frankie asked.

"I wouldn't know him if it was a hundred," the kid said. "You cops need to get a new routine."

"What makes you think we're cops?" Frankie asked.

"Because I wasn't born yesterday. You might as well leave 'cause you're not getting anything out of us." The kid turned to the rest of the guys on the court. "Listen up," he yelled. "These cops want information on people. Don't give it to them."

I tapped Frankie on the arm. "We might as well go," he said. "We're not getting anything out of this group."

"I agree," Frankie said, and headed for the car.

We made a few more stops, asking people who lived in the area, but nobody admitted to knowing Danny or anybody named D'Agostino.

We got in the car, and I slumped in the seat behind the steering wheel. Bugs glared at the kids on the basketball court. "Sons of bitches," he said.

I smiled at Bugs. "Stop acting insulted. You did the same thing when you were young; in fact, you might have been the worst."

"Don't try to push that shit on me, Rat. Besides, what the hell are we going to do now. D'Agostino's not just going to come up and introduce himself, and it's obvious we're not getting anything from those kids."

"Remember what Doggs said—that he went to Pat's Steaks almost every day, and he said he walked there."

"That only works if he's home, Rat. If he's down in Wilmington or somewhere else, he's sure as shit not coming up here for a sandwich."

I tapped Bugs on the arm. "Try sitting a little lower. Just in case."

"Okay, I'm sitting lower. Now what?"

"Now we wait for him to show. If he's like most good Italian sons, he won't go long before visiting his mother."

"Won't go long? That could be days or more."

"I know, but what's a couple of days if it means we solve a string of murders?"

Bugs sighed and pulled out his phone to play games. "Wake me if you see him."

"Get your ass up and do something," I said. "Study that picture we have of him so you'll know him when you see him."

"What do you mean by 'study the picture'? How much studying can you do on a picture?"

"How'd you ever make it as a cop without me, Bugs? You look at every person and figure out why they're *not* who we're looking for. Nose too big or small. Eyes too close or too far. Color of hair. Before long, you've got D'Agostino's image ingrained in your mind, and when you see him, you'll know. You won't have to study the face to tell if it's him."

Bugs looked over at me. "Pretty good, Rat. I'll work on what you said."

"All right, sit back and watch," I said. "If you need to sleep, let me know. We can take turns."

"In that case, I'll catch a quick nap now. Wake me in an hour or so."

I watched everyone come and go at both Pat's and Gino's, but after two hours, there was no sign of D'Agostino. I let Bugs sleep until mid-afternoon, then we exchanged watch, with him looking out for Danny and me napping. "Wake me if anything happens," I said, and rested my head against the window.

Bugs woke me around five. "Nothing, Rat. I've checked every guy who walked by, and D'Agostino wasn't one of them."

I punched the dashboard. "Damn! I was hoping he'd show."

"What now? Go home and come back tomorrow?"

I thought for a moment, then shook my head. "I think we should rent a hotel room in the city and get here early in the morning. We might as well make the most of being up here."

"All right, Rat. I'll buy that. How long do you want to stay here?"

I checked the time on my phone and looked to Bugs. "Let's give it another hour or so. If nothing happens, we'll return early in the morning."

We checked into a hotel near the airport and settled in for the night. I called Angie as soon as we got a room.

"Nicky, how's it going? Did anything happen?"

"Not yet, babe, but it will. I'm sure of it. Listen, I don't want you staying there tonight. I'd feel better if you spent the night somewhere else."

"Dear God, Nicky, I'm fine."

"Angie—"

"All right, all right. I'll go to Brenda's until I hear from you."

"Great, that will make me feel better. I'll call when we're on our way home."

Bugs grabbed a drink from the mini-fridge and sat on the edge of the bed. "Everything good, Rat?"

"Now it is. Angie's staying at Brenda's house until we get back."

Bugs ordered room service, adding a bottle of Chianti to two orders of pasta. "You can relax now, Rat. At least until tomorrow."

Chapter Forty

DANNY CASES THE HOUSE

Shortly after dark, Danny D'Agostino parked on DuPont Street, a block away from Nicky's house. He turned on some music and sat back to listen, affixing his earbuds firmly to each ear.

By eleven o'clock, no one had shown, so Danny started the engine, put the car in gear, and drove off. There was always tomorrow.

The next morning, Danny left early and once again drove down DuPont Street. He turned onto Beech Street and parked in the first empty spot he saw. He once again listened to music while he kept watch on Fusco's house.

After an all-day stakeout, no one showed at the house. Danny wrapped up the earbuds and put his phone away. Once again, he started the engine and drove off. *No matter what, Fusco will pay for what he did.*

On the way down Front Street, Danny's phone rang. He glanced at Caller ID, then answered it. "Yo, Ma. What are you doing calling so late?"

"I tried calling you twice today. Mrs. Emiliano told me she saw two men who looked to be policemen watching our street."

"Watching our street? You sure?"

"That's what she said. She said they were parked near Gino's almost the whole day. Two of them."

"What were they doing?" Danny asked.

"Mrs. Emiliano said all they did was sit in the car and stare down our block."

"Shit. All right, Mama. Don't worry about it. I'll take care of it."

I did my best to remain calm, but with nothing happening, it was difficult to stay cool. I didn't mind sitting still as long as I knew something was going to happen.

Bugs tapped my shoulder around noon, and then he whispered.

"Rat, check out this guy coming in from the west, by the basketball court."

I sat up and looked, squinting as he approached, but as he got closer, it was obvious it wasn't Danny. "Not him," I said. "Look at the hairline. No way that's Danny."

Bugs sat silent and assessed the people passing by. "You know, Rat, if we spot this guy, you've got to let me take him into custody. I don't want the guy shot."

"I hear ya," I said.

"I know you heard me. I need you to acknowledge what I said."

I didn't say anything for a moment, just thought of all the grief D'Agostino had put me through. I thought of the men he killed, but most of all, I thought of how he tried taking Rosa, and the more I thought about it, the more angry I got.

"Rat?" Bugs chimed in again with his nagging.

Despite my feelings, his continual reminders worked. I snapped out of it and nodded. "Okay, Bugs. You have my word. When we find him, he's yours. I won't kill him."

Danny turned at the next block and headed back toward the smoke shop. He'd give Fusco a reason to get his ass back to Wilmington, and then he'd finish him for good. Screw all this frame-up shit; he'd just kill him. *Or kill his wife and kids.*

He waited for Doggs to exit the smoke shop, and as he locked up, Danny lowered his window and took aim. He was about to squeeze the trigger when the beam from a cop's flashlight shined through the passenger window.

"Everything okay in there?" the cop asked.

Danny quickly tucked the gun under his leg. "Fine, Officer. I was just enjoying the fresh air."

"Fresh air? I don't know what you're breathing, but there's not much to call fresh about mine."

"I guess I'm just dreaming," Danny said. "Anyway, thanks for checking on me. You can't be too sure these days."

"That I'll agree with," the cop said. "Have a good night."

Danny waited for the cop to leave, then he grabbed his gun again, but Doggs was gone. He'd already driven off too, so there was no chance of following him. *What now?*

Danny lit a smoke while he thought, but by the time he finished it, he had a plan. He'd get Paulie "the Deuce."

Danny knew where "the Deuce" lived because he'd dropped him off several nights when Paulie drank a few too many.

At the first break in traffic, Danny pulled out and turned on Front Street, then again on Lincoln. It wasn't far to his house.

Paulie "the Deuce" got his name from his penchant to hoard two-dollar bills. Every time he could, he'd get as many as possible—from the banks, the track, anywhere. No one knew why he did it, but those who knew him said it began at an early age, and regardless of *how* it started or *why*, it was now what distinguished Paulie from anyone else. And if he thought someone did a good job for him, he'd tip them using the bills, as if it were some big deal.

Danny slowed down as he approached Paulie's house. He was sitting on the porch with his wife.

Danny pulled into a space almost directly in front of his house, rolled down the window, and fired.

The first shot grazed the Deuce's left arm. He moved lightning quick to the side and pushed his wife's chair over. At the same time, he pulled a .38 caliber gun he always carried in his waistband and fired.

He continued firing until he emptied his gun. He hit Danny's car several times, but he didn't hit Danny.

Knowing the shots would bring the police, Danny sped off, cursing. *I can't believe I missed him.*

An hour later, Mrozinski got a call while he helped his youngest with homework.

"Detective, you said to call if anything happened involving people from the smoke shop."

"What happened?"

"Someone took a shot at Paulie DiFranco up on—"

"The Deuce? That DiFranco?" Mrozinski asked.

"That's him," the officer said. "They grazed his arm, but he seems okay. He's at the hospital now."

"He might be okay, but there will be hell to pay when he gets out. The Deuce is not a man to mess with. Shit! We've got to find this guy."

"Anything else, sir?"

"No, that's all," Mrozinski said.

He disconnected the call and dialed Frankie. "Donovan, where are you?"

"And fuck you, too," Frankie said.

"I'm sorry," Mrozinski said. "Let me start over. Someone took a few shots at the Deuce and—"

"And you want to know where Nicky is?"

"That's what I need to know, yeah."

"I'm up in Philly at a hotel, and Nicky's sitting right next to me. Been here since early this morning and plan on being here for another day or so. Aside from that, is Paule all right? He get hit?"

"Grazed on the arm from what I know so far. I haven't talked to him yet, but I plan on it. Donovan, ask Fusco if he knows anybody who has a beef with Paulie or any kind of grudge?"

"I don't, Mrozinski. Other than the same nut job who killed those other people. That's what we're doing up here—trying to catch him."

"Well, it looks like you're in the wrong place. If it's the same guy, he's down here."

"All right, Mrozinski, we'll take that into consideration. In the meantime, how about getting out there and catching a *real* bad guy?"

———

Bugs hung up and looked over to Nicky. "What do you think? Should we go back?"

Nicky nodded. "Assuming it was D'Agostino who did that—and I'm sure it was—there's no reason to stay here. I can't think of anyone who would want Paulie dead. He's not the kind that pisses people off."

"Not like Doggs does," Bugs said.

"Not even close," Nicky said. "And as I think about it, there's no sense in spending the night. You okay with checking out now and driving back?"

"Fine by me," Bugs said. "You're the one driving."

We checked out of the rooms, then we hopped into the car and headed home. "We didn't do shit up here, Bugs. I think we need a new plan."

"I didn't know we had a plan," Bugs said.

"Screw you. I didn't hear you offer any advice."

I got in the left lane as we approached Chester, hoping to bypass the traffic at the exits. "Maybe we should get Monroe to stake out his place in Philly. They wouldn't suspect a black person to be watching them."

"I don't know," Bugs said. "I think those people would suspect anyone not born there. We need something more than that as a plan."

I grabbed my phone and dialed Monroe. "Monroe, I need help."

"Name it, Rat."

"I need a pair of eyes on a place in South Philly. Bugs and I tried it, but I think we might have been made. Anything you can think of will be great."

"Count yourself taken care of, my man. I'll think something up. Tomorrow good enough?"

"If you get an idea, it will be perfect," I said. "Stop by my place in the morning. I'll have breakfast."

I hung up the phone and looked over to Bugs. "Monroe's going to work on it. He'll come up with something."

"I hope so," Bugs said. "This guy Danny is getting more brazen."

"And he'll continue to do so until we stop him," I said.

Bugs nodded. "Just remember what we talked about, Rat. No killing. I'm gonna take him in."

"I hear you, Bugs, but that's assuming we have that option. If he gives us no choice, he's going down."

Chapter Forty-One

CHEESESTEAKS FOR LUNCH

Nicky pushed his chair back from the table and got up to answer the door. "Must be Monroe," he said.

Nicky opened the door, and Monroe and DuPree walked in.

"Somethin' smells pretty damn good," DuPree said.

"I don't know what in the hell you're smelling, DuPree, because I don't have a damn thing cooking."

"Fill me in on what you need, Rat. I got a few plans."

Nicky sat at the kitchen table and sketched the neighborhood around Pat's. "He lives here," Nicky said, pointing to a string of row houses about a block from Pat's. "The trouble is, I don't know which one. All I know is it's about a block or two from Pat's, and we think it may be this block."

"I'm guessing you did the obvious like checking the phone book," Monroe said.

"Christ's sake, Monroe. What the hell do you take me for. Of course I did that. Lots of D'Agostinos in Philly, but none in this area."

Frankie got up to get some water. "We never even got to check it out closely. They made us from a block away, and we were just sitting in the car."

"See, that's the problem," Monroe said. "You can't go casing a joint and just sit in the damn car. You've got to be legit, have a reason to be there."

"I can't think of many reasons why a couple of brothers would be in South Philly," Nicky said.

Monroe laughed. "There you go with your prejudice, racist shit again. Leave it to me, Rat. I'll think of something."

DuPree looked over at his cousin. "So you're doing this, Monroe?"

"Hell yeah, I'm doing this. Shit, I been wantin' a cheesesteak, anyway.

Monroe turned to Nicky. "Give me what you've got on his address, Rat, or anything you got on where he hangs out, and I'll do the rest."

"Just be careful when you do," Nicky said. "South Philly isn't your stomping ground."

"I know that, Rat. Now tell me what you've got."

"From the little we know, he lived within walking distance of Pat's Steaks—like I said. But even if we figure a few blocks, that's a lot of houses."

"That ain't nothin'," Monroe said. "Leave it to me."

Monroe left and gathered up a crew of loyal members, then they headed to South Philly with Wilson driving.

"What's the plan?" DuPree asked. "We're a little too dark to pass for paisans, and those people don't take kindly to our color."

"Not to worry. We just need to make a stop in the west section to pick up some PECO uniforms."

"What the hell are PECO uniforms?" Wilson asked.

"Willie, you don't know shit," DuPree said. "That's why you're driving and not sitting in the back giving orders."

"Well, smart ass, what are they?"

"PECO's the damn electric company, fool. Stands for the Philadelphia Electric Company."

"What good's that gonna do us?" Wilson asked.

"We'll go door-to-door and say we have a potential refund," Monroe said. "All we need from the homeowner is ID and proof of address."

"And they'll give that up in a minute," DuPree said. "Ain't nobody turning down free money."

Monroe stopped and got the uniforms from a guy he knew, then they dressed and moved on to South Philly.

"Just remember to be polite," Monroe said. "We don't need anybody calling the electric company on us."

"Park the car here," Monroe said. "We'll each take a different direction away from Pat's, but there's no need to go west."

Wilson and DuPree started walking away when Monroe called them back. "You assholes better get the instructions right. Hit every house. If nobody's home, make note of it. If the person answers but doesn't give us what we ask, take note of it. In fact, unless the person gives us what we ask for, take note of it."

DuPree knocked on the door of the first house he came to. He waited until an older woman answered.

"Yes?"

"Ma'am, I'm with—"

"I don't care who you're with. I'm not interested," she said, and started to close the door.

"Ma'am, you may want to hear me out. I'm with PECO."

"I don't know any PECO," the lady said.

"PECO," he said. "You know, part of Excelon. We're the company that lights your house." He pointed to the logo on his coveralls as proof.

The old woman sighed but stopped closing the door. "What do you want?"

"Like I started to tell you, we're employees giving out refunds for when the electricity was out in certain parts of town. All you have to do is show ID and proof of address. After that, I'll mark your name down, and when I report back, you'll get a check issued. The ID can't just be a credit card, though; it's got to be something that shows your name and address on the same card."

"How much is it gonna be?" she asked.

"I don't know. I've seen it be as little as forty-five dollars and as much as two hundred dollars. They calculate the amount based on how much electricity you use and how long you've been a customer."

"If that's the case, I should get a lot. Been with those damn people almost as long as they been around. Hang on, and I'll get what you need."

She closed the door and returned a moment later with an electric bill and an official ID card. "This should do it," she said.

DuPree smiled as he wrote her name down next to her address. "I think it will, Ma'am. Thank you."

"When will I get the check?" she asked.

"I'm not sure, ma'am, but it won't be long."

———

Jackson and Wilson worked different sides of the same street, but neither of them had any luck. Wilson got five answers in a row, but none of them were D'Agostino. Jackson fared no better.

———

About three blocks away from Pat's, Monroe hit pay dirt. He looked at the ID card when the woman handed it to him: Lena D'Agostino. As he wrote the information down, he smiled. "D'Agostino? I knew a guy with that name. I think it was Denny or Kenny or something like that."

The woman perked up. "Danny?"

"Yeah, that was it, Danny. I met him in Atlantic City when I was losing all my money one weekend. And he's the one who took it from me, dealt me nothing but losing hands. Nice guy, though."

Pride showed in her smile. "That's Danny. He used to work at one of the casinos down there dealing cards." She shook her head. "I don't know why he ever quit that job."

"I've heard people say it's tough work—a lot of pressure. Anyway, say hi to him when you see him. In fact, I'll probably be in this neighborhood for two more days. If he's gonna be home, I'll stop by."

"Sorry, young man, but he won't be. He's out-of-town looking for work. He said he couldn't find anything here." She frowned and shook her head again. "I don't know that he tried hard enough, but who am I? Just his mother. What's your name? I'll tell him you came by."

"Monroe, ma'am. My name's Monroe."

Monroe gathered everyone, and they piled in the car and headed back to Wilmington. Monroe and DuPree in the back seat, and Jackson in the passenger seat, with Wilson driving.

"So you found him?" DuPree asked.

Monroe held up a slip of paper. "Got the address right here, and if asshole up there slows down and pays attention to the road, we just might make it home."

"Fuck, Monroe, I'm only doing sixty-five," Wilson said.

"But you're all over the damn road; besides, I don't want you to get stopped. I'm sure one of you assholes is holding drugs. That's all we need. Some peckerwood cop stopping us and finding drugs. Bein' black will be the least of our troubles then."

Wilson let off the gas, and the car slowed. "There, sixty miles and hour," he said. "Satisfied?"

"I'll be satisfied if you stay in one lane," Monroe said.

After five or six miles, Monroe dialed Nicky. "Got it, Rat. Not two blocks from the steak joint."

"And you're sure it's him?"

"Talked to his mother for damn near fifteen minutes. Couldn't shut her up when I told her I met her son dealing at the casinos."

"Son of a bitch! That's fantastic, Monroe. Thanks."

"You got it. We'll be leavin' PA in a few, but we're hittin' a lot of traffic. You want me to come by?"

"No, but I do have another favor to ask. A big one."

"Spit it out," Monroe said.

"I know we got his house, but we still don't have him, and based on what happened with 'the Deuce', I'm guessing he's still in Wilmington."

Monroe laughed. "So you need a tap?"

"Damn, Monroe, I knew there was a reason I liked you. You think you can manage it?"

"Gotta call my man at PECO again and see if I can bribe him 'cause sure as shit I don't know how to tap a line. I'd end up frying myself."

"Do it and don't worry about what he charges. It's my debt."

"He's probably gonna want a grand, maybe more."

"Go for it, even if it's two grand."

"I'll let you know, Rat."

Monroe had his man turn around and drive back to the city. He found the guy he was looking for in West Philly and explained what he needed. "Can you do it?"

"Doin' it isn't the problem," Shaky said. "Doin' it and not gettin' caught is the problem."

"I got ten C-notes if you can make it happen."

"Ten? If I get caught, I'll lose my job."

Monroe thought for a minute. "All right, how about this? If you lose your job, I'll pay your salary until you find a new one, and either way you get the Cs."

"Suppose it takes me two or three months to find a job?"

"I said 'until you find a new one.' That means until you do."

"All right, but I can't do it until tomorrow."

"Needs to be early," Monroe said. "How you gonna do it?"

"Not sure yet," Shaky said, "but I'll probably have to cut service for a few minutes from the next block, then go in there like somebody reported it. That way, I can get up on the poles to hook a tracing device without them suspecting anything. Once we're through with that, I'll rewire the break on the other block, and we'll be done."

"Sounds simple. Just make sure it works," Monroe said. "I can't have any problems."

Shaky wrapped everything up by two in the afternoon. Monroe paid him, then dropped him off near his house.

"Thanks, my man. That helped."

Shaky stuffed the cash into his pocket and smiled. "Anytime. I like earning the extra green."

"All right," Monroe said. "Let's head home. We're done here." On the way, he called Nicky and gave him the news.

Nicky was ecstatic. "Hey, Monroe, you never gave me his address."

"No biggie. I'll stop by and give you the address. I don't want to text it 'cause I don't want a record of me having it."

"I agree," Nicky said. "You never know what might happen to old Danny."

"I hear that," Monroe said, and laughed.

"I heard that," DuPree said, "but I'm gonna pretend I didn't hear it."

Monroe smacked him on the side of the head. "Some day—maybe—you'll get some brains. The way to have handled that would have been to shut up, not to say you heard it, but pretend you didn't. You know how stupid that is to admit you heard it?"

"Sorry, Monroe."

"Don't say you're sorry to me. Save that for your mother when she's weeping over your coffin."

"Ain't no way he'll find out anyway," DuPree said.

Monroe tilted his head and gestured toward the front seat. "You trust those two with your life?"

DuPree looked at Jackson, then Wilson. He pulled his gun and stuck it against Jackson's head. "You two motherfuckers say anything about this, and I'll put a cap in each of you. Shit, I'll put two caps in you. Got it?"

Jackson gulped, then said, "I hear you, DuPree. What the hell, man? Chill the fuck out. We ain't saying nothin'. Damn."

"Better not," DuPree said. "I hear 'bout this from anyone, and both of you are dead. I don't care which one said it, you'll both die."

"All right, shit," Wilson said. "You made your point."

Chapter Forty-Two

WHERE IS DANNY

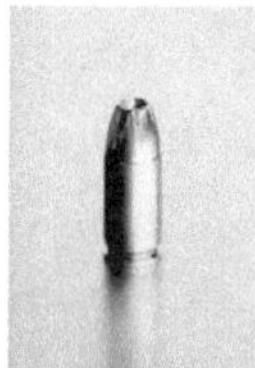

Monroe walked into the house, DuPree close behind. "Rat, how's it going?"

"Good to see you, Monroe. You did good."

"I don't know about *good*, but we tapped the line just like I told you we would. All we got to do now is wait for his mom to call him or him to call her."

"With him using a burner, which I'm sure he is, all we're going to get is a location, and a general one at that, unless he stays on the phone long enough."

Monroe filled a glass with water. "Even a general location will do in a town as small as Wilmington. I guarantee he's somewhere close by. He's not going to be chillin' out in the suburbs."

"I think you're right, Monroe. I don't see him in suburbia, even for a hiding place."

Monroe sat down. "Then I guess we sit back and wait. Nothing else to do."

"Anybody want more coffee?" I asked. "I'm putting more water on."

"Count me in," Monroe said, and Bugs joined in.

DuPree said, "I've had that shit, Rat. It's too damn strong for me."

"I'm sorry, DuPree. All you need to do is say 'I'd like some pussy coffee.' Say that, and I'll fix it."

Monroe laughed his ass off, and Frankie joined in. DuPree slouched and sulked.

We sat around playing cards and shooting the breeze until about five o'clock, then we got word from Monroe's contact that a call had come in. "Hey, dude, I'm going to put this on speaker," Monroe said. "And don't worry, no one from your work will find out. These are all my men in Wilmington."

"Okay," the guy said. "The call came from a Philadelphia number, but it originated from a location in Wilmington."

"Were you able to pinpoint the location?" Monroe asked.

"Not exactly, but when we checked the coordinates, it came back close to somewhere between Chestnut and Maple Streets and Van Buren and Franklin Streets."

"Damn, dude, there are a lot of houses in that area. You can't get any closer?"

"I'm not a magician, Monroe. If another call comes in that lasts longer, I might be able to narrow it down, but as it is, this is what you get."

"Keep a watch on it and let me know if anything changes," Monroe said. "It'd be nice if we could narrow it down."

"I'll let you know," the contact said. "If I get anything better, I'll call."

Monroe turned off the speaker, made sure the call was disconnected, then put the phone away. "You heard him," he said. "That's about a six square block area with a lot of row houses. It's not gonna be easy."

"Nothing's easy," Bugs said. "But we have a good likeness with Frisco's drawing. If we space out and use four people—one on each side—we should be able to spot him. He's got to leave the area sooner or later."

"I don't know," I said. "That puts him square in the middle of Hedgeville, the Polack section, and they're about as tight-lipped as the people in South Philly. I don't think flashing a picture around will get us anything other than rousing his suspicions."

"What's you plan, Rat?" Monroe asked.

"I think we're going to have to do a major stakeout, so everybody better get more coffee."

I looked at DuPree and said, "You too, DuPree. We're likely going to be up late planning this out."

"All right, Rat. I'll suffer through it. Count me in."

I put more water on and waited for it to boil, then ground the beans and put the coffee in to let it sit. "Anybody got a plan yet?"

"You're an ass, you know that, Rat?" Bugs said. "We'll have a plan when we get one. Nobody asked you if that damn coffee was ready yet."

I laughed. "All right, Bugs. You made your point."

I walked into the living room with coffee and served it to the guys sitting there. "Now, I'll ask. Anybody got a plan?"

"By the way, Rat, where's your wife and kids?" Monroe asked.

"Angie's with a friend, and the kids are in New York. You should know, your boys are with them."

Bugs pointed to his computer. "I've been looking at this on Google maps, and it seems clear cut based on how the streets run."

I took a seat on the sofa. "Let's see."

Bugs pointed to the streets as he explained. Monroe and I went through this already. "Maple Street is one way heading west, so we'll position someone at Maple just north of Harrison. From there, they can see anyone going either way. We'll put somebody else at Chestnut and Van Buren and another at Elm and Franklin. Finally, we'll put someone at Linden and Harrison. With those four, we should be able to spot D'Agostino when he leaves the area, and he's

going to leave some time. Whether it's going to church or going to
the corner store, we'll have him."

I looked at the maps carefully, then went over the plan Bugs laid
out again, tracing each of the streets, making note of which direction they ran one way on. When I was finished, I nodded. "I think
you've got something here, Bugs. It wouldn't hurt to have a few
more people so we have partners in each car, but we could make do
with what we have."

"I'll talk to Mrozinski," Bugs said. "I'm guessing he'll want in on
this, and if he does, we could get Viola and Borelli. That'll give us
three cars with two people each."

"I can get another," Monroe said. "DuPree, get Santos to sit with you. I'll sit with the Rat, and Donovan can take his pick of the detectives."

I thought a moment, then nodded. "Make the call, Bugs. See if Mrozinski goes along with it. But tell him it's our plan. If he doesn't like it, he doesn't need to come. And if he has a plan he thinks is better, he's got to get our approval."

Bugs laughed. "He's gonna love that, Rat."

"I don't care whether he loves it or not. I think you and Monroe have a good plan, and I'm going with it. D'Agostino's got to be stopped."

Bugs called Mrozinski, and he not only went along with the plan, he got Borelli and Viola to agree to the stakeout.

Maddy showed up at the house by seven. She was followed minutes later by Borelli and Mrozinski.

"Where's everybody else?" Mrozinski asked.

"Monroe and his men are already in position," I said. "They went down earlier. They're at Maple and Van Buren, which leaves us Elm and Linden Streets."

"Donovan and I will take Linden," Borelli said.

"I guess that leaves Elm for Maddy and I," Mrozinski said. "Who's going to be with you, Fusco?"

"Monroe's got an extra guy with him, so he'll join me when we get there."

Before we left, I addressed them one more time. "Remember not to let other factors fool you," I said. "He might be walking with a woman, an older couple, or a few kids. Hell, he might be pushing a baby carriage. No matter the company a person keeps, check out the man with them. And don't forget that a hat or a pair of glasses makes a person look different. Don't let it fool you. If you see someone wearing a hat or glasses, look at him harder. Look *through* the disguise and see him for what he is."

By seven forty-five we were in position on all the streets, and everyone had two copies of the sketch Frisco had drawn.

All we had to do now was wait.

Chapter Forty-Three

I'VE GOT YOUR WIFE

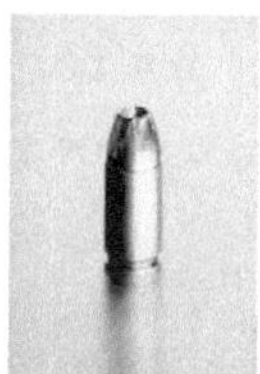

We watched for two days but got no results. A couple of times, when someone thought a person might have been Danny, we had someone else double-check, and it proved not to be D'Agostino.

On the third day, I kept watch while Monroe played games on his phone. After a few hours, I tapped him on the shoulder. "Time for you to take over. I'm going to nod out."

"Go ahead, Rat. You can sleep tight knowing Monroe is awake."

I leaned against the window, head cushioned by a jacket. "Make sure you're awake *and* alert, Monroe."

Danny pushed the blinds aside and stared out the window.

"What's it look like?" Debbie asked.

"It looks the same as yesterday did, which was the same as the day before—the cops or Fusco or both are watching.

"I had an idea," Debbie said.

Danny turned to her and stared. "What?"

"I can leave the house, take the car, and park it a few blocks away, far enough so they can't see it. Then I'll come home, but use the back door. They won't see me come in. After that—some time tonight—you leave by the back door and take the car, then you're outta here."

"I'm sure they've got a car somewhere out back. They wouldn't leave an open gap like that."

"I'm sure they do too, but they won't be looking for a woman by herself, so it should be easy for me to slip by. And if you go at night and be careful, you should be able to make it across the street to where I put the car."

"I don't know. It might be better if I left during the day. They'll be on the lookout more at night. At least I think they would. Let me think on it," Danny said, then he opened a beer and sat on the edge of the sofa.

"Why are they watching you?" Debbie asked.

"None of your damn business. Just do like you're told."

Debbie tossed a shoe at him. "And you can go to hell too. I'm trying to help you."

Danny got up and walked to Debbie. He hugged her and stroked her hair. "I'm sorry. I didn't mean it. This shit's got me nervous, that's all."

She stepped back. "I told you, do like I said. It'll work."

Danny went to the window and pulled the blinds aside again. "All right, we'll do it." He tossed her the keys, and said, "Park the car just across Porter by Linden. Any spot you can. I'll find it."

Debbie started out the door, but Danny called her back. "Don't forget to be gone for an hour or more so they don't suspect anything. And I'm doing it during the day; I've decided on that."

Debbie shot him the finger. "You do your part. I'll do mine. Just be ready to leave after lunch."

Debbie walked out the door and got in the car. She drove to a friend's house and sat with her for more than an hour, then she asked the time and said she had to go. She drove back toward home, but turned onto Porter and found a parking spot right away. Afterward, she walked home by going up Elm Street, then down Harrison.

She opened the door and walked to the fridge to get a drink. "I'm home, Danny. You can leave whenever you want."

"Where's the car parked?"

"Right where you said on Porter. You can't miss it."

"Which way do you think is the safest?"

Debbie finished her bottle of water, then threw the empty into the trash. "If you go by Linden and Van Buren, you should get by with ease. Just walk casually and keep your head down, but nothing obvious, don't try to be no damn 1940s detective."

Danny leaned in and kissed her. "Got it, doll. See ya' later." After that, he walked out the back door and down the alley.

Danny sneaked into his car, started it up, then drove slowly until he got out of sight. Even afterward, he was sure not to break the speed limit for fear of being picked up and identified. He drove to Fusco's house and parked near the corner of Clayton and Beech, where he still had a good view of Fusco's front door.

He waited several hours, and his diligence paid off. Angela pulled up Beech Street and parked in front of the house, then she got out and walked inside.

Danny opened his car door, walked up, and knocked. When Angela answered, he pointed a gun at her. "Inside," he said, and stepped in behind her.

"What do you want? I don't have any money."

Danny laughed. "Honey, I don't want your money or your ass. Just get on the phone and call your husband."

"What? No way. You're crazy."

"You either call your husband, or I'm gonna shoot you. It's that simple."

Angela hesitated, but then took out her phone and dialed Nicky.

He answered right away. "Hey, babe, what's up?"

Danny grabbed the phone from her. "This ain't babe, but I *am* with her. And if you don't do exactly as I say, I'm going to rape her, then kill her. Understand?"

I didn't know what true fear and panic felt like until I heard that. It never bothered me when my life was threatened, but this was different—this was Angie.

"I hear you," I said. "What do you want?"

"Much better," D'Agostino said. "Now do everything I tell you.

Instruct whoever is in the car with you, that you have to leave. Make up some excuse, but make it a believable one. After that, I want you to drive home *by yourself* and come inside. Any foul-ups, any mistakes at all, and she dies. In fact, I'll make sure she suffers before she dies. Got it?"

"I understand," I said. "It won't take me long."

I hung up and turned to Monroe. "That was D'Agostino. He got out somehow and, he's got Angie. Tell Bugs I'm going there, but tell him when he comes to make sure he's not seen. I'll stall as long as I can."

"I'm comin' with you," Monroe said.

I shook my head. "Won't do any good, Monroe. I've got to do this myself, or he might hurt Angela."

Monroe opened the car door. "Go on then. Get movin'. I'll tell Donovan."

I drove like a maniac all the way home, praying the whole time that Angie was all right.

The car had barely stopped moving when I switched it off and hopped out. I ran to the house and went inside, gun drawn.

"Put the gun down, Fusco."

To the side stood D'Agostino with Angie in front of him. He held a gun to her head, and his arm was around her neck.

I evaluated the situation and decided to place the gun on the table. If it had been anyone but Angie, I might have risked a shot, but I couldn't gamble with her life.

"What do you want, D'Agostino?"

"How'd you find me?" he asked.

"It doesn't matter how," I said. "It was inevitable."

"I guess so," he said. "Just like her, dying is inevitable. The best part of this is you're going to have to watch."

"That sounds threatening and all, but it doesn't hold water. In order for you to do anything other than put a bullet in her head, you'll have to take your focus off her for at least a second or two. If you do that, you're mine."

"You think so, huh?"

I smiled. "I *know* so, little Danny. Even your perverted father, good as he was, proved to be no match for me. You should have heard him in the end, crying like a baby."

D'Agostino shook and pressed his finger to the trigger. "Shut up, you hear me. You better shut the fuck up."

"And you know what, Danny boy. When I finish with you, I'm gonna go up and take care of your mother and all your siblings. And yes, I know where they live. I was just there."

"I'll have to make sure you're dead too."

I shook my head again. "It won't matter if I'm dead. I've got friends who will do worse than I ever would."

Danny laughed. "Nice try, Fusco, but I don't believe a word of it. *You* might do something to my mother, but I'm pretty sure your friends won't."

"Then you don't know all my friends," I said. "One of them will not only kill her, he'll make sure his men do other things to her before she dies."

Danny stepped forward and hit me with the butt of the gun. "You should have shut up, Fusco. All you did was give me a new idea of what to do with your wife."

I glared. "You say anything like that again, or if I get the indication you're even thinking about it, I'll make you use the other end of that gun."

"Not a good idea, Fusco. If I use the gun, it won't be to wound you."

"Doesn't matter. It will be one more count of murder they'll charge you with. Two if you kill Angela."

"Somehow I doubt you're willing to die just to get me convicted, or should I say on the chance of convicting me."

"You underestimate me, D'Agostino. I've got no problem giving my life if that's what it takes to bring you down. As to the chance of convicting you, let's just say it will be difficult for you to place the blame on me if I'm dead."

"They'd still have to catch me."

I smiled. "I'm not counting on Mrozinski catching you, but I *know* Monroe won't stop until he nabs your ass. And if he can't get you, he'll get your mother, your brother, and any other family you have."

D'Agostino looked as if he may say something when my cell phone rang. I instinctively reached for it.

"Leave it," Danny warned. "You're not going to be giving signals to anyone. Just let it ring."

The phone rang a few times, then quit. I assumed it may have been Bugs and hoped it was.

D'Agostino talked for a few more minutes, then said we were going for a short ride.

"Where are you taking us?" I asked.

"None of your damn business, Fusco."

"Afraid, Danny boy?"

"Afraid of what?"

"Everything. Afraid I may get to you, which would be your worst nightmare. You'd squeal more than your sissy father did."

He struck out like a snake, hitting me with the gun again.

I wiped the blood from my forehead and smiled. "Afraid Monroe might get to you if I don't. That wouldn't be as bad as me getting you, but it'd be the next worst fate. And it definitely would be the worst fate for your family."

D'Agostino fixed his eyes on me and gestured to Angie. "Say anything about my father again, and I'll kill her now."

"Stop bluffing and get on with the ride," I said. I figured it had been enough time if that call had been Bugs. I prayed he'd be outside waiting.

———

Monroe filled Frankie in on what Nicky told him right after he left. Bugs jumped into action and told Borelli what needed to be done.

On the way to the house, he called Nicky, but when he got no answer, he hung up. Frankie turned to Borelli and said, "No answer. Something's up."

"You don't know that, Donovan. It could be anything. He could be in the damn restroom."

Frankie shook his head. "Even if he did go to the restroom, he'd have taken his phone with him, especially in a situation like this."

"If you really think that, we better get an alert on his house. Or better yet, just get a SWAT team there."

"No," Frankie said. "If something's wrong, having them show up may panic D'Agostino into doing something rash. I say we go to the house right now and check it out."

Borelli stepped on the gas. "Let's go, then. Time's wasting."

Borelli drove up Maple Street, crossed South Clayton, and turned left on South DuPont. He put on the signal to indicate another turn on Beech Street when Frankie took hold of his arm. "Hold on, Borelli. Why don't you park here, and we'll walk the rest of the way in case D'Agostino is there."

Frankie and Borelli walked up the street, making sure to remain out of sight if someone were looking out the window from Nicky's house.

"Better move in closer," Borelli said. "If we go much further, he'll be able to spot us."

Frankie and Borelli cut across the grass and hugged the brick walls of the houses. When they got two houses away, Frankie tugged on Borelli's arm. "Get behind the next stoop, and I'll sneak past Nicky's house and use that tree for cover. If it's D'Agostino in there, it won't be long before he comes out."

"Maybe I should call his phone again. It might make him do something rashly."

Frankie thought for a moment. "If he plans on killing him, the phone ring could be the trigger; on the other hand, if he plans on leaving with them, it might force his hand on that."

"So?"

"Let's go for it," Frankie said. "Wait until I'm behind the tree though."

Borelli nodded. "Got it."

———

"Let's go," D'Agostino said. "Time to leave. Just remember, if you try anything, she dies."

He held his arm around Angie's throat with the gun pointed at her head. "Get the door, Fusco. And move slowly."

I opened the door and stepped onto the stoop, then took the steps one at a time.

D'Agostino followed me out the door, looking both ways as he exited. "Don't try anything, Fusco. I know you're quick, but you're not quick enough to stop me from putting a bullet in her head."

"Take it easy, D'Agostino. I'm not going to try anything." I caught a glimpse of Borelli behind the stoop next door and assumed Bugs was here as well. I slowed and let D'Agostino get closer.

"Why are you stopping?" he asked.

"I'm not stopping," I said. "I didn't know what you wanted me to do. You want me to get in *my* car? *Your* car? Walk down the block? What?"

"Your car. And no tricks."

"Okay, got it. That's all you needed to say." As I turned to go toward the car, I grabbed Angie's hand and yanked as hard as I could. "Now, Bugs!"

Angie broke free of D'Agostino and fell to the ground. Seconds later, two shots rang out, then two more. I rolled on top of her, covering her with my body as I risked a glance to the rear."

D'Agostino's head exploded, blood spraying in all directions. A millisecond later, two shots hit his chest close to the heart. D'Agostino never had a chance to fire his gun.

He lay on the sidewalk, blood pooling. He wasn't breathing. I stood and checked his pulse as Borelli approached, still holding his weapon. I looked to the other side where Bugs was approaching, gun in hand.

"He gone?" Borelli asked.

I nodded. "You did him in, Jimmy."

"I guess mine didn't count, then?" Bugs said.

I laughed, got on my feet, and hugged Bugs. "As bad as you shoot, I'm almost convinced there was another shooter 'cause sure as hell you couldn't have hit him from that far away."

Bugs laughed and pulled out his cell.

"Who are you calling?" Borelli asked.

"Somebody needs to call Mrozinski. If he hears about this from someone else, he'll have a cow."

I held Angela tight and walked her inside. "It's over, babe. Nothing to worry about now."

"I can't believe it's over," she said. "Now the kids can come home."

Chapter Forty-Four

MROZINSKI SHOWS UP

Mrozinski pulled up as Borelli and Donovan stood by the body. He and Maddy got out of the car and quickly walked up to them.

"What happened? Fusco do this?" Mrozinski asked.

Borelli shook his head. "Learn to be a detective, Ed. Just because it's his house doesn't mean he did the shooting."

"Did he?"

"I did," Frankie said. "He had a gun on Angela, and I had no doubt he was going to shoot her. Jimmy and I were hiding when D'Agotsino came out of the house with Nicky and Angie. He held a gun on her and was forcing Nicky toward the car. Nicky must have seen one or both of us, so he grabbed Angela and yanked her free. When he did that, I took the shot at D'Agostino."

Mrozinski looked at Borelli. "Is that how it happened?"

"You heard him," Jimmy said. "It was exactly like that. What Donovan didn't tell you is that there are other bullets in D'Agostino too. Mine. I took two shots—got him in the chest."

"What?"

"I shot when Nicky grabbed his wife. I figured it might be our only chance."

"You're telling me Fusco had nothing to do with this? That you two shot this guy, and he's clean?"

"Check the ballistics, Ed. It's what good cops do. You'll see that everything we told you is true. And if you do the report right, you'll probably even get credit for solving a bunch of murders, but if you keep being a pain in the ass, I might have to stick around and straighten things out. Let them know it was Fusco and Donovan who did most of the work."

Viola knelt beside D'Agostino's body and seemed to bury her smile. "Ed, I think it looks like they said. We've got two shots in the head and two in the chest."

She stood and moved beside Mrozinski, then whispered. "You're probably better off listening to them. I think it might play better that way."

Mrozinski looked around as if someone were missing. "Where's Fusco? Where's his wife?"

"I'm right here," Nicky said as he exited the house. "And Angela is inside. Why? What do you need?"

"I have a few questions."

"Ask away," Nicky said. "But my wife is too upset to talk now."

"I want to know how this went down, Fusco. All of it. Every detail."

Nicky smiled. "It went down exactly how Bugs and Jimmy said it did. *Exactly*."

Frustrated, Mrozinski closed his notebook and stuffed it into his pocket along with his pen."

Mrozinski got in his car but yelled to Borelli before he left. "Jimmy, I'm going to need a full report before I close this. I mean a *full report*."

"You'll have it, Ed. Just go home and savor your win."

Nicky put his arms around the shoulders of Bugs and Jimmy. "I can't thank you two enough. If anything had happened to Angie, I'd have died."

"Now you know what I felt like years ago," Jimmy said. "Every time I look at my boy, even when he's being a pain in the ass, I thank you for saving him."

"It's all about the neighborhood," Bugs said. "We look out for each other."

"Always," Nicky said. "Always."

Nicky walked up the stoop. "Now I've got to take care of getting my kids back before Angie kicks my ass."

"Good luck with that," Frankie said. "And I've got to get back home before Kate kicks mine."

"I'll let you pussy-whipped guys be on your way then. I've got a long way to go home—and that's *after* I give Ed 'the ass' Mrozinski his *full report.*"

Bugs laughed, then he and Jimmy walked to the car.

I went in to sit with Angie and found her sitting on the sofa crying. I rushed over and sat next to her. "What's wrong? Did something happen to the kids?"

She sobbed but shook her head. "No, I'm just glad it's finally over."

I almost laughed. "Sitting here crying is no way to show you're glad. Cheer up. Things are better. The clouds are gone."

"I know. I know."

Chapter Forty-Five

WE CAUGHT THE KILLER

Mrozinksi got the report from Borelli, and he and Maddy turned it in.

"You did a good job on this," the captain said. "We haven't had so many dead bodies since that mess up in Hockessin a while back."

"Thanks, Captain. I'm just glad it's over and done with. Even more glad that the man's dead. I never like seeing a man killed, but this one deserved it."

The captain put the report on the side of his desk. "Detective Mrozinski, I'm putting you in charge of all homicides from now on. I hope we don't have enough to keep you busy, but those we get, you'll be heading up."

Mrozinski shook the captain's hand. "Captain, I appreciate it, but you've got to know that Detective Borelli—or ex-detective Borelli—along with a detective from New York had a lot to do with this; in fact, if it weren't for them, we wouldn't have caught the killer. The credit goes to them."

The captain returned the smile from Mrozinski. "I'm more

convinced than ever I made the right decision to promote you, Detective. Don't let me down."

"I won't, sir. I definitely won't."

Mrozinski left the captain's office and returned to his desk. He had to organize for his new position. Mrozinski worked through most of the day, then a call came in from the coroner.

"Hey, doc. What can I do for you?"

"I heard about the killer. I also heard about my mistakes regarding the analysis of the bodies."

"It's a mistake anyone could have made," Mrozinski said. "I wouldn't worry about it."

"But I am worried, Detective. I've been considering retirement, anyway. I'm getting old. When you're so old you make mistakes like that, it may be time."

"Doc, why are you telling me this? It's none of my business."

"I'm telling you because I turned in my resignation today. I wanted to let you know it was nice working with you, and I wish you well."

"All right, doc. I appreciate it. Good luck."

———

Kate walked in the front door, stopped, and sniffed the air. "That smells like seafood ravioli from my favorite restaurant."

Frankie walked to her and gave her a peck on the cheek. "It's even better than that; this is Manny's seafood ravioli. And we have the house to ourselves; Alex is staying over at Tommy's house."

Kate looked at Frankie with narrowed eyes. "Seafood ravioli from Manny? To what do I owe this gift?"

Frankie led her to the table by the elbow. "Let's eat first."

"No," Kate said, "I prefer to know now."

Frankie shook his head. "Kate, I quit my job. I'm done with the department."

Kate laughed. "Is that all? I knew that already, and I didn't figure it would change; besides, I saw that coming ages ago. And we can live off what I make, which leaves you free to watch Alex."

Frankie got up and hugged Kate, then he kissed her hard. "I love you, Kate. You're the best."

"I've always known that, Donovan. It's about time you learned it."

Frankie sat back down and dished out the meal, then he opened a bottle of wine, and he and Kate enjoyed the meal. About halfway through, Kate's phone rang, and she answered.

"Kate Donovan."

"Yes. Yes, I'm familiar with it. I did work on comparing the cases."

She covered the mouthpiece and whispered to Frankie. "It's about the coroner in Wilmington."

Kate nodded a few times, then said, "Yes, I might be. Okay, you let me know."

When she hung up the phone, Frankie said, "What was that all about?"

Kate smiled. "It was a call from Wilmington. They want me to interview for the medical examiner's position."

"What? Are you interested? Would you consider it?"

Kate smiled at Frankie. "I know how much it would mean to you to be back there with Nicky, so yes, I'd consider it. And I wouldn't mind moving from this rat race. I think it would be better for Alex too."

Frankie scooped a mouthful of ravioli and sipped his wine. "This meal is gonna taste a whole lot better now."

———

Rosa burst into the house carrying Dante. She set him down and ran to her mother. "Mom, I'm so glad to see you."

Nicky walked in and Dante screamed and hugged him. "Dad!"

Nicky kissed on Dante, making raspberries on his cheeks. "Did you have a good time?"

"We did, Dad. Uncle Manny let us do a lot of really neat stuff."

"Uncle Manny?" Angela almost fell over. "Who told you to call him Uncle Manny?"

"Uncle Manny did," Rosa said.

"You too?" Angela said.

"Oh, Mom, stop being so fussy. Manny's a nice man, and you know it."

"Sit down and tell me all about your visit with Uncle Manny," Nicky said.

Rosa laughed and kissed Nicky on the cheek. "We had a good time, but I'm glad to be home."

"And it's good to have you home," Nicky said. "Don't worry. Everything's all right. All of our troubles are over. At least for now, they are."

"If that's the case," Rosa said, "I think it calls for a vacation."

"And I think I've missed enough work already," Nicky said. "I need to get back in there before Johnny either messes things up or does so good I've got to hire him."

Chapter Forty-Six

DO YOU WANT THE JOB?

Kate finished out the day and was ready to leave when the phone rang. "Kate Donovan."

"Ms. Donovan, this is Douglas Slobov. I'm in charge of hiring the new medical examiner for the county. We'd like to talk to you about that position since you expressed an interest in it."

"They said they'd call for an interview."

"Ms. Donovan, we're in a hurry, and I've been authorized to make the offer without the interview based on the work you did on the recent murders and on recommendations we've received."

"I'm listening."

"We can't do much on salary, but we can match what you're getting now, and we can offer a full relocation package with standard benefits. Vacation will be four weeks per year. And keep in mind that even though the salary would be the same, the cost of living is much lower here."

"I have to discuss this with my husband, Mr. Slobov, but my inclination is to say yes. I'll let you know in two days."

. . .

Kate walked in the front door wearing a sour expression. Alex ran over and hugged her, and Frankie blew her a kiss from the kitchen.

"It's not Manny's seafood ravioli, but I'm making eggplant parmigiana with meatballs on the side."

"That's good," she said, and walked straight to the bedroom.

Frankie looked at Alex and whispered, "What's wrong?"

Alex shrugged and started to say something, but Kate came out of the bedroom.

"What's wrong?" Frankie asked with genuine concern.

"Nothing. I was surprised when I saw you cooking. I thought we could go out to celebrate my new position."

It took a second to sink in, but then Frankie set down the spatula and raced to her side. "New position? They gave it to you? How? You didn't interview?"

Kate was all smiles. "I got a call from the director. He said they were in a hurry and had examined my work on the autopsies I sent down. They also did some referencing."

"Oh, my God. I can't believe it. The hell with eggplant parmigiana. Let's go to Cataldi's. I'll call for a table."

Alex looked from Kate to Frankie and back. "What's going on? What position?"

Kate bent down and hugged him. "I got a new position, Alex. We'll be moving."

Alex's face dropped to the floor. "Moving. Where?"

"To Wilmington, where Rosa and Dante live."

He lit up immediately. "You mean it? For real?" He ran to get his phone, then he picked it up and dialed.

"Whoa," Frankie said. "Who are you calling?"

"I'm calling Rosa."

Frankie was going to nix it, but then said, "What the hell, go ahead and tell her."

Chapter Forty-Seven

A SURPRISE GUEST FOR DINNER

Sherri parked her car a half a block from Manny's house and walked down the sidewalk, looking left and right with cautious glances. When she was sure no one noticed her, she walked to his front door and knocked.

Manny opened the door in a few seconds and gave her a hug.

Sherri flashed a quick smile. "Manny, I just came by to thank you for your help. It was the first case I closed by myself."

Manny brushed his hand in the air. "Think nothin' of it. It needed to be done; besides, you saved me the trouble of taking care of it."

"I don't want to know about any of that," Miller said.

"Yeah, I know," Manny said. "But come in and have some espresso. Besides, you saved me a trip."

Sherri looked confused. "Saved you a trip? How?"

"I was going to invite you for dinner—Manny's famous seafood ravioli, but for obvious reasons—yours and mine—I didn't want to visit you at work."

Manny walked into the kitchen and put the espresso pot on the stove. "Sit down. It'll be ready in a minute."

Sherry sat, then tilted her head and smiled. "Manny, I don't know what to say."

Manny leaned on the stove as he laughed one of his big-belly laughs. "You can say *yes*, and you can be here Friday night at seven. Bring someone if you like."

"Manny, I . . . I can't."

"Why not?"

Sherri lowered her head and shook it. "I'm a cop, for God's sake. I can't be seen here."

Manny tapped Giorgio on the elbow. "You hear that shit, Giorgio? She can't eat here because she's a cop."

Giorgio and Manny laughed, then he reached over and pinched her cheeks. "*Dolcetta*, if you knew how many cops have eaten dinner here, you'd die. And if any of your bosses give you any shit, tell me, and I'll remind the Chief of Detectives that he's been here with his wife, and that Captain Pallelo and his whole family have been here. I have pictures to prove it."

"Yeah," Giorgio said. "And if they try to tell you not to eat with any gangsters, half the Italian restaurants in Brooklyn would be off limits. And you know they won't do that."

Manny brought the espresso to the table, then opened a jar with biscotti inside. "Grab a couple; they're good for you."

"Thanks," Sherri said, and took out a biscotto which she nibbled on while she drank espresso. "As usual, Manny, this is great."

"Won't be half as good as that seafood ravioli."

"All right, you convinced me. I'll be here at seven on Friday."

"You coming alone?"

Sherri smiled. "No, I'll bring someone. He's never had good seafood ravioli."

"Good," Manny said, and slapped her on the back. "I'll see you Friday."

Sherri finished her espresso, then stood. "Time for me to go, Manny. Thanks."

Manny walked Sherri to the door. "You go home and plan on being here on Friday. I'm counting on it. By the way, you've got a nickname now—*dolcetta*—it means *sweetie*. Anyone who eats dinner here gets a nickname."

"I know what it means, Manny." Sherri stopped and stared. "You know, you're a nice guy, Manny. You could—"

Manny placed his finger on her lips, leaned down and kissed her cheek. "*Dolcetta,* you know those religious people who try to convert everyone? Don't be like that. Accept things the way they are."

"But, Manny, what you do is against the law."

Manny laughed. "Whose law? Did you ever think that maybe what you do is against my law. I accept you for what you are. I don't ask you to be a carpenter or plumber."

Sherri shook her head. "Okay, Manny, but don't expect me to cut you any slack if you do something wrong."

"I wouldn't think of it," Manny said. "Now get out of here. I'll see you on Friday."

Chapter Forty-Eight

A PROPOSAL

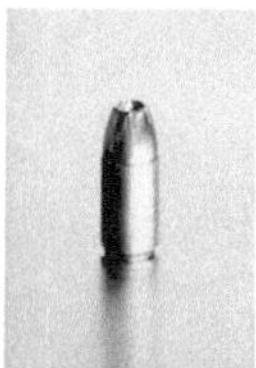

A week went by and everything was back to normal. That was the good thing, but it was also the bad thing. As much as I loved what I did, I missed the action more.

I thought about the thrill of the hunt—when we were looking for someone who did something—and the even bigger thrill when we caught them. Even the excitement that built when a clue was found—like a dog picking up a scent.

I sat back in the chair and folded my hands behind my neck. *Damn, it's exciting.*

As I sat in the chair daydreaming, Sheila called over the intercom.

"Mr. Fusco, someone is here to see you."

"Who is it, Sheila?"

She whispered. "I don't know, sir. He won't give his name."

Curiosity, more than anything, got the best of me, so I got up and went to the front desk.

Sheila pointed to someone dressed in a blue suit and sitting in the corner with their back to me.

I walked over, cleared my throat as I approached, and said, "Excuse me, sir. May I help you?"

The man stood and turned. "I hope so, Rat, but who knows."

"Bugs!" I embraced him. "What the hell are you doing here?"

"I needed some advice from my best friend, so I came on down."

"Well, shit, come in the office; in fact, let's go to Casapulla's and get a sub. I'm always up for a sub."

As we walked past Sheila's desk, I pointed my finger at her. "You damn devil. You knew who this was."

She smiled. "I know, Mr. Fusco, but Mr. Donovan asked me not to say anything."

I laughed. "Well, I'm glad you didn't."

Bugs and I left the office and drove to Casapulla's. As we ate on the bench outside, Bugs's expression got serious. "Nicky, I've got a proposal for you."

"What, fed up with Kate already?"

"Shut up, you ass. I'm serious. I quit my job, and Kate has a new job she'll be starting in a few weeks."

"Damn, Bugs, I didn't know. What do you need, some bucks? I can probably handle ten grand or so. If you need more, I'm sure I can get it from Doggs."

Bugs waved his hand in the air. "No, nothing like that. Kate's new job is down here, in Wilmington."

I damn near knocked my sandwich off the table. "What? Where? Doing what?"

"She's going to be the new medical examiner. Fred is retiring."

"Son of a bitch! I can't believe this. When did you find out? Why didn't you call?"

Bugs took a bite from his sandwich, waited till he swallowed it, then said, "I was going to, but then Alex called Rosa, and I figured she'd tell you."

"That little shit never said a word," I said. "Wait till I get my hands on her."

"Anyway, Kate's all set and ready to go, but I'm looking for something to do."

I hesitated for only a second. "Think no more, Bugs, you can be my new old-as-dirt apprentice estimator."

Bugs flushed. "No, you don't understand. I'm not looking for work. Not in the sense you're thinking. And besides, we can make do on what Kate earns. I'm going to open up a private detective agency."

"Well, damn, Bugs. I think that's great."

"And I want you to join me," Bugs said.

I didn't say anything for a moment, then said, "Bugs, I don't know. I've already got a business to run, and unlike you, I've got no one else taking care of the bills."

"I thought you'd say that, Rat. Since that's the case, how about helping me part-time? I'll set the business up, and you help me with cases."

I hesitated. "I don't know, Bugs. I—"

"Come on, Rat. It'll be a blast, and it's sorely needed. From what I've been told, there's not a good detective agency in the city."

I laughed. "I wouldn't go that far, Bugs."

"None that could hold a candle to the two of us."

"I don't know. I—"

"I know. You need to check with Angela. Well, check with her. I'm betting she'll say okay. She'd rather have you working with me than playing cards at the smoke shop."

That made me smile, knowing he was right. "I'll think about it."

"Sounds good," Frankie said. "That means yes."

"Like hell. That means I'll think about it and nothing else."

ACKNOWLEDGMENTS

It is with great honor that I give eternal gratitude to my wife and all four of my grandkids. They give me the inspiration to keep going.

ABOUT THE AUTHOR

Giacomo Giammatteo is the author of gritty crime dramas about murder, mystery, and family. He also writes non-fiction books including the No Mistakes Careers series, No Mistakes Publishing, No Mistakes Grammar, and No Mistakes Writing.

When Giacomo isn't writing, he's helping his wife take care of the animals on their sanctuary. At last count, they had forty-five animals—eleven dogs, a horse, six cats, and twenty-six pigs.

Oh, and one crazy—and very large—wild boar, who takes walks with Giacomo every day and also happens to be his best buddy.

nomistakespublishing.com
gg@giacomog.com

ALSO BY GIACOMO GIAMMATTEO

You can see all of my books here.

And you can buy them on the platform of your choice.

This brings up a thought: with more than eighty books out now, it is becoming difficult to try to update the list at the back of all of them. If you want to know what books I have out, use the link above, which takes you to my website, or download the latest copy of my GG recommended reading list, which is free.

Nonfiction

Careers

No Mistakes Resumes, Book I of No Mistakes Careers

No Mistakes Interviews, Book II of No Mistakes Careers

Grammar

Misused Words, No Mistakes Grammar, Volume I

Misused Words for Business, No Mistakes Grammar, Volume II

More Misused Words, No Mistakes Grammar, Volume III

Visual Grammar (this is a compilation of volumes I–III with a bit of new information added. It also includes pictures and is the world's first visual grammar book)

Misused Words and Then Some, No Mistakes Grammar, Volume V

Simply Put: The Plain English Grammar Guide

How to Capitalize Anything

More Grammar

No Mistakes Grammar Bites, Volume I, Lie, Lay, Laid, and It's and Its

No Mistakes Grammar Bites, Volume II, Good and Well, and Then and Than

No Mistakes Grammar Bites, Volume III, That, Which, and Who, and There Is and There Are

No Mistakes Grammar Bites, Volume IV, Affect and Effect, and Accept and Except

No Mistakes Grammar Bites, Volume V, You're and Your, and They're, There, and Their

No Mistakes Grammar Bites, Volume VI, Passed and Past, and Into, In To and In

No Mistakes Grammar Bites, Volume VII, Farther and Further, and Onto, On, and On To

No Mistakes Grammar Bites, Volume VIII, Anxious and Eager, and Different From and Different Than

No Mistakes Grammar Bites, Volume IX, A While and Awhile, and Envy and Jealousy

No Mistakes Grammar Bites, Volume X, Could've and Should've, and Irony and Coincidence

No Mistakes Grammar Bites, Volume XI, "Quotation Marks and How to Punctuate Them" and "Plurals of Compound Nouns"

No Mistakes Grammar Bites, Volume XII, "Latin Abbreviations"

No Mistakes Grammar Bites, Volume XIII, "Redundancies" and "Ax to Grind"

No Mistakes Grammar Bites Volume XIV, "Superlatives and How We Use them Wrong"

No Mistakes Grammar Bites Volume XV, "Shoo-in and Shoe-in" and "Horse Racing Sayings"

No Mistakes Grammar Bites Volume XVI, "Which and What" and "Since and Because"

No Mistakes Grammar Bites Volume XVII, "Hyphens, and When to Use Them" and "Em Dashes and En Dashes"

Uneducated

Whiskers and Bear—Volume I, Sanctuary Tales

A Collection of Animal Stories, Volume II, Sanctuary Tales

More Animal Stories, Volume III, Sanctuary Tales

Surviving a Stroke—Or Two

Life and Then Some

Fiction

Friendship & Honor Series:

Murder Takes Time

Murder Has Consequences

Murder Takes Patience

Murder Is Invisible

Murder Is a Promise

Murder Is Immaculate (coming soon)

Blood Flows South Series

A Bullet for Carlos: A Connie Gianelli Mystery

Finding Family, a Novella

A Bullet from Dominic

The Good Book

The Ranger

Redemption Series

Necessary Decisions: A Gino Cataldi Mystery

Old Wounds

Promises Kept, the Story of Number Two

Premeditated

The Ranger

Rules of Vengeance Series (Fantasy)

Light of Lights (the beginning, a novella)

A Promise of Vengeance

Undeniable Vengeance

Consummate Vengeance

Vengeance Is Mine (2019)

Note: The Light of Lights is a novella. It's about 100 pages long and sets the stage for the series. The other books in the series are between 650 and 850 pages long.

OTHER BOOKS

You can always see the current and coming-soon books on my website.

Fiction

***Memories for Sale* (mystery/sf)**

***The Joshua Citadel* (SF novella)**

Children's Books

No Mistakes Grammar for Kids, Volume I—Much and Many

No Mistakes Grammar for Kids, Volume II—Lie and Lay

No Mistakes Grammar for Kids, Volume III—Bring and Take

No Mistakes Grammar for Kids, Volume IV, "Would've, Should've" and "Your and You're"

No Mistakes Grammar for Kids, Volume V, "There, They're, and Their" and "To, Too, and Two"

Shinobi Goes to School—Life on the Farm for Kids, Volume I

Fiona Gets Caught, Life on the Farm for Kids, Volume II

Coco Gets a Donut, Life on the Farm for Kids, Volume III

Squeak Gets a Home, Life on the Farm for Kids, Volume IV

Biscotti Saves Punch, Life on the Farm for Kids, Volume V

The Adventures of Adalina, Volume I, Adalina and the Five Tiny Bears

Coming Soon

The Adventures of Adalina, Volume II, Adalina and the Underwater Bears

Get on the mailing list and you'll be sure to be notified of release dates and sales.

<u>Mailing list</u>

And don't forget to leave a review!

www.ingramcontent.com/pod-product-compliance
Lightning Source LLC
Chambersburg PA
CBHW061306190726
48288CB00002B/374